Voice of Evil

The new latches were strong and secure. We'd left a light burning in the hall downstairs as well as upstairs. I must have gone to sleep almost immediately. . . . There was a sharp, piercing clamor —the telephone, shrill, insistent. I picked up the receiver. "Hello."

"Lynn—" It was a low, hoarse whisper. "Baby, this is Daddy—"

The shock registered on my face: I couldn't say a word. "You've come home, Baby. At last you've come home. *Wherever you go, I'll be there* . . ."

THE BOOK TREE
rade your averbac
-ave up to 50%
188 St Georges Ave Ranway
(201) 381-2665

QUANTITY SALES

Most Dell books are available at special quantity discounts when purchased in bulk by corporations, organizations, and special-interest groups. Custom imprinting or excerpting can also be done to fit special needs. For details write: Dell Publishing, 666 Fifth Avenue, New York, NY 10103. Attn.: Special Sales Department.

INDIVIDUAL SALES

Are there any Dell books you want but cannot find in your local stores? If so, you can order them directly from us. You can get any Dell book in print. Simply include the book's title, author, and ISBN number if you have it, along with a check or money order (no cash can be accepted) for the full retail price plus $2.00 to cover shipping and handling. Mail to: Dell Readers Service, P.O. Box 5057, Des Plaines, IL 60017.

Wherever Lynn Goes

Jennifer Wilde writing as
BEATRICE PARKER

A DELL BOOK

Published by
Dell Publishing
a division of
Bantam Doubleday Dell Publishing Group, Inc.
666 Fifth Avenue
New York, New York 10103

Copyright © 1975 by Tom E. Huff

All rights reserved. No part of this book may be reproduced or trans-
mitted in any form or by any means, electronic or mechanical, including photocopying, recording, or by any information storage and
retrieval system, without the written permission of the Publisher,
except where permitted by law.

The trademark Dell® is registered in the U.S. Patent and Trademark
Office.

ISBN: 0-440-20905-6

Printed in the United States of America

Published simultaneously in Canada

May 1991

10 9 8 7 6 5 4 3 2 1

OPM

1

THE DESK DRAWERS were cluttered with five years' accumulation, and it was with great satisfaction that I finished clearing them out. Not a single paper clip remained. Old lipsticks, half-finished short stories, stale chocolate bars, torn and tattered snapshots: All had been disposed of now, and the drawers were beautifully empty, ready for the next aspiring young career girl who was willing to work under horrendous stress for starvation wages. I pulled the cover over the battered old typewriter and took a last look at the office with its flaking plaster walls and dusty gray file cabinets. I hoped my replacement had a sense of humor. She'd need it. She'd also need nerves of steel and Herculean stamina.

Five years is a long time. There should have been tears and sad farewells, nostalgia and a sense of loss. There wasn't. I was elated to be leaving. There would be no more gossipy articles about Lady Cynthia's swank garden parties, no more chatty features about new dress lengths and revolutionary eye make-up, no more interviews with zany eccentrics who raised pet ocelots or planned to swim the Channel at eighty-five. Nor would I be faced with shattering deadlines and rampaging editors with volatile tempers and astounding vocabularies. I was on my own now, and in my purse was a perfectly lovely contract and an even lovelier check signed by Philip Ashton-Croft himself. The Sunday Supplement would have to do without me.

Someone else could cover the next axe murder from "the woman's point of view."

At twenty-six, Lynn Morgan was retiring from the newspaper world, moving on to bigger and better things at long last. Fleet Street would survive the loss, I thought, smiling to myself. Any bright young thing with a fair education and a way with words could do as well, so long as she didn't take herself too seriously. One needed a sense of proportion. I had known all along that the job was a stopgap, providing bread and butter—the latter in very small quantities. Now I could say good-bye to it all without even the tiniest regret.

It had all come about in quite a remarkable way. History was my first love, and in my spare time I had written a series of articles on the Court of Louis XIV— character studies, really, filled with spicy anecdotes and loving period details. There was absolutely no demand for them, but after dozens of rejection slips they had finally been accepted and published by a totally obscure historical quarterly whose circulation was practically nonexistent. So far as the world was concerned, their publication remained a deep, dark secret, which had made the message from Philip Ashton-Croft which had arrived three weeks ago all the more startling.

Philip Ashton-Croft was one of the most prestigious publishers in London—frightfully distinguished, formidably intelligent. The books he published were the very last word in scholarship and impeccable taste. He wanted to meet me, the message read, and I went to the interview nervous and on edge. I was astounded to learn that not only had he read the articles, he thought they were "glorious." He felt they could be expanded into a highly readable book, and was offering me a contract forthwith—including a more-than-generous advance upon signing.

That had been three weeks ago. All details had

been se
today
pres
be
co
the
the
that 3
cubl
final
ished
strand
succes
those l
silver f
the offic
hind me. M.
be scratched

Typewriter
main newsroom.
angry, morose. Clerk
copy, fetching scissors,
the distance came the om.
The chaos was perpetual,
only an occasional lull after t.
filed, the last copy read and ready
were very few farewells. As feature
day Supplement, I had had little to de
paper. Though I had been on friendly t
eryone, I had not been close to the rowdy,
frantic types that generally inhabit the ne
world. A few of the secretaries flocked around,
ing appropriately, wishing me well, and in a matte.
minutes I was outside. The clamor within was mi.
compared to the screech of brakes, the blast of horns,
the shouts of newsboys heaving fresh bundles of news-
print off the curb and into the backs of vans.

I went to my bank immediately, deposited the

um, stuffing the bills into
. I'd never had so much
ughly intended to splurge
absolute orgy of shopping:
efore, new shoes and dresses,
ber Mandy had eyed so long-
one of the boutiques. For the
in heaven. I was much too real-
y tales, had worked too long and
losing all the standard illusions
today I felt exactly like Cinderella
e ball. Gloriously exhausted, sur-
ls, I had tea in the restaurant of one
t stores and thought about my incred-
e.

ather well for myself, I decided. I had
wn for such a long time. My mother died
five, and Daddy and I went to live with
ne in her big, rambling house in Devon, a
us Victorian mansion completely sur-
by dense woods. Shortly thereafter, Bill Mor-
rted for Australia, leaving me with Daphne, a
ccentric old spinster with a great fondness for
wsuits, blood sports, and vociferous quarrels
servants, neighbors, local authorities, and anyone
who happened to come within range. Although
ddy sent a letter once a month, I never saw him
ain, and when I was thirteen we received word of his
eath. I was immediately packed off to boarding
school, heartbroken at my loss but secretly glad to be
getting away from my colorful but decidedly unlovable aunt. I had seen the cantankerous old lady only a
few times since, enduring each occasion with remarkable patience. For all purposes, I had been on my own
since I was thirteen years old, and I had come a long
way.

The waitress brought more tea and a platter of
tiny frosted cakes. I smiled at her, intending to leave a

generous tip. I'd worked as a waitress myself in the old days, before the position with the Supplement, and I knew the grueling hours and strenuous work involved. I remembered that crowded, noisy tea shop, popular with plump matrons and brawling children. That's where I had met Mandy, who worked there too. Soon we were rooming together, the struggling actress and the aspiring author. We had gone through some rough times together and were closer than sisters, our life styles complementary instead of clashing. Mandy was going to be elated when I told her about the book, for I hadn't mentioned it to her, wanting to be certain of the contract before springing the news.

I hadn't even told Lloyd.

I smiled again, thinking of Lloyd Raymond. If I was Cinderella, Lloyd was definitely Prince Charming. I had met him three months earlier, at the opening-night party for one of Mandy's plays. The play was an unmitigated disaster, but the party was riotous, a merry wake with champagne in profusion, dozens and dozens of people crowded on stage, laughing, drinking, making new connections. Mandy was surrounded by a bevy of males, as always, and I was left alone. I detest noisy crowds, and this had to be the noisiest crowd on record, so after a while I slipped out into the back alley, standing on the rusty fire escape, thankful for the solitude and fresh night air. I'd been there for only a minute or so when the door opened behind me and Lloyd stepped out, looking as relieved as I had felt.

He was a lawyer, I discovered, connected with a very prominent firm, and had been dragged to the party against his will. He was thirty years old and six foot two, dressed in a silky black suit that fit his athletic body to perfection. He had clean-cut, virile features, dark brown eyes, and brick-red hair clipped unfashionably short. His heavy black-rimmed glasses only emphasized his stern, manly good looks. His manner was grave and polite, and he spoke in a beauti-

fully modulated voice. Quiet, reserved, he nevertheless radiated strength and vitality. One had the impression of great energy carefully channeled, of force
under tight control. We talked for two hours there on
the flimsy iron fire escape, and then he took me to an
all-night restaurant. Later, when he drove me home,
we sat in his car for another two hours, talking, watching the sky lighten from black to gray to a misty violet.
After years of trying to match me up with one or another of her scores of admirers, Mandy was delighted
that I had finally found one of my own. "And *such* a
beautiful specimen," she added, in her blithe, carefree
manner.

Lloyd and I had been seeing each other three or
four times a week ever since. He was wonderful to be
with—thoughtful and considerate, perhaps a bit too
stern and reserved, yet wonderful just the same. If he
was rather dictatorial at times, that was merely part of
his nature, the strong, silent male. Although he was
only four years my senior, he seemed much older, and
when I was with him I felt very secure. I was very fond
of Lloyd Raymond, very fond indeed, but I was too
inexperienced to know if that feeling was love. I wondered what my answer would be when he asked me to
marry him, for I knew it was only a matter of time
until that question came up. Lloyd had some rather
old-fashioned ideas about a woman's place, a man's
role, and I wondered if I would be willing to give up
my independence.

Gathering up my parcels and placing a large tip on
the table, I left the tea room, excitement still like a
heady wine, wonderfully inebriating. An enormous
red bus rattled past outside, discharging noxious
fumes. The din of rush-hour traffic was deafening.
Taxi horns blared loudly. Tires squealed at the inter-
section. An irate driver leaned out the window of his
Bentley to shout an obscenity at a long-haired youth
who zoomed past on a motorcycle. Shops and stores

disgorged crowds of flushed, irritable clerks and secretaries who stampeded for the nearest Underground entrance. I might feel madly reckless, but not enough so to throw away money on a taxi, and at this hour the buses would be better suited for sardines than people. I decided to walk. Smiling, filled with a sense of well-being, I turned a corner and, a short while later, found myself in the peaceful little cul-de-sac where weathered, ancient flats overlooked a tiny square with leafy green trees behind a wrought-iron fence. The building where Mandy and I lived was the most dilapidated of the lot, tall and narrow, painted a dingy blue, crowded between a dusty brownstone and a Victorian relic that looked like a soot-stained marble wedding cake.

I was relieved to find Mrs. Wellington temporarily away from her post. Once she caught you in the foyer she was good for thirty minutes, rattling away interminably about her health, her cats, the state of the nation and the scandalous cost of pork. Mrs. Wellington, our landlady, was a plump, fussy, insatiably curious old dear given to horoscopes, scandal magazines, and other people's business. Her flat was on the ground floor, the door always open so she could see anyone who stepped into the building, and little escaped her eagle eye. She frequently informed Mandy that she ran a respectable house and refused to tolerate all these *men* trooping up and down the stairs at all hours, but in truth she tolerated everything but unpaid rent. As Mandy and I always paid promptly, we could have entertained Gypsies all night without risking anything more than a severe tongue-lashing. Mrs. W. adored us, said we gave the place "class." That was hardly a compliment, considering some of the other tenants.

Mrs. Wellington was so cheap she could hardly draw breath without being tipped for it, and she certainly didn't intend to waste good money on electricity before nightfall. The stairs were dark, and the place reeked of corned beef and cabbage and stale beer. We lived on the top floor, and by the time I reached.our landing I was genuinely exhausted. Shifting the parcels, I took out my key and opened the door. I dropped the parcels on the living-room table and sighed with relief.

We occupied the entire top floor, and the flat was large and roomy, perfect for Mandy's parties. It was furnished with wildly mismatched furniture, littered with books and magazines and various feminine paraphernalia, and, always, dusty, as neither Mandy nor I was domestic. The wallpaper was hideous, faded green roses against a faded blue background, and the dismal gray carpet was threadbare. There was a constant draft from a window that refused to shut, the kitchen was gloomy, with dark brown linoleum and shockingly outdated appliances, the bathroom plumbing was madly unpredictable, but the place was homey and, best of all, quite inexpensive.

"Lynn?" Mandy called from her bedroom.

"You home already?"

"I've been home for *hours*, pet. I need a six-letter word for mysterious. Four down is prey. That makes the second letter r."

"Arcane?" I suggested.

"A, r, c—that's it! You're a *wonder*, luv. There! I'm finished with the silly thing. I don't know why I bother."

If Mandy wasn't experimenting with cosmetics or trying on clothes, she was reading or doing crossword puzzles. The closet shelves were piled high with hundreds of thrillers. I had received free review copies at the office and brought them to her by the dozen. Mandy devoured them with relish. She had once gone with a handsome inspector from Scotland Yard, and crime had fascinated her ever since—the bloodier the better.

"What about the play?" I called, slipping out of

my shoes and moving over to the mirror to brush back a wave of long, glossy brown hair. "Did you get the part?"

"The afternoon was sheer disaster, luv. The producer, I use the word loosely, wanted . . . well, he took me out for a nice cozy drink and suggested a nice cozy arrangement. Poor man, he looked rather silly sitting there with Scotch dripping all over his bald head . . ."

Mandy stepped into the room, smiling a wry smile.

"You threw your drink at him?"

"The waiter was *scan*dalized. It was a very proper bar. I didn't really want the part, anyway. I'm no good in heavy drama. Light, frothy farce is my thing. If only Noel Coward were still alive . . ."

Amanda Hunt was tall and lanky, with enormous brown eyes and dark tawny gold hair that swirled around her shoulders in disorderly locks. Not really beautiful, she had a dry, sophisticated style that was distinctly her own. Men found her fascinating, and with her powerful magnetism and individuality she could have been quite successful had she really tried. Mandy was singularly unambitious—rather lazy, in fact, far more interested in being amused than in having a career. Her chief claim to fame thus far was her appearances on the telly as Maisie the Milkmaid in a series of commercials for Delicious Dairy Milk. Flippant, lighthearted, invariably cheerful, she was also shrewdly intelligent—something few of her merry companions ever suspected.

"Lynn!" she cried, seeing the parcels for the first time. "Have you gone berserk? The rent's due next Friday, we're both flat, and you buy out half the shops in London! I knew you'd crack one of these days, luv. Years of necessary penny-pinching have finally driven you over the edge—"

"I have something to tell you," I said calmly.

"You've robbed a bank. I'll be a character witness, darling. We'll get you out of this some way—"

Smiling, I told her about Philip Ashton-Croft, about the book and the advance I'd already deposited. Mandy was very cool about the whole thing, taking the contract from me, carefully going over the fine print I'd merely skimmed myself.

"It seems like a fairly decent contract," she said, handing it back to me, "although I'm not too sure about that clause concerning foreign rights. Don't expect me to seem surprised, pet. Didn't I tell you those articles were as good as anything Nancy Mitford ever wrote? I *knew* something would come of them."

Mandy was my biggest fan. She felt my work for the Supplement was unworthy of my abilities, and had been after-me for years to write a thriller. She was constantly giving me plot ideas—smashingly clever ones, too—but fiction was not my metier.

"I suppose you've chucked your job?"

I nodded, sitting down on the lumpy green sofa. "It's going to be a big job, expanding those articles into a book-length manuscript. I'll have to do tons more research, reorganize everything. I'm thinking of doing a whole section on Louise de La Valliere—"

"More about Madame de Thianges, too," Mandy said. "I've always thought she got shortchanged by history, overshadowed by her sister. She's a fascinating woman." Mandy had read all the books I brought home for research, had gone to the library on her own, and knew almost as much about the period as I did myself. "Darling, it's going to be *fun!* I'll help you with your notes and—"

Mandy chattered blithely, working up more and more enthusiasm for the project, and then we opened the parcels. She was elated with the sexy black dress, and tried it on immediately. The bodice fit like a glove, and her back was virtually bare. I wouldn't have dared wear such a dress, but on Mandy it looked sensational. She whirled around, her dark-gold locks flying in all directions.

"I feel ever so wicked! George will go out of his mind."

"George? The trombone player?"

"No, luv, that's Craig. George is that darling croupier I brought up last week, the one who had the bit part in the Fellini film."

Mandy had so many beaux it was almost impossible to keep them straight in one's mind. They ranged from a Member of Parliament to a handsome young stevedore, and she treated them all with a casual, merry disdain. They loved it. Mandy was always entertaining, always fun to be with, never demanding. With her, even a simple excursion like walking in the park took on the aspects of a madcap adventure. Though she frequently pretended to be bored by all this male attention, it was as necessary to her as air.

An hour later, surrounded by empty boxes and sacks and clouds of tissue paper, we were contemplating dinner. Lloyd was working late, and Mandy had turned down several invitations, planning to stay in and read the newest thriller. Although she adored pub-crawling and parties and the theater, she could be just as happy in housecoat and slippers, knocking around the flat. We had just decided to open some tins and heat up some leftovers when the telephone rang. Mandy tensed, giving me a nervous glance.

"There's no need to look so worried," I said lightly. "It's probably one of your friends."

"What if it's *him?*"

"He hasn't called for almost a week."

"Lynn, I just have a feeling—"

"Nonsense."

I got up and answered the phone.

"Hello?"

There was silence on the other end of the line.

Then, after several seconds, a low, hoarse voice began to whisper.

"Lynn? Lynn, this is Daddy—"

"Sorry," I said brightly, "wrong number."

I hung up immediately. Mandy, standing beside me now, her cheeks a bit pale, said, "It *was* him."

I nodded, not at all alarmed. The phone calls were irritating, and in *very* poor taste, but I refused to let them bother me. Someone with a sick sense of humor was playing a prank. That was all it amounted to. Mandy, however, found the calls terribly distressing, certain that they had some deep significance.

"Did he say anything *new?*" she asked in a strained voice.

"No, just the same old thing. 'This is Daddy.' The chap hasn't much imagination, I'm afraid."

"Lynn, it's—well, *obscene* phone calls I could understand, but this is *spooky!*"

"You read far too many thrillers."

"He's been calling for over two months now, and it's always the same, like . . . like a voice from the grave."

I smiled, moving over to the table and beginning to gather up the tissue paper. "My father died in Australia in 1959, I assure you. Besides, ghosts are hardly likely to utilize the London Telephone Exchange. I wish you'd forget about it, Mandy."

"I wish I could. It gives me the shivers! Lynn, who could it possibly *be?*"

"I have no idea."

"None of our friends—"

"I used a by-line on all my stories in the Supplement. He probably saw my name over one of them and looked me up in the telephone directory."

"But our number's unlisted," she protested. "We had it changed after the first couple of calls."

We'd been over this several times before, and I knew it would be useless to argue with her about it.

Addicted to thrillers, her mind cluttered with ideas for more, Mandy obstinately maintained that the calls were part of some intricate plot. I believe she actually expected me to end up on some dark street in Soho with my throat slit. At her insistence, I had informed the police, who, bored and wearily tolerant, suggested we get an unlisted number. We had, but somehow or other my caller had discovered it. There had been no threats, no mysterious warnings in the mail, no sinister-looking men in dark glasses who followed me on the street. The prankster would grow tired eventually and find another victim. Until then, I would continue to ignore the calls.

"Lynn," Mandy said, "are you—are you *sure* your father's dead?"

"Of course I'm sure."

We were in the kitchen now. The oven crackled ominously as part of a leftover casserole heated, and eggs boiled noisily on the ancient gas burner. As I set the table, Mandy tried to open a tin—for her a highly dangerous process which might well result in a surprise appendectomy. Still wearing the sexy black dress, looking as out of place in the kitchen as a duchess, she gouged at the tin, apprehensive but determined. Finally succeeding without bloodshed, she dumped the herring onto a plate, gave a sigh of exhaustion, and leaned against the scarred zinc drainboard.

"They always turn up in books," she remarked.

"Who?"

"The deceased. He died in Australia under mysterious circumstances—"

"A heart attack," I amended.

"—when you were thirteen years old. He'd been away from England for years. You didn't actually *see* the body, and—"

"Don't be ghoulish."

"Lynn, I just *know* those phone calls mean something. I don't see how you can be so casual about them."

"I try to be sensible, and I don't read thrillers."

"Go ahead, make fun of me, but he *could* still be alive. He probably discovered a gold mine in Australia, or . . . or maybe he was involved in some nefarious scheme, innocently involved, of course, and found it necessary to disappear—"

Mandy cut herself short as great clouds of black smoke began to billow from the oven. There was a noise like machine-gun fire. She dashed to open the window. Grabbing a pair of tattered pot holders, I flung open the oven door and pulled out the charred remains of the casserole. As I dumped it into the trash bin, the eggs exploded, geysers of hot water spewing over the stove. I turned off the burner, feeling terribly frustrated. When the smoke cleared, Mandy shrugged her shoulders philosophically.

"You know, luv, one of us really *should* learn to cook."

"I know," I said bitterly.

"Oh well, who needs food?"

Stepping over to the icebox, she pulled out a tall, slender bottle with gold foil around the cap and then fetched two mismatched glasses from the cabinet over the sink.

"*Where* did you get that champagne?"

"Stevie brought it along last night, the lamb. I knew it would come in handy. Let's celebrate the contract, luv. In fact, let's get gloriously plastered!"

2

THE RESTAURANT was charming. Sitting at a table on the patio, we could look beyond the graceful stone balustrade at the park, trees in full leaf now, in early April. Daffodils bloomed riotously in untidy beds, and farther away, through a partial screen of clipped yews, part of the pond was revealed. Noisy little boys sailed toy boats along the edge of the water. A week had passed, and, as he would be unable to see me tonight, Lloyd had arranged to meet me here for lunch. Rays of sunlight spilled down, gleaming on silver and china, making bright yellow pools all around us. Waiters moved around with hushed efficiency, discreet and rather formidable.

"More coffee?" Lloyd asked in his deep, quiet voice.

I shook my head, watching a group of young people who were sitting on blankets spread over a sloping bank. One of them was playing a guitar, and the music wafted toward us with gentle melancholy. I was in a pensive mood, satisfied with life, enjoying the fresh air, the music, a sense of well-being. Lloyd was preoccupied, a serious look on his stern, handsome face. Behind the heavy black glasses, his eyes looked grave.

"Dessert?" he said.

"I dare not. Thank you for a marvelous lunch, Lloyd."

"The pleasure was all mine."

"Do you have to get back to the office soon?"

"Not immediately. I have another thirty minutes or so."

"Let's walk in the park. It's such a glorious day . . ."

Lloyd signaled for our waiter, scrutinized the bill closely, and then placed several bills on the tray. As he stood up, I marveled again at his tall, muscular frame. Today he wore a leaf-brown suit, spotless white shirt, and carefully knotted rust-colored tie. He looked the successful young lawyer, all right, needing only a black leather briefcase to complete the picture. Several women at nearby tables turned to glance at him. They always did, for Lloyd had that subtle magnetism that is far more interesting than overt sexiness. I felt a glow of pleasure as he took my arm, leading me down the low white marble steps and into the park.

Although far more conventionally dressed than most of the other people sauntering through the park, we must have made an attractive pair nevertheless. I wore a white cotton dress printed with tiny brown and green leaves. While not beautiful, I was at least arresting, with high, sculptured cheekbones, dark blue eyes, and long brown hair gleaming with chestnut highlights. Men looked twice, had done so for several years now, and Lloyd seemed pleased to have me walking beside him. I held on to his arm, matching my stride to his.

"How's the book coming along?" he inquired.

"Creaking. I spent the whole afternoon in the library yesterday, hunting down an obscure reference to Scarron, Madame de Maintenon's bizarre invalid husband. I'm doing a chapter on their marriage, including a bit about their rather unusual sex life."

"I can hardly feature you writing about sex," he said.

"Why not?"

"Because, luv, you're so defiantly virginal."

"Is that bad?"

"It's bad for me," he remarked.

"You could easily find another girl. I can think of several who—"

"So can I, but I happen to want you."

"You've got quite a problem."

"How well I know. I'm happy about the book, luv. I'm glad you have something to amuse yourself with."

"Is that what you think I'm doing, *amusing* myself?"

Lloyd smiled, the corners of his wide mouth turning up. "No need to take offense," he said. "I didn't mean it that way. I'm glad you've got brains."

"But you'd rather I be a clinging vine."

"Not especially," he drawled.

"I'll never be that way, Lloyd."

"I know, luv. You're a fiercely independent, thoroughly liberated woman, sharp, shrewd, and, incidentally, gorgeous in that dress. Do you want to argue about equal rights or would you rather neck?"

"Neither," I said irritably.

Lloyd chuckled, dropping his arm around my shoulder. We walked to the pond and stopped beside a mound of huge gray boulders at the edge of the water. Sunlight danced in shimmering silver threads over the surface. Above thick green treetops, we could see brown and gray buildings rising, pigeons fluttering about window ledges. London was touched with a springtime magic today, as charming and exhilarating as the poets claimed. Watching the pond's waves lapping, I felt Lloyd beside me, strong and silent and very male.

"Angry?" he said.

"Why should I be angry?" I snapped.

"No reason."

"It's just that—you refuse to take me seriously."

"You're wrong about that. I take you very seriously."

"You think—"

"I think you're delightful."

Pulling me into his arms, Lloyd kissed me for a long time, his mouth caressing mine with expert skill. Then, arms resting heavily on my shoulders, he stared down at me, a faint smile curling on his lips and a touch of amusement in his dark brown eyes. He was in an unusually affable mood, I thought, some of his earlier preoccupation gone. I studied his clean-cut, chiseled features, his face so close that I could see the tiny pink scar at the corner of his mouth where he had cut himself shaving. The heavy black-rimmed glasses set off his good looks, I thought, adding character and maturity and saving him from being merely conventionally handsome. I touched his lean cheek, mollified. He kissed me again, lightly this time.

"You're an enchanting creature, Lynn, far too enchanting to be turned loose on mankind. What am I going to do with you?"

"I know what you're *not* going to do."

He grinned. "So liberated in some ways, so old-fashioned in others."

"I'm not old-fashioned," I protested. "I just happen to believe—"

"I know what you believe. But you can't blame a chap for trying."

"Keep trying, by all means. It gives a girl confidence."

"That's one thing you don't need any more of. I'm sorry about tonight, Lynn. I know we'd planned to go to the new Tom Stoppard play, but something came up—"

"You don't have to apologize, Lloyd. I understand."

"You always understand. That's another thing I like about you. I've exchanged the tickets. We're scheduled to see it next Thursday night. That all right with you?"

"Fine," I said.

"After the play, we'll go to the Garden for dining. I've made reservations. Then I thought we'd pop over to Sybilla's for a couple of drinks. Everything's set."

Everything was set. Everything was neatly arranged, down to the last detail. It always was. Lloyd sighed, stepping back and staring across the pond. He was preoccupied again. Having filed me away in a neat little compartment, he was thinking of something else —some lawsuit, perhaps, or some new will he had to draft. I stared at his handsome profile. Lloyd was so thoroughly in control of every situation. I often wished he weren't quite so efficient and predictable. Life with Lloyd would be very stable, very well-organized, even the lovemaking. There would be no crises, but neither would there be any surprises. Perhaps I was being too hard on him, I thought, rather ashamed of myself. Dashing, mercurial heroes are all very well in books, but I imagined they would be extremely taxing in real life. Lloyd Raymond was everything a woman could hope for, and it was a wonder some predatory female hadn't snapped him up already.

"Lynn," he said abruptly, turning to me. "Have there been any more phone calls?"

"Why—" The question took me by surprise. "Yes. There was one last week, the day I got my contract, and another one on Wednesday. Why do you ask?"

"It's been on my mind. I worry about you."

"There's no reason to. It's just some crank—"

"I'm not so sure," he said grimly. "There're a lot of freaks running loose in this city. Those calls have bothered me from the very first, particularly after you changed your number and he kept right on calling. Have you any idea who it could be?"

"Not the foggiest. It's really not worth discussing, Lloyd. *I'm* not worried. I don't see why you and Mandy should—"

"Tell me about your father," he interrupted. "What kind of man was he?"

"Lloyd, I'd really rather not."

"I think this is important, Lynn."

His voice was firm, his tone clearly indicating that he intended to brook no argument. I sighed, accepting the inevitable. When Lloyd wanted to discuss something, it was discussed.

"I don't remember very much about him," I said, trying to recall that vague presence who had been there in the early years of my life. "We moved to Devon when I was five, and he left just a few months later. I couldn't have been more than six years old. He was a large man, and gruff, with dark black hair and a flushed face. He loved me dearly. I was heartbroken when he went away—"

"He went to Australia, you say?"

"Yes. I have no idea why he left England. Daphne never told me. He sent me a letter once a month, regular as clockwork, and then he died. I was thirteen at the time."

"Do you still have the letters?"

"I have no idea what happened to them."

Lloyd frowned, thrusting his square jaw out. He looked very much the lawyer on a case. We might have been in a courtroom instead of in the park. I resented his attitude. I wasn't on trial, and I had already told him everything I knew about my father a long time ago, after the first call. He folded his arms across his chest, head tilted to one side.

"Can you remember what was in any of those letters?"

"Of course not. It was years ago."

"Look, Lynn, I know you think I'm being unreasonable, and maybe I am, but I want to get to the bottom of this thing. The phone calls could be the work of a prankster, as you say. They very likely are, but if there's the least possibility . . ." He hesitated, his brown eyes grave. "It's just that I'm concerned about your welfare," he added.

"I appreciate that, Lloyd, but I can assure you it's entirely unnecessary. You and Mandy have blown this thing all out of proportion."

"Maybe so," he said. "You're probably right. Nevertheless, if you remember anything pertaining to your father, anything at all, I want you to tell me about it."

As he peered at me through the glasses, I realized that his concern was genuine. I should have been flattered. Lloyd did mean well, even if his manner was sometimes overbearing. Standing there with his arms folded, his hair a sleek copper-red cap, he looked like a stern parent, all sober dignity. I found that suddenly humorous and utterly endearing. That lighthearted glow came back, and I smiled, touching his jaw with my fingertips.

"I will," I said. "I promise."

"I guess we'd better start back. I have an appointment at two. Sorry if I was rough on you, luv. I guess I spend too much time in the courtroom. Am I forgiven?"

"There's nothing to forgive."

"You mean a lot to me, Lynn, a hell of a lot."

He took my hand, and we followed one of the shady walkways that led to the street.

"I wish you didn't have to go back," I said wistfully.

"I wish so, too, luv. There's nothing I'd like better than to spend the whole afternoon with you."

"Do you mean that?"

"Of course I do. I'm not the most gallant suitor on earth, but that doesn't mean . . . I'm no good at romantic dialogue, Lynn. Let's just say meeting you is about the best thing that ever happened to me. Will that do?"

"It'll do nicely for starters."

We were standing on the busy pavement now, the

park behind us. Across the street, ponderous gray
stone buildings rose up, seeped in age and tradition,
their white marble porticos streaked with soot. Secretaries on their way back from lunch bustled through
the doors, and serious-looking men with briefcases
moved along briskly, causing the sidewalk pigeons to
scatter. I sighed, holding on to Lloyd's arm, reluctant
to have him join the ranks. He glanced at his watch,
mentally already among them, my presence a mere
hindrance now.

"What'll you do for the rest of the day?" he
asked.

"I'm going to the library. I have my notebooks
here in my purse, and I intend to—"

"Well, luv, it's getting on. I've got to dash. I'll try
to call you tonight if I get a chance."

He pulled his arm free, gave me a quick, perfunctory kiss, and hurried across the street. He moved vigorously down a side street and disappeared into one of
the buildings. I stood there for a moment, wishing he
were a carefree bohemian in sweater and jeans who
had nothing better to do than shower me with attention. Then, realizing the absurdity of the thought, I
laughed aloud and dashed to board the bus that would
take me to the library.

I spent several hours in those solemn, vaulted
rooms, prowling among the dusty stacks, tracking
down elusive volumes. Notebooks spread out over an
ancient wooden table with peeling varnish, I forgot all
about Lloyd, completely caught up in that glittering
world of rakish courtiers, vindictive courtesans, and
gossipy old men. I was doing the chapter on Madame
de Thianges, Montespan's sister, a frivolous, amoral
creature who bounced on satin sofas with the Sun
King, kept her friends up all night with vivacious chatter and, when they deserted, brought in her servants
for rowdy card games and snacks. I filled several pages
with cramped handwriting, quite pleased with my

progress. The book was going to be much longer than I had originally planned, but it would be a labor of love.

Twilight was descending when I stepped outside. Tired and content, I caught my bus home, settling down beside an open window and staring out as we passed across the city.

For no apparent reason, I began to think about Aunt Daphne, perhaps because I had mentioned her to Lloyd earlier in the day. I wondered how the old girl was. Months had passed since I had last seen her, and that had been an extremely trying occasion. She had come up to London on some vague business, and by the time I met her for lunch she was already well soused with gin. Her hair was newly hennaed, and she wore high-buttoned shoes and a purple crepe dress. Around her neck was wrapped a tattered fox furpiece, one fox biting the tail of the other, both incredibly dusty, and she carried an ebony cane. As cantankerous and shrill as ever, determined to be a character, she had downed three more gins, ranted about her malicious neighbors in Devon, and informed me, bluntly, that I looked like a harlot in my too-short skirt. Realizing that she was a lonely old woman with little to do, I could be tolerant of her now, even fond of her after a fashion, but life had been sheer hell when I had lived with her as a child.

The bus rumbled ponderously down a cobblestone street with much shifting of gears, stopping in front of a pub to take on more passengers and let others off. As we moved on, I thought about those distant days when I had run wild through the woods, hunting birds' nests, climbing trees, studying nature and responding to it like some wild creature. Aunt Daphne had been delighted to have me out of the way. If she wasn't writing vicious letters to the local newspaper or filing a lawsuit against someone who'd irritated her, she was riding to hounds in scarlet jacket and ancient jodhpurs, her face bright pink, her voice ringing lustily over the countryside. She was a local character, something of a legend in the nearby village, a raucous, indomitable, flamboyant old girl who was a colorful figure in an age of conformity.

I had had few friends, for, while not an aristocrat, and certainly not wealthy, I was, according to Daphne, much too good to associate with the village riffraff. My days were spent in the woods or curled up in front of a crackling fire with a book. Although she never read anything but the racing sheets, Aunt Daphne housed a splendid library, inherited from a distant relative who had been a professor of history. It was in that dusty, leathery-smelling room that I had first developed my love of the past. If I couldn't play with the local children, I could at least associate with kings and countesses and knaves, however vicariously.

There *had* been one boy, I recalled, an insufferable young savage who roamed the woods as freely as I did, looking like a Gypsy child with his deep tan, unruly black locks, and lithe, slender body. I couldn't remember his name, but he had been four years my senior and, I seemed to recall, the son of a neighboring Lord. He teased me without mercy, delighted in creeping up behind me and letting out a pirate yell, waving his wooden sword in the air with bloodthirsty relish. I had avoided him whenever possible, and when he finally went away to school I had the woods to myself again and was able to roam freely without fear of being seized in muscular arms or chased across the river. What was his name? Oh well, it wasn't important. I hadn't thought about him in years. He would be thirty now, probably a solid member of the House of Lords.

When I got off the bus, three blocks away from the flat, it was already night. Hugging my books against my breast, large purse swinging from my arm, I walked down the murky street. Lights burned in only a few windows, and cats prowled around shadowy front steps. Up ahead a street lamp burned, shedding a warm yellow pool over the corner, intensifying the darkness. The neighborhood wasn't terribly respectable, but neither was it dangerous. No one had ever bothered me when I came home late from work.

Deftly eluding Mrs. Wellington, who lurked behind her open door, I went upstairs. As it was after dark, dim electric light seeped over the stairs, with just enough illumination to reveal the worn blue carpet and faded gray wallpaper with violet nosegays. The living-room lights were blazing as I opened the door, and Mandy was pacing up and down, looking terribly upset.

"I've been *distraught!*" she cried.

"Whatever for?" I asked calmly. Mandy was frequently dramatic.

"It's so *late,* Lynn, and when you didn't come—"

I shook my head, relieving myself of books and purse.

"I lost track of time at the library," I told her, "and the bus was unusually slow. There was no need to *worry,* Mandy."

"I expected you back hours ago. You mustn't *do* these things. You know how nervous I've been since those calls began—"

I raised my eyes heavenward. Mandy pushed back a lock of tawny gold hair. She was wearing a girlish pink dress with puffed sleeves, low neckline, and tight bodice, the skirt full and swirling. On her it looked chic and sophisticated.

"I thought you were going out," I remarked.

"I'd planned to, but last night was too much. I phoned Reggie and told him to tell Dave and Michael to count me out tonight. Riverboat parties are rather old hat. Besides, I get seasick every time the deck tilts the least little bit. I thought we'd eat in this evening."

"You don't plan to *cook?*" I asked, alarmed.

"Of course not, pet. I popped down to that funny little restaurant on the corner and had them box up some things. There's sliced pork and chicken and the most peculiar-looking little sausages, two kinds of salad, potatoes, bread, and cheesecake, too. I was feeling madly extravagant. The postman brought another check—residuals.''

Maisie the Milkmaid might never bring her thunderous applause or critical acclaim, but the commercials did bring in a steady if unspectacular income that permitted her to remain unemployed for long periods of time without fretting. They also brought in a steady supply of Delicious Dairy Milk, which both of us had learned to hate.

We had a festive meal, strewing the table with cardboard boxes and wax paper. Mandy chattered on about a visit to her agent's office. He was highly respected, with a string of very successful clients, but Mandy's cavalier attitude drove the poor man wild with frustration. When her bank balance was sufficient, she constantly turned down lucrative jobs that would have given her career a boost, only to take on a small part in a certain flop when funds were running low. Since Maisie, she had worked even less, while less-talented actresses made great strides in roles she'd rejected.

I spent the next two hours typing up the notes I had taken that afternoon, putting them away in a mottled gray cardboard filing box. I sat at my desk a while longer, toying with pencils and a blue glass jar, thinking about the immediate future. In a short while all my research would be complete and I could get down to the actual writing. I contemplated renting a small cottage on the Cornish coast where I could work in peace. Thanks to Ashton-Croft's generous advance, I could afford it, and it would be lovely to take long strolls over the moors early in the morning and devote my days to a routine of hard work and blissful solitude. Sighing, I pulled the cover over my decrepit old typewriter, tidied up the desk, and prepared for bed.

Freshly showered, I stepped into the living room in pajamas and robe. Mandy was lounging on the sofa, long legs propped up and her head resting on a cushion. An empty teacup and a box of sweet biscuits were on the floor beside her, and, still wearing the pink dress, she was reading contentedly. The front of the book jacket depicted an amazingly proportioned blonde being strangled by a dark, handsome chap in black overcoat, while the photograph on the back showed an author sinister enough to have posed for the villain, with disheveled raven hair, brooding eyes, and wide, cynical mouth.

"Kill Me with Kindness," I read. "Is it good?"

"Smashing. Brad Carter's ever so clever. I adore his books."

"He's certainly attractive."

"Isn't he though," she replied, glancing at the photograph. She sat up and put the book aside.

"Did Lloyd call while I was in the shower?"

"Afraid not, pet."

"It's just ten thirty. Perhaps he'll still call."

"Well, pet," Mandy said, getting to her feet and stretching lazily, "it's a long hot bath and then bed for me. I have to look especially fresh and wholesome in the morning. They're opening a new Dairy Bar at eleven and want Maisie to put in a personal appearance and cut the ribbon. It'll be absolute chaos, of course, packed with gabbing matrons in flowered hats and nasty, noisy children with balloons and lollipops, climbing all over the platform and trying to ride the papier-mâché cow. It never fails. Anyway, I mustn't disappoint my public."

The telephone rang before I could reply. Certain that it was Lloyd, I hurried to answer it. Screeching, buzzing static met my ear, as though I were listening in on a distant electrical storm. "Hello," I said, but there was no reply, just that scratchy, crackling noise. I frowned, puzzled by the uproar, and when she saw my expression Mandy grew tense, hurrying over to stand nervously at my side:

"Who *is* it?" she whispered.

"I don't know. No one—"

"Hang *up*, Lynn!"

"Long distance," a metallic voice said over the storm. "Am I speaking to Miss Lynn Morgan?"

"This is she."

"One moment please."

The static grew worse. It sounded like a roomful of yowling cats now, rising and swelling until I had to hold the receiver away from my ear. Then I heard a voice that managed to be slurred and shrill at the same time. "Are you *there!*" it cried. "Answer me!"

"Aunt Daphne?" I said, barely recognizing her voice.

"These operators are totally shiftless! Took me forever to get through, and this is an emergency! Lynn, I've got to—" The line crackled worse than ever, completely drowning out her voice. I couldn't understand a word she said, but she kept right on talking, muffled and distant, a mere background to the static.

"Aunt Daphne," I interrupted. "I can't hear you. What is it? Are you in some kind of—"

The static stopped abruptly. The line was absolutely clear. Her voice rose with hysteria. "—here now. I have to talk to you. I have to tell you about—"

There was a loud bang, then nothing but the dial tone.

"We were cut off," I said, frowning. "I'll call her back. Maybe the line will be clearer."

I placed the call, patiently waiting to get through. The phone rang at the other end, and rang, and rang. There was no answer. I placed the receiver back in its cradle and turned to look at Mandy. Her velvety brown eyes were wide.

"Why didn't she answer?" she said nervously.

"I have no idea. She's probably drunk."

"Lynn—what did she say? Do you—do you think there could be some connection with the other calls?"

"Of course not," I retorted.

I desperately wished I could be sure of that.

3

Mrs. wellington finally caught me two days later. I had finished early at the library, and it was shortly after three when I stepped into the foyer of our building. As it was daytime, the candle-shaped bulbs in the brass wall sconces were unlit, and the only light came through the uncurtained glass panels on either side of the front door. Hoping to find a letter from the American bookseller whom I'd asked to locate some elusive volumes, I paused to examine the mail spread out over the battered Regency table. That was a bad mistake. Mrs. Wellington came bustling out in old felt slippers and soiled print dress, plump and robust, her steel-gray hair tightly rolled on old-fashioned tin curlers.

"There's *men* in your flat!" she exclaimed.

"Really?"

I wasn't at all surprised. Mandy's handsome male chums had a habit of dropping in at odd hours, making themselves right at home if we happened to be out. One unemployed actor had camped a whole month in our living room, sleeping on the sofa. As he was cheerful, amusing, and a marvelous cook, I hadn't complained. Mandy and I had eaten splendid meals that month, and the flat was always spotlessly clean when we got home.

"Oh, not the *usual* kind," Mrs. Wellington added hastily. "These two are wearin' suits and 'ave *haircuts.* You could have knocked me over with a feather when they marched in and asked for you. I told 'em you weren't in, but they insisted on waitin'."

"Indeed?"

"Miss Amanda wasn't in, either, but I showed 'em up to your flat and let 'em in with my passkey. I run a perfectly respectable 'ouse, always 'ave, and I didn't want 'em 'anging around my foy-yeah, alarmin' the other tenants. Sober-lookin' chaps, both of 'em."

"Do you know who they are?"

"One of 'em's a lawyer—not that good-lookin' Mr. Raymond what calls for you now 'n' then. This one's much older. The other one's a *copper!* Ever so grim-lookin', a big, blond brute. I wasn't goin' to let 'em into your flat, you see, and then he flashed his *badge!* Stunned, I was. You could 'ave knocked me over with a feather!" Feathers presented a constant threat to Mrs. Wellington. "My 'ealth isn't all that strong, you know, dear, and when 'e flipped out 'is wallet and showed me that badge, I felt palpitations in my chest. I thought 'e was going to *raid* the place—"

"I wonder what they want," I said, frowning. That was a mistake, too, giving my redoubtable landlady an opportunity to launch into another of her monologues.

"I wouldn't know, dear, but they look like they mean *business.* I do hope you're not in any sort of trouble, but coppers don't come callin' just to pass the time of day. It probably 'as somethin' to do with those friends of Miss Amanda's. Rowdy lot, they are, and anything but respectable. One of 'em stole my doormat just last week—I'm addin' the cost of it to your rent, incident'ly. Always stompin' up and down the stairs like a bunch of 'ooligans, that lot, drinkin' and carryin' on. That one who wears leather jackets and rides th' motorscooter, a criminal type if I ever seen one. I've told 'er over and over again, I run a respectable 'ouse, and—"

"I'd better go up and see what they want, Mrs. Wellington."

"Want me to come with you?" she asked eagerly.

"That won't be necessary."

"Oh . . ." Her small pink mouth pursed with disappointment, a crestfallen look in her wide blue eyes. "Well, dear, if you need any 'elp, you just 'oller and I'll come runnin'. Coppers 'ave no respect these days, clubbin' them students night and day and menacin' the public. They 'ave no right to come bargin' in 'ere to terrorize a sweet child like you. I feel I should warn you—that blond brute looked mean. 'E probably 'as a billy club 'idden under 'is jacket—"

Paying no heed to Mrs. Wellington's dire warnings, I hurried upstairs and opened the door of our flat. I had never seen either of the men before. They were sitting on the sofa, talking quietly, and both of them rose as I stepped inside—the blond giant in one athletic bound, the older man with considerable effort. He was at least sixty, tall and gaunt, with thinning silver hair, a complexion like wrinkled parchment, and sober brown eyes. His lips were thin, pressed in a grim line, and in his neat black suit and navy blue tie he looked like nothing so much as a prosperous funeral director.

"Miss Lynn Morgan?" he said.

"Yes?"

"Niece of Miss Daphne Morgan?"

"That's right."

"I'm Clive Hampton," he said in a sepulchral voice, "your aunt's solicitor, and this is Sergeant Duncan from our local police station."

Sergeant Duncan nodded, looking extremely ill at ease. He was a towering six foot four, with wavy blond hair, celestial blue eyes, and an embarrassed expression on his handsome young face. The tweedy brown suit fit his lean, muscular frame much too tightly, straining at the shoulders, and his gaudy red-and-maroon tie was improperly knotted. Although he was undeniably manly, and possessed enough strength to subdue the most formidable opponent, there was, nevertheless, an air of schoolboy innocence that was as charming as it was refreshing.

"I'm very pleased to meet you," I said.

A delicate pink flush mounted Sergeant Duncan's lean cheeks. He lowered his heavy brows in an effort to look suitably stern, but succeeded only in appearing all the more boyish and endearing. Clive Hampton cleared his throat. He looked uncomfortable, too.

"You're both from the village?"

"That's right, Miss Morgan," Hampton said.

"Is it about Aunt Daphne?"

"I'm afraid so."

"So she's gotten into another of her scrapes," I said. "I thought as much when she called, but I didn't expect the police to be involved. What is it this time? Poaching? Disturbing the peace? Assault and battery? Am I expected to provide bail money, or—"

"It's a bit more serious," Hampton said grimly.

"Oh?"

"Murder."

"She's killed someone?"

The sergeant shifted his weight uneasily, looking as though he wished the floor would open up beneath him. Hampton gave him a questioning look, and Sergeant Duncan nodded, his blue eyes filled with misery.

"I'm afraid there's no way to break it gently, Miss Morgan," Hampton began. He hesitated, wondering how to phrase it.

"She's dead, isn't she?" I didn't recognize my own voice.

He nodded. "Her body was found night before last, after midnight. She had been stabbed several times. She was in the front hall, at the foot of the stairs . . ."

I didn't say anything. I merely smiled. This was exactly like a scene from one of Mandy's thrillers, I thought, quite unreal. Aunts aren't murdered, not in real life. They were just playing an elaborate joke, and in a moment they would both burst into gales of hearty laughter.

Neither did. Clive Hampton looked funereal, and Sergeant Duncan seemed extremely distressed.

My knees seemed to give way. Duncan took my arm, led me over to a chair, and pushed me into it with gentle firmness, carefully avoiding my eyes. Several minutes of strained silence ensued, and then I looked up at them.

"Are you all right, miss?" the sergeant asked. It was the first time he had spoken. His voice was deep, and he had an unmistakable Scots brogue.

"I'm fine now. Please forgive me for—"

"We understand, miss. Perfectly normal reaction."

"She—she was *murdered?*"

"I was assigned to bring you the unhappy news, miss."

"Do they have any idea who—"

"The inquest will be held tomorrow, but it's just a legal technicality. We know who did it. One of her neighbors, Colonel March. They'd been quarreling for weeks, the whole village knows that, and night before last he popped over to her house and . . ." He hesitated, looking pained. "After he did it he went home and blew his brains out. We found the murder weapon at his side, still smeared with her blood. It's an open-and-shut case, no question about it."

"I—I see."

Sergeant Duncan fell silent, and Clive Hampton took over. Reaching for a briefcase I hadn't noticed before, he sat down, opened it, and spread a sheaf of paper over the table. I only half listened as he told me about my aunt's will. With the exception of a few bequests to rather eccentric charities, she had left me everything, including the house and all its contents. He explained in a clear, precise voice, but I simply couldn't concentrate. After several minutes of his dry, monotonous rambling, I must have looked exceedingly distracted, for Sergeant Duncan frowned and laid a hand on Hampton's shoulder.

"Can't you see she's in no shape to listen to this dribble?" His voice was firm, full of surprising authority. "The lass has had a shock. You can give her all the particulars later."

"Of course," Hampton muttered. "Thoughtless of me . . ." He began to stuff the papers back into his briefcase.

"Thank you," I said quietly.

I got out of the chair, slightly dazed but steady on my feet. There was an air of unreality about all this. I knew it wasn't a joke, knew my aunt had indeed been murdered in that particularly horrible fashion, but I was unable to assimilate it. I had been thinking about her constantly ever since that hysterical telephone call, and I realized with a shock that the murderer might well have been there in the house at the very moment she had called.

"Colonel March," I said in a strained voice. "I—I think I remember him. Was he a blustering old gentleman with a hearing aid?"

Sergeant Duncan nodded, miserable.

"He was always riding his bicycle up and down the lanes, and—and he bred Pekineses, I remember. He wanted to give me one when I was seven, but Aunt Daphne wouldn't let me keep it. He and Aunt Daphne were always fighting, but he was terribly fond of her. I just can't believe he—"

"He went berserk, miss," Sergeant Duncan said gently. "This has been a very unpleasant task. I'm sorry we had to be the bearers of such unhappy news, but my superior felt it would be better this way."

"I understand."

"You'll probably want to sell the place," Hampton said, fastening his briefcase and standing up. "The house isn't much, tumbling down, in fact, but the property itself is quite valuable, with real estate selling for what it does today. I may be able to find a buyer for you. We can discuss that when you come down to Devon."

I looked up, confused.

"For the funeral," he added.

"Oh—yes, of course. What—"

"I took it upon myself to make all the arrangements, feeling you would probably want it that way. Your aunt left specific instructions. If you'd care to—"

"No, I'm sure you've handled everything properly."

"Day after tomorrow," he informed me. "Three o'clock, at the Chapel. Vicar Peckinpah will be officiating."

"We'd best shove off," Sergeant Duncan said uncomfortably. "When you get to the village, Miss Morgan, my superior would like to have a few words with you. The inquest will be over by then, and he'll . . . uh . . . give you all the details."

"I'll stop by the station," I promised.

"Would you like me to make reservations for you at the inn?" Hampton inquired.

"No. I—I'll stay at the house. I don't suppose there's any reason why I can't?"

"None at all. You'll probably want to take inventory, anyway. Much of the furniture is antique, might fetch a good price on the market. If you'd like for me to contact some buyers . . ."

"I'll think about that later, Mr. Hampton."

I showed the men out. Sergeant Duncan was apologetic, more than ever like a shy, overgrown schoolboy who just happened to have the physique of a soccer star. His wavy blond hair was unruly, and relief

showed all over his handsome face as he stepped out
onto the landing. He tugged nervously at the gaudy
red-and-maroon tie. Hampton looked slightly disappointed, much more concerned with his documents
and deeds than with my aunt's demise. Although he
was undoubtedly efficient, I was surprised that someone as bombastic and vitriolic as Daphne had tolerated
him.

I closed the door behind them and turned to stare
vacantly at the living room. The shock had worn off,
and a curious calm possessed me. I was deeply sad-
dened by Daphne's death, and horrified at the way it
had happened, but I felt no sense of great loss. During
the past thirteen years she had been almost a stranger
to me, a pathetic old woman who barged noisily into
my life only on rare occasions. Frowning, I stepped
over to the telephone. I would have to leave for Devon
almost immediately. There was much to do, no time to
brood. I phoned Lloyd at his office, and my voice
seemed to belong to someone else as I told him about
the murder. I might have been reciting a weather bul-
letin.

"You sound peculiar," he said in a worried voice.

"I'm perfectly all right, Lloyd."

"Look, I've got several things that have to be
taken care of here before I can get away. I'll come as
soon as I can."

"Marvelous."

"Lynn, I think you should go to bed. You
sound—"

"Don't be absurd. I have to start packing."

I hung up. Mandy came in a short while later.
Clothes were spread all over my bed, and I was stuffing
them into a suitcase.

"Sudden trip, pet?" she inquired, leaning in the
doorway of my bedroom.

"Very sudden. Aunt Daphne's been murdered."

Mandy was marvelous. She didn't so much as

raise an eyebrow. Nor did she bombard me with questions.

"I have to go down to Devon," I explained.

"You can't make the trip alone, Lynn. I'll go with you."

"I don't know how long I might be there, Mandy. I'll have to dispose of the house and sell the furniture and—"

"I have nothing but time. One of the joys of being unemployed."

"It—it won't be much fun."

"That's what you think," she said lightly. "You know how I adore murders. At last I'm actually involved in one. Let me help you with the packing, pet. You're botching it up."

"I—I feel rather strange."

"That's what's known as delayed reaction. Why don't you go brew us a pot of tea? I'll do this. Such lovely undies, darling. When did you buy them? Don't just *stand* there, Lynn. Go make the tea."

Later, sitting in the living room with our teacups, I told Mandy all I had learned. She was quiet and thoughtful, an intelligent look in her velvety brown eyes. She made no comment, but I could tell that she was examining the story from every possible angle.

"The phone call," I said quietly. "She must have been . . ." I couldn't finish the sentence.

"Yes," Mandy replied.

"What a terrible thing to have happened. She was a hateful, thoroughly unlovable old woman, constantly involved in lawsuits, constantly feuding. Many people must have longed to murder her over the years, but . . ." I shook my head, staring down at my teacup without seeing it.

"They're certain who did it?" she asked.

"Sergeant Duncan said it was an open-and-shut case. Colonel March must have gone berserk, he said. They—they found the knife at his side."

"Very tidy," she remarked.

"What do you mean?"

"Nothing, pet. Nothing at all."

"At least this proves there was no connection between Aunt Daphne's phone call and the—the others."

"I suppose it does."

She sounded unconvinced.

Setting her teacup down, Mandy still wore a thoughtful expression. A tiny frown made a delicate line between her brows, and her eyes seemed unusually dark. After a moment she stood up, sighing, tossing her long golden hair like a cinema queen.

"Well, I guess I'd better start my packing. I've no *idea* what to carry. Incidentally, how are we going?"

"By train, I suppose. I hadn't really thought—"

"Why don't we drive? I can borrow Brent's car. He never uses it, and we might need one after we arrive. You said the house is isolated."

"Very. It's over a mile from the village, surrounded by woods."

"Lovely."

"Mandy, you're not actually worried?"

"Of course not. I *adore* isolated old houses."

"It isn't as if the murderer were still—"

"Such a shame, really," she said gaily, "but perhaps we'll find something else to amuse us."

"You're incorrigible, Mandy." I smiled despite myself.

"I know, pet, but is there really any reason why we should be solemn and *grim?* There's no need to be hypocritical about it."

"None whatsoever."

"We must keep up our spirits."

"Definitely," I replied, playing along.

"I'd better call Brent right away. His Rolls is ancient and dreadfully battered, but it runs like a dream. I'll have him bring it around tonight so we can pack it.

He can help us with the luggage. We'll take a picnic lunch and eat on the road, and you'd better bring along your typewriter, too, since you don't know how long we'll be gone. I wonder if I'll need my bikini." The trip already began to sound like a lark, with Mandy's bright enthusiasm erasing the reason behind it.

It was after seven when Lloyd arrived, and although he did his best to conceal it, I could tell that he was extremely worried. In dark gray suit and navy blue tie, he looked even more sober than usual. Still holding the briefcase he had brought directly from the office, he solemnly explained the unexpected conference that had kept him so late. Lloyd's mouth tightened with disapproval when he spied the lanky, raven-haired fellow in sweatshirt and jeans who lolled casually on our sofa.

Brent grinned. His ugly, magnetic face was instantly recognizable to millions because of his success on television as Roger Stone, the hard-hitting private eye who treated his women rough, his enemies even rougher. The role required considerable skill, as Brent was, by nature, lazy, amiable, and, in Mandy's words, an absolute lamb. He had arrived early in order to take Mandy out to dinner before helping us pack the car.

I performed introductions. Brent waved breezily, and Lloyd gave a curt nod. He was dismayed to find me so calm. I had taken a long, hot bath and changed into one of my nicest dresses. Mandy's chatter had been therapeutic, as she had intended it to be, and I felt almost normal as Lloyd and I left to go to a quiet restaurant nearby. He was silent in the taxi, preoccupied. It wasn't until we had taken our table and ordered that he finally questioned me about the murder. My voice was calm. The shock was over, and I could be objective now. Lloyd frowned. Although he realized it was necessary, he didn't like the idea of my going to Devon, particularly after I told him about Aunt Daphne's incoherent phone call.

"I'll be perfectly all right," I assured him.

"This disturbs me, Lynn."

"It's not very pleasant, granted, but there's no reason why you should be disturbed."

"What if the police made a mistake? What if this Colonel March didn't murder her after all? It's possible, you know. These country police aren't nearly as efficient as they should be. Bumpkins, most of them, sloppy in performing their duties. No, I don't like it. Two girls alone in an isolated house—"

"You're being absurd, Lloyd."

"I keep thinking of those damned phone calls."

I sighed wearily. He reached across the table and took my hand.

"Look, I'm sorry. I can't help worrying about you. You're all I've got, luv. I feel responsible for you."

"I can take care of myself."

"I seriously doubt that. You're far too innocent and trusting."

"You're wrong. I'm perfectly—"

He released my hand as the waiter brought our food. We talked about inconsequential things during the meal, but there was an underlying tension that made us both uncomfortable. The night was lovely as we stepped out of the restaurant, the pavements damp, reflecting blurred pools of color from the red and green and blue neon lights. As it was only a few blocks back to the flat, I suggested we walk. Lloyd agreed, wrapping an arm around my shoulders. An old woman in a shapeless gray dress and tattered blue shawl was selling violets on the corner. Lloyd paused to buy a bunch, but he handed it to me without comment, and his manner robbed the gesture of much of its intent. Romantic Lloyd would never be.

We walked on in silence. A group of bright, chattering young people spilled out of a discotheque, scat-

tering around us like a flock of colorful birds. Lloyd
gripped his briefcase firmly. We passed a row of cine-
mas with garish posters, passed pharmacies and tightly
locked shops with rolled awnings and steel mesh
stretched across dimly lit display windows. Lloyd's
arm tightened around my shoulders as we walked
down the dark street that led to the square. We
stopped beside the wrought-iron fence, directly across
the street from the flat. Behind us the dark trees rustled. We stood just outside the radius of light from the
street lamp, but I could see his face clearly.

"I guess we won't see the Stoppard play after all,"
I said.

"You think *that* matters?"

"You went to so much trouble, making all those
arrangements."

"That's unimportant. I still don't fancy the idea
of your going down there, Lynn."

"It's something I have to do."

"I realize that. Damn, if only I didn't have to be
in court for the next two days. There's no way I can
get out of it. If it weren't for that, I'd go with you. I'll
come down as soon as I can."

"There's no need for that."

"Someone has to look after your interests. I don't
trust this Hampton chap you told me about. I'll want
to study the documents before you sign anything, and
I'll need to examine the property, too, and see that it's
properly evaluated before you make any move to sell.
These things can be tricky."

"You're all business, aren't you?"

"What's that supposed to mean?"

"Nothing. I was merely being bitchy."

"You think I'm unfeeling, don't you?"

"I didn't say that."

"You damned well implied it."

"I'd better go in," I said.

"Not just yet!"

Lloyd set down his briefcase, pulled me into his arms, and kissed me angrily, displaying a vigor he'd never shown before. I was startled and, ultimately, pleased. His arms held me tightly, his mouth seeking and demanding. When he released me, we were both a little breathless. Lloyd scowled and held me away from him.

"I'm human, you know! Dull, stodgy, serious-minded, granted, but I happen to love you. I may not come on like that actor who was lounging about upstairs. I may not be devastating and clever, but I do love you, and don't you ever forget it!"

"I won't, Lloyd."

He let go of me, looking suddenly helpless and thoroughly miserable. I was surprised, for I had never imagined there was anything vulnerable about Lloyd. He kept tight control over himself, but I had just glimpsed another Lloyd, one not nearly so rigid, not nearly so sure of himself. The glimpse was a fleeting one. Smoothing down the lapels of his jacket and picking up the briefcase, he stepped back into character. A few locks of hair had fallen across his forehead. I brushed them back. He stood stiffly unresponsive.

"I haven't been very good company tonight," I said.

"That's perfectly understandable, under the circumstances. We've both been on edge."

"I do appreciate you, Lloyd. Honestly."

He did not reply, still a bit sullen.

"Are you coming up?" I asked.

He shook his head. "I have some briefs to go over. I want you to call me tomorrow night without fail, and I want you to keep me informed of any new developments. I'll try to get down." He unbent enough to give me a quick, perfunctory kiss. "No need to call a taxi. I'll catch one at the thoroughfare. Good-bye, luv. Be careful."

He walked briskly away, vanishing into the dark-

ness, his footsteps ringing loudly in the night silence. I
went on upstairs, deftly eluding Mrs. Wellington, who
had several dozen questions to ask. Mandy and Brent
came in around ten, along with three other hearty
males they'd picked up somewhere or other. Brent carried a huge wicker basket brimming over with expensive gourmet items. Mandy had a bag of oranges. With
four robust males to assist, packing the car was simple.
Then, somehow or other things got out of hand.
George arrived, and then Craig, and then Randy, and a
short while later the male cast members of a West End
revue came trooping up the stairs. The farewell party
lasted until one. At five o'clock in the morning,
Mandy and I climbed sleepily into the car. We reached
the outskirts of London just as dawn began to break.

4

MANDY TOOK an orange from the bag and began to peel it with studied nonchalance. "I don't mean to *nag*, pet, but we've been on this wretched back road forever. I realize this is your old stomping ground and all that, but are you quite sure you know where you're going?"

"Of course. Cooper's Green is just a few more miles."

"I'll believe it when we get there," she said lazily. "You *do* see that lorry, luv?"

"I see it."

"Just wanted to be sure. Try not to run it off the road."

As we rumbled past, Mandy waved at the startled driver. Finishing her orange, she settled back in her seat, and sighed contentedly. It had been a pleasant trip, the day sun-spangled, the sky a clear, pure blue. It was good to be getting away from the city, and, despite our reason for leaving, there was a holiday air. In the decrepit, much-battered Rolls, the back seat piled high with food, books, baggage, a typewriter, and bulging gray cardboard files, Mandy and I might have been highly sophisticated Gypsies. As her driving was highly erratic and extremely hazardous, Mandy had been happy to let me take the wheel. After declaring herself enchanted with the countryside, she promptly ignored it—and picked up another Brad Carter thriller. We had lunched at the side of the road, snacking in between, and neither of us had so much as mentioned the murder.

It was almost five before we reached Devon. We drove past a sprawling, majestic gray stone mansion set far back from the road, surrounded by formal gardens. It was over three hundred years old, festooned with turrets and battlements, rich with history and tradition. Bright red flowers grew in pots placed at intervals along the marble balustrade around the patio, and several giant oaks cast cool shadows over the lush green lawns. It looked like something out of a guidebook, and, indeed, tourists could tour it for a fee during certain months of the year.

"What a lovely place," Mandy remarked, turning to look back. "Do you know who owns it?"

"The local Lord. He owns most of the land around here, as well as the textile mill that employs many of the villagers. I don't remember his name, but I *do* remember his son."

"Oh?"

"A perfectly horrid little boy. He used to chase me through the woods at least once a week. One time he tied me to a tree and left me there to starve."

"Really?" She was fascinated. "Whatever happened to him?"

"He eventually went away to school. I think there was an older brother, but I never met him."

"It must have been lovely growing up around here," Mandy said thoughtfully. "All these trees, everything so quaint—"

"It was hell, believe me."

We rounded a curve and, in the distance, caught our first glimpse of Cooper's Green. The textile mill was over a mile away, its chunky gray bulk and huge smokestacks hidden behind a hill. Fortunately, it did nothing to mar the beauty of the town. The river that twisted its way through Cooper's Green had several old stone bridges spanning it, and there were many trees to shade the pavements. Small and thriving, the village was undeniably modern, but there was a turn-of-the-century charm, despite the cinema, the Wool-worth's, the television antennas perched atop roomy Victorian houses and cottages mellowed with age. There were two historic old churches, and the shops and business establishments surrounding the square were uniformly faded, brown and yellow and tan, adorned with peeling white gingerbread woodwork. People turned to stare as we drove through the village. We must have presented an incongruous sight in the battered old Rolls.

"What a divine little tea shop," Mandy ex-claimed. "I'll bet they actually serve cucumber sand-wiches and frosted cakes. Look at that character strolling into the pub. This is enchanting, Lynn, so serene. Of course, I wouldn't want to *live* here."

"Perish the thought."

"Where are we going?"

"I promised Sergeant Duncan I'd stop by the sta-tion house. I think the constable wants to talk to me."

"That should be interesting."

"Mandy, you—you'll behave, won't you?"

"Whatever do you mean?"

"You won't ask a lot of questions, play private detective?"

"*Me?* I just came along for the ride, pet."

The red brick station house with its sloping roof was surrounded by oak trees. Untidy beds of daffodils grew in front. Although there were bars over the rear windows, it looked cozy and inviting with the bicycles parked at one side and a shaggy brown-and-white sheepdog snoozing contentedly on the front steps. He lifted his head and gave us an inquisitive look as we got out of the car, then yawned and went back to sleep. Mandy stretched, the skirt of her yellow dress billowing. She looked fresh and glorious, whereas I was travel-worn and weary, my own dress deplorably wrinkled. We had to step over the dog as we entered.

The tan plaster walls were adorned with sundry official notices, clipboards hanging on nails, and two homemade posters, one announcing the jumble sale to be held in the basement of the church in two days, the other proclaiming an amateur-theater production of *She Stoops to Conquer* opening May first at the school auditorium. A tarnished silver coffeepot perched on a marble-topped table, a bag of doughnuts beside it, and there were two desks littered with papers and telephones and wire baskets. A huge, dusty green short-wave radio stood behind one of them. A door opened onto a hall leading to the back rooms and cells. The place seemed empty. Through the open windows we could hear bees buzzing. The dog snored loudly.

"Overwhelming activity," Mandy remarked, "but then, I don't suppose a village like this has much crime, the murder notwithstanding."

"They have the usual trouble with teen-agers, I imagine, and Saturday-night brawls. The mill hands sometimes get restless, if I recall, and of course there are feuds."

"Charming place," Mandy said. "Not at all what I expected. Look at that divine calendar. I adore kittens who play with yarn."

"Don't be bitchy."

"But I *do*, I assure you."

There was a rattling noise from the back of the building, then heavy footsteps sounded in the hall. Mandy and I looked up as a plump, middle-aged man stepped into the office. He wore baggy brown trousers and a rumpled brown-and-tan checked sportcoat, his green tie askew. His plump cheeks were rosy, his blue eyes amiable, and his short sandy hair was liberally sprinkled with gray. He undoubtedly loved dogs and children, I thought, and probably spent a great deal of time puttering about in his garden.

"Thought I heard someone out here," he said. "Miss Morgan?"

"I'm Miss Morgan. This is my friend Amanda Hunt."

"Pleased to meet you both, though I'm sorry it had to be under these unhappy circumstances. I'm Constable Plimpton, out of uniform, I'm afraid, but it's being let out. Doughnuts are my downfall. Sergeant Duncan's just popped out to fetch a fresh bag. These are stale. I was in back, taking Old Mike his tobacco. He's our only lodger at present. Likeable old chap, but he *will* go setting his traps in Lord Cooper's woodland. Been a poacher all his life." Constable Plimpton shook his head. "I 'spect you'll want to know all the details of the case, Miss Morgan. Dreadful thing, dreadful, first murder we've had in Cooper's Green since 1948. Old Colonel March seemed such a harmless fellow—eccentric, of course, but then, most oldsters are. Bred Pekineses, he did, won several prizes. Collected old china. Who would have thought he'd go off his rocker like that . . ." A deep frown furrowed his brow. "Reggie March was the last person I'd nominate as likely to murder someone, but facts are facts."

"Are you quite sure he did it?" Mandy inquired casually.

"Oh, no question about it. He was seen tearing out of the house that night—young Cooper saw him. Cooper found your aunt's body, Miss Morgan, told us over the phone he'd seen the Colonel running away, and by the time we reached his cottage Reggie March had already shot himself. Put a bullet through his head, he did, not a pleasant sight to behold. Sprawled out in front of the fireplace, his gun on one side, the knife he'd used to stab Miss Daphne on the other."

"Did he leave a note?" I asked.

"No need for one, miss, not hardly. The facts spoke for themselves. They'd been quarreling, you see, him and Miss Daphne. Had a big feud going for weeks.

He was . . . uh . . . more or less courting her, took her to all the church socials and so on. They'd had a falling out because she wanted to go to an auction and he insisted on staying home to tend to one of his bitches who was having pups. Uh . . . when Miss Daphne was crossed she could be pretty vindictive. Quite a few people have cause to remember that, myself included. No disrespect, Miss Morgan, but your aunt wasn't exactly the most endearing lady in these parts."

"I'm well aware of that."

"The inquest was held this morning. They reached the same verdict we did. Not much question but what they would. Case closed. There are a few details I need to discuss with you, Miss Morgan, and a couple of papers I'd like for you to sign. Sit down, both of you. Here, let me clear the magazines off that chair. Young Doug *will* leave them scattered about . . ."

He gathered up a stack of magazines devoted to health foods and weight lifting, dumped them on the table, and then sat down behind his desk. Putting on a pair of reading glasses, he began to search through the piles of paper in front of him. I sat down at the chair he had cleared, but Mandy preferred to lean against the other desk, a speculative look in her eyes. She wasn't at all satisfied. That was quite obvious. She listened carefully as Constable Plimpton explained several points and read various reports in a tedious, official voice. When he finished, I signed the required papers, as relieved as he was.

"Unpleasant, this, most unpleasant," he muttered, slipping off the glasses and shaking his head slowly. "Reggie March, the last person in the world I'd have thought . . . You just never know. Seen a lot of peculiar things in my time, miss, and that's a fact." He shook his head again, ruffled the papers on his desk and sighed. Business behind him, social amiability replaced it. "Are you going to be staying long, Miss Morgan?"

"I don't know. I'll have to see about selling the house."

"I reckon Clive Hampton will help you there. Not the most cheerful man I know, but quite efficient. He told you about the funeral arrangements, did he?"

"Yes—yes, he did."

"The whole village'll show up, I suspect. Not much happens in a place this small, and the murder caused quite a sensation, as you can imagine. Everyone knew your Aunt Daphne, of course, and everyone knew the Colonel. Both of 'em were more or less local characters. Both will be missed. Your aunt had her faults, miss, that I won't deny, but she kept things lively with her shenanigans."

"I imagine she did."

"Great sportswoman. Sat a horse with real distinction. Of course, that was a long time ago, but how well I remember her in that red coat, hair flying in all directions as she jumped a fence. I think I remember you, too, Miss Morgan. Didn't you live with her a while?"

I nodded. "My father and I came to live with her when I was five. He left for Australia soon after, and I stayed on with Aunt Daphne until I was thirteen."

Constable Plimpton gave me a peculiar look, as though what I said had puzzled him. "Uh . . . yes, seems like I remember that. Was a long time ago. Will you and your friend be staying at the inn?"

"We plan to stay at the house."

He looked slightly dismayed. "Well . . . I reckon there's no reason why you shouldn't. Perfectly safe. Young women these days have a lot more gumption, aren't so easily shook. Everything's in working order, lights, water, gas, and . . . uh . . . the bloodstains have been removed. I think young Cooper stayed on to keep an eye on things—"

Before I could ask him who young Cooper might

be, the dog outside gave a happy yelp and bounded heavily into the office. He was followed immediately by a handsome blond giant carrying a bag of fresh doughnuts. I hardly recognized Sergeant Duncan, so different did he look in his tailored dark blue uniform. It fit glove-tight, emphasizing broad shoulders and slender waist, trousers displaying long, muscular legs. His black leather boots were highly glossed. His silver badge was shiny. He had an air of authority and confidence that had been missing when he was in civilian clothes. He took the dog by the collar and put him back outside, heaving a manly sigh. Turning around, he stared in confusion when he noticed Mandy leaning nonchalantly against his desk.

"So there you are!" Plimpton cried. "It took you long enough to fetch 'em, lad. I suppose you were flirting with that flashy piece at the bakery. What's her name—Alice? Up to no good, that one. You'd best watch your step, Duncan."

Mandy's yellow dress was cut exceedingly low, and Sergeant Duncan was unable to take his eyes off her. He merely nodded, not hearing a word his superior said. Mandy smiled as only she could, lifting one brow in a pronounced arch.

"You've met Miss Morgan," Plimpton continued. "This is her friend, Miss Hunt."

"Hello," Mandy said.

Sergeant Duncan lowered his brows, trying to look stern. He gave her a curt nod and marched over to the table to put down the bag of doughnuts. He missed the table. The bag plopped loudly onto the floor. Blushing, he bent to retrieve them.

"What kept you, lad?" Plimpton asked.

"I stopped by the school auditorium to see how they were coming along with painting the backdrop. It's almost done. Lady Cooper's lending us some authentic period furniture. Sporting of her, considering how clumsy some of us are."

"Doug's an active member of our amateur theater group," the constable explained. "He has the leading role in the new play, this boy. Not much of an actor, but the ladies like to look at him. Did Mark Antony last year, and three women swooned when he came out in 'is short tunic and sandals. I expect him to be leaving the force for the film studios any day now."

"Not bloody likely," Duncan said gruffly, painfully embarrassed.

Although he was in his late twenties, Douglas Duncan had a clean, boyish freshness that would be vastly appealing to any woman. Perhaps it was those innocent blue eyes and the thick, wavy blond hair. Perhaps it was his shyness, so unusual in a man his size with such obvious physical prowess, and the total lack of sophistication. There was something immediately endearing about him, and I could tell that Mandy was enchanted.

"I'm sure you're very talented," she said.

Another blush tinted his cheeks. "It's just something I do to pass the time."

"Quite the ladies' man, Doug is. Comes on shy and helpless, but don't let that innocent look fool you, miss. He's got half the lasses in town breaking their hearts over 'im."

Sergeant Duncan scowled, giving his chief an angry look.

"Come on, lad. A little razzing never hurt anyone. A fine boy, this one. Best man on the force, takes his work very seriously. Judo expert, too, though he rarely gets a chance to use it. You can feel safe with Douglas Duncan on the job." Clearly, the constable was very fond of his young sergeant.

Plimpton got to his feet. I reached for my purse and stood up. Mandy leaned against the desk. The sergeant's arms were folded across his chest, his head tilted to one side. He looked at Mandy as a small boy might look at a shiny new toy in the window of a shop.

"You going to be at the old house?" he inquired.

Mandy nodded.

"I'll come out after I get off duty and have a look 'round, see that everything's all right."

"How sweet of you."

"What'd I tell you?" Plimpton said, a twinkle in his eyes. "Very fast worker, Sergeant Duncan. If he starts pestering you too much, Miss Hunt, you just give me the word. I'll keep him in line."

Sergeant Duncan followed us outside. Opening the car door for Mandy, he watched her climb in. She accomplished this with considerable grace, showing an inordinate amount of leg.

"How tall *are* you?" she asked.

"Six foot four," he said proudly. "You like tall men?"

"I *adore* them."

No one opened the car door for me, but I was accustomed to being ignored when Mandy was around. Sergeant Duncan closed the door on Mandy's side and stepped back, looking very stalwart and impressive in his uniform. The sheepdog bounded about him, trying to get his attention, but young Douglas had eyes only for Mandy. She rolled down her window and waved as we pulled away, and then she sat back, extremely pleased with herself.

"Divine," she said. "Utterly."

"He's quite attractive," I agreed.

"*Sweet*. That's the only word to describe him. Maddeningly sexy, of course, and not nearly as innocent as he looks."

"Interested?"

"Not this trip," she said firmly. "I intend to relax and do a lot of reading. It gets rather tiresome—all these men hanging about. Naturally I'll be *polite* to him . . ."

I smiled, certain we would be seeing quite a lot of the sergeant during the time we were here.

We passed the green with its bronze horseman rearing on a marble pedestal, pigeons roosting cozily behind him, colorful flowers blooming in neat square beds. Across the way stood the vast brown church with shadowy courtyard and a copper spire rearing above the oak boughs. A sign in front announced the jumble sale, and several busy-looking women were unloading a wagon heaped high with old lamps and birdcages and discarded clothing. We drove over a stone bridge and down a lane of small cottages, several with thatched roofs, each with its own garden. Mandy was amazed to see a flock of geese waddling imperiously along the side of the road, but I assured her it wasn't an unusual sight in these parts. Many of the villagers still kept poultry, and grew their own vegetables as well.

Leaving the village behind, we followed a poorly paved road that led through cultivated fields with cows grazing behind low stone walls. In a few minutes the fields were behind us, too, and heavy woods lined either side of the road. I drove slowly because of the bumps, but even so the Rolls groaned in protest. Peculiar noises came from beneath the floorboards. I hoped we would be able to return Brent's car with all its parts still intact. Mandy sighed, smoothing down her yellow skirt.

"What did you think of Constable Plimpton?" she asked casually.

"He seemed rather nice."

"Very," she agreed, "but I wouldn't say he was the last word in efficiency. Would you?"

I had to agree that I wouldn't.

"Even *he* seemed to find it hard to believe that Colonel March murdered your aunt. Nice old gentlemen who collect china and breed Pekineses rarely butcher people, no matter how hard they're pressed."

"Evidently he did."

"Evidently," she repeated. "Things aren't always what they appear to be, Lynn."

Swerving to avoid a hole in the middle of the road, I shook my head in resignation, knowing full well that Mandy would have all sorts of theories about the murder. It would be too much to expect for her to accept the obvious solution, the one the authorities had already agreed upon.

"Too many weapons," she said firmly.

"Oh?" I might just as well humor her, I thought.

"If he planned to kill her, why didn't he shoot her? Why did he *stab* her, take the knife back home with him, and then shoot himself? It doesn't add up, Lynn."

"Perhaps not, if this were one of your thrillers. Things aren't always so tidy in real life."

"This is *too* tidy," she continued. "By the time the police got there, everything was neatly wrapped up. An open-and-shut case of murder-suicide, with nothing left dangling. If there had been a note, I might buy it, but there wasn't."

"He didn't need to leave a note. His reasons for killing himself were obvious."

"The motive isn't there, either. *Why* did he kill her? Because they'd had a falling out. Totally absurd. If he were a hot-blooded Latin thirty years old and passionately in love, perhaps, but I hardly think escorting her to a few church socials and bingo games constitutes a grand passion. If even half the things you've told me about your aunt were true, the Colonel was probably relieved to be rid of her. How old *was* he, by the way?"

"I don't know. Seventy, at least."

"A seventy-year-old man commits a crime of passion and then kills himself in a fit of self-remorse? Really, Lynn, someone has to be joking."

"Passion had nothing to do with it," I said. "She

was giving him a very hard time. Aunt Daphne could be extremely vicious. She probably drove the poor man to the point of desperation."

"That's still not motive enough for such a brutal crime."

"He was seen leaving the house that night."

"I know."

"The knife was at his side when they found him. What's more, his fingerprints were on it."

"That doesn't prove a thing," she said stubbornly.

"He went berserk, Mandy."

"That's a very pat explanation. There's no real motive, so everyone simply assumes he went berserk. The police didn't really *investigate*, Lynn. They just accepted things at face value."

Reluctantly, I had to admit that she was right. I tried to make light of all she had said, attributing it to her addiction to sensational fiction, but Mandy was an extremely intelligent person, and there was much food for thought in what she had said. Constable Plimpton was an amiable, easygoing chap, no doubt very popular with the villagers, but he hardly inspired confidence. What if they had made a mistake? What if the Colonel hadn't murdered her . . . Of course he did, I told myself firmly. It was absurd to think otherwise. Mandy could chatter all she liked, but one of us had to remain sensible.

"One other point," she said.

"What's that?"

"The telephone call. That's what really bothers me. She was incoherent, hysterical. She said it was an emergency, that she had something to tell you. Lynn, if she was afraid for her life, why did she call *you?* Why didn't she phone the local police?"

"I don't know, Mandy. The—the call probably had nothing whatsoever to do with the murder."

"Perhaps not."

"I wish you wouldn't carry on like this."

"I suppose I *do* read too many thrillers," she said lightly. "It probably happened just the way they say it did. I certainly hope so. I wouldn't want to think the murderer was still roaming around, not if we intend to stay way off out here." She glanced through the windshield at the thick, leafy trees, their trunks almost hidden by underbrush. "We *are* going to be isolated, aren't we?"

"Very," I said cheerily.

"So many trees—"

"Would you like to turn back?"

"Of course not."

"We could always take rooms at the inn."

"I wouldn't think of it, pet. I'm dying to see the house. Is it really as dark and gloomy as you've described it?"

"It was thirteen years ago. By this time it should be in even worse condition."

"Marvelous. There'll probably still be bloodstains in the hall, too. Do hurry, Lynn. I can hardly wait . . ."

5

THE HOUSE was exactly as I remembered it, only more weathered from thirteen additional years of exposure to sun and damp night air and seasonal storms. Built shortly before the turn of the century, it had all the architectural indulgences of that era, and none of the virtues. Five ornamental gables reared up for no purpose, and the spacious veranda was festooned with Victorian gingerbread woodwork. The house, once white, was now a dismal gray, and the multi-level slate roof was more bronze than green. The drive led around the right side to the carriage house in back, which was in slightly better condition. The lower half had been converted into a modern garage, and an outside wooden staircase led to rooms above it.

I parked the car in front, and Mandy and I climbed out. She seemed enchanted with the place, while admitting that she expected bats to come swooping out of the windows. As we stood there looking up at the house, a distant roll of thunder sounded ominously. The sky, so vividly blue before, was growing darker as gray clouds began to congregate.

"It's got atmosphere," Mandy said, "definitely. It looks like a setting for an old-fashioned horror movie. I do hope there's a damp, shadowy old cellar."

"There is," I assured her. "Attics, too. Are you sure you want to stay here, Mandy?"

"Of course. I think it's ever so exciting, luv. I've never been in a house where a murder was committed.

There's a flash of lightning. It's going to storm. Perfect."

"We don't *have* to stay here, you know."

"I know."

Although she spoke in a light, merry voice, I could see that she had reservations. The house was indeed desolate-looking, and what had happened here just a few days ago made it seem all the more forbidding. It had been sheer folly to come, I realized, but for some perverse reason I was reluctant to go back to the village. That would have been an admission of defeat.

Another rumble of thunder sounded as we moved up the worn wooden steps and onto the shadowy veranda. The floor creaked alarmingly, and there was the sour smell of mildew and decay. The veranda ran around all four sides of the house, with French windows opening onto it. A tarnished brass knocker was attached to the center of the wide, dark oak door. I suddenly realized that I didn't have a key. Mandy solved that problem by turning the brass doorknob and pushing the door open. It swung inward with much groaning of its hinges. As we stepped into the hall, I wondered why the door hadn't been locked.

Enough light streamed through the front windows to reveal the dark parquet floor, the mahogany wainscoting and hideous William Morris wallpaper of brown, orange, and maroon swirls. A chandelier with a blue and red glass shade hung from the high ceiling, and along the right wall the dark staircase with its shabby maroon carpet rose up into shadows. A narrow hall beside the stairs led back into the kitchen regions. I stared at the huge grandfather clock, the heavily carved table, the wingback chairs, one purple, one maroon, both faded. How well I remembered the curtains of heavy burnt-orange velvet looped back on either side of the archways leading into adjoining rooms, the dusty green plants in their Oriental brass planters, the general impression of gloom.

"Cozy," Mandy said blithely. "The table's Jacobean, by the way, and worth a fortune. So is the chandelier. Cecil would go wild." Cecil was an antiques dealer who had an exclusive, frightfully expensive shop in London. Mandy ran her finger along the highly varnished table top. Both of us were tense, though Mandy was trying her best to hide it.

"The house is full of old furniture and Victorian knick-knacks," I remarked in a conversational tone. "There's even a glass case in the sitting room filled with stuffed birds—"

I cut myself short. Mandy was staring at the rusty brown stains near the foot of the staircase. I stared at them too, unable to look away. They were barely discernible against the dark wood, but they were unmistakable. Mandy's cheeks were slightly pale, and I felt suddenly cold. The house seemed to engulf us, walls pressing closer. The grandfather clock ticked with a steady, monotonous rhythm. We both started as the floorboards on the veranda groaned loudly. Mandy seized my hand. We stared at the open door in horrified fascination.

Someone was walking along the veranda. There could be no mistake about it: The footsteps were loud and clear. Whoever it was was making no effort to be stealthy. He was whistling a merry little tune, and the sound was jarring here in the dim hall. He paused a moment, then stepped into the doorway. The light was behind him, making him no more than a dark silhouette. Mandy's hand was crushing mine, and I felt as though my heart had stopped beating.

"Hello, Lynn," he said in a rich, jovial voice. "It's been a long time, what?"

"Who—who are you?" My own voice was trembling.

"Surely you're not frightened? I know you had an

aversion to me when you were a child, but you're a big girl now. I'm actually a rather genial chap. I don't chase girls through the woods any more, I promise." He gave a soft chuckle. "That hasn't been necessary for years and years."

He leaned over and flipped a switch. The chandelier streamed down rays of light that banished the shadows. The man was tall, with a lean, powerful build and unusually wide shoulders. He wore scuffed tennis shoes, black denim trousers, and a loose navy blue jersey with the sleeves shoved up over his elbows. His dark hair was disheveled, tumbling over a tanned forehead, and the full mouth curled amiably at one corner. His eyes were a deep, deep blue, his dark brows oddly slanted, giving him a wry, quizzical look. I remembered that face all too well, but I didn't remember its being quite so devastatingly handsome.

"Remember me?" he inquired.

"I certainly do," I said coldly.

"Is he the one who—" Mandy began.

"He's the one," I told her.

"Bartholomew Cooper, ladies, at your service."

"Bartholomew," Mandy said. "Surely not?"

"My friends call me Bart," he added.

"I'm Amanda Hunt. You seem to know Lynn."

"That I do."

"What are you doing here?" I demanded.

"I happen to live here. Over the carriage house, actually. Your aunt was kind enough to rent me the rooms. I'm paid up until the middle of May, and I saw no real reason to leave. You plan to throw me out?"

"I certainly do."

"My, you *do* hold a grudge, don't you? Yours is a most uncharitable attitude, I must say. After all I've done."

"What have you done, Mr. Cooper?"

"Bart. We're going to be friends. What have I done? For one thing, I've been a marvelous watchdog, running off hordes of teen-agers and curiosity seekers determined to see the scene of the crime and carry off a souvenir or two. For another, when I found out you intended to stay here, I had a crew of women come in and give the place a good cleaning—it still looks like hell, but at least the cobwebs are gone. I also drove to the village and bought a fresh supply of groceries."

"How very generous of you," I said dryly.

"Oh, I made a complete list of my expenditures. I expect to be reimbursed to the penny."

"You will be," I retorted. "How did you know I was coming?"

"Everyone did. Word gets around in a place like Cooper's Green. Duncan and Hampton hadn't been back fifteen minutes before the whole village knew. Hampton told his secretary, who told her best friend, who told her sister, who happens to run the local telephone exchange. You know how it goes. Hard to keep anything a secret in these parts."

"Something puzzles me, Mr. Cooper."

"What's that?"

"*Why* are you living in the carriage house? Aren't you the son of—"

"The second son, alas," he said with mock sadness. "When my dear dad passed on, he left the estate to my brother, Edgar. Rather unsporting of him, I thought, but then, Edgar is level-headed and industrious and solemn, and I've always been something of a black sheep. I needed a place to stay, and the village was too noisy and nosy, so I rented the rooms from Daphne. She was delighted to get the extra money every month. Edgar, I might add, was utterly horrified, though I think he was secretly relieved that I didn't intend to hang around the big house and scandalize the servants."

"That gorgeous home we passed?" Mandy asked.

"Cooper House," he told her. "Great barn of a place, actually. Impossible to heat properly. Really,

Lynn, I wish you'd reconsider. I can be of great service. Besides, I should think you'd feel safer with a man about the place."

"He has a point," Mandy said.

I was forced to agree with her. After seeing the house in all its decaying gloom, I would feel much safer knowing there was a man around, even one as audacious as Bartholomew Cooper, but I had no intention of letting him know that. I didn't like his chummy familiarity, nor the way he stood there with his hands thrust into his pockets as though he owned the place. He had a breezy charm, true, and a raffish, amiable manner most, women would find disarming, but I was, fortunately, immune. I remembered the way he had pursued me through the woods, waving his wooden sword. He hadn't changed all that much, I thought. With his tumbling raven locks, those comically slanting brows and that wide, curling mouth, he still had that devilish look. The deep blue eyes were decidedly sexy, I noticed, irritated at myself.

"What's the verdict?" he asked.

"I—I don't suppose it would do any harm for you to stay on for a few days until I decide what I'm going to do with the house."

"Ripping," he said.

"Understand, you'll stay out of the way."

He grinned, one brow arching. "Worried I might try to revive some of our childhood games?"

"I'm not amused, Mr. Cooper."

"Bart. I told you, I don't chase girls through the woods any more, not unless they're thoroughly amenable to the idea. Quite a few are. You'd be surprised."

"I doubt that," I said crisply.

Bartholomew Cooper brought out all my worst qualities. He made me feel stiff and prudish, which I certainly wasn't. I was on the defensive with him, and I sensed I would always have to keep my guard up. He was obviously accustomed to having women melt into his arms any time he cared to snap his fingers. It was plain to see that women had spoiled him deplorably, and I could understand why Aunt Daphne had taken a fancy to him. She would have found his flippant, irreverent manner utterly delightful. I found it outrageous.

"I had the women get your room ready," he said affably, "the one you stayed in as a child. I took it for granted you'd want that one. The guest bedroom next to it has fresh linen too."

"You took quite a lot for granted, didn't you?"

"Just trying to make myself useful," he replied. "Daphne talked about you quite a lot when she was in her cups, you know. The old girl didn't approve of your life in the wicked city. Mini-skirts. Lipstick. Parties. She left the impression you were something of a swinger."

He was obviously baiting me. I didn't deign to reply. I wondered just what his relationship with Daphne had been. He was certainly familiar with the house. It didn't make sense that such a healthy young man would choose to live way off here, completely isolated, with only a boozy old woman for companionship.

"How long have you lived over the carriage house?" I asked.

"Over a year, off and on."

"Off and on?"

"I spend a lot of time in London," he explained. "Hate the place, I must say, but I keep a flat there out of necessity. When I'm not in London, I stay here."

The answer was evasive, but I didn't pursue it. Mandy was standing with one hand resting lightly on her hip, studying Bartholomew Cooper with a puzzled expression in her eyes. Something was bothering her, I could tell. He had paid very little attention to her, but that wasn't it.

"Let's go on up, Lynn," she said in a rather weary

voice. "Look, luv, why don't you be a lamb and put those muscles to good use? Unload the car for us."

"Glad to," he replied.

I flipped the light switch by the staircase, and we started up. As we reached the landing, I turned to look back. Bartholomew Cooper was watching us with an infuriating grin. In the tight black trousers and navy blue jersey, he looked like a robust college lad just coming in after a rousing game of soccer. He definitely needed a haircut, and those scuffed tennis shoes were preposterous for a man his age. He nodded at me impudently, one brow crooked.

I took Mandy's hand and led her down the dim hall.

"What do you think of him?" I asked.

"A most enigmatic young man," she replied.

"That's for sure."

"I've seen him somewhere before, Lynn."

"Where?"

"I can't remember. It—that face. I've seen it before in connection with something vaguely sinister. Like . . . well, like a movie actor who's played a gangster, only of course he hasn't. The minute I saw him, I knew that face was familiar."

"Are you sure?"

"Positive. Those eyebrows. I wish I could . . . oh well, it'll come to me eventually."

"Maybe I should have—"

"Thrown him out?" she interrupted. "Not at all. I'm rather relieved he's here, if you want to know the truth. This place is definitely Hitchcock, like that house in *Psycho.* I may have my doubts about Mr. Cooper, but he *is* a healthy specimen. A most effective watchdog, I'd say."

"I don't trust him."

"No?"

"His being here doesn't make sense."

"He explained that," Mandy said airily.

"Not to my satisfaction."

"Not to mine either, actually, but then, perhaps we don't know the full story. He might have perfectly logical reasons for wanting isolation while he's in Cooper's Green. He might be writing a book, or—"

"Fat chance," I said acidly.

"Anyway, I'm sure we'll find out more about him. He's rather intriguing."

"That's hardly the word I'd use."

"I know, luv, but then, you're prejudiced."

Mandy could be perfectly maddening at times.

My old bedroom was at the end of the hall, directly across from an enclosed staircase that led up to the attics and down to the back hall. I opened the door and reached for the light switch. Faint yellow light blossomed in the old-fashioned brass wall sconces. The light blue wallpaper with its lilac flowers and jade green leaves was a bit more faded, perhaps, and the polished hardwood floor was darker with age, but the Aubusson runner was just as I remembered it, as were the heavy antique furniture, the tattered blue silk bed canopy. A tarnished silver candelabrum stood on top of the wardrobe, stubs of candles still in its holders. I used to read by candlelight, because Aunt Daphne, ranting about wasting electricity, ordered lights out at eight sharp. A bay window with a window seat covered in lilac velvet looked out over the herb gardens in back of the house. A bookcase stood to one side, crammed with worn, much-read children's books.

I felt an odd sensation, something like nostalgia but with none of the wistfulness, none of the pleasant associations. The skinny little girl with her long braids and enormous eyes who had lived in this room was a stranger to me now, separated by many years. Lonely, restless, fiercely individual, she had been a pensive creature, longing for wider horizons, longing to be noticed by an indifferent world. I wondered how much of her still remained in the woman.

"You look like you've just seen a ghost," Mandy said, breaking into my reverie.

"I think I have," I said pensively.

"I'm not surprised," she replied. "This house is undoubtedly full of them. Let's go see my room. I'm prepared for anything."

"It's really not so bad . . ."

A door opened onto a large dressing room and bath that connected with the adjoining guest room. As we went through, Mandy admired the dark golden fixtures and rust-streaked white marble tub. The guest room was all done in yellow and ivory, musty yellow draperies over the windows, a yellow velvet chaise longue at the foot of the bed. The embossed ivory wallpaper was splitting at the seams. Bed, wardrobe, and dresser were of aged golden oak, the varnish peeling, and the large oval mirror was a murky blue. The room had been lovely once. Now it was funereal.

"Charming," Mandy said lightly. "I already feel right at home." She parted the drapes and threw open the windows.

"There's another bedroom on the other side of the house—"

"This will do nicely. Besides, I want to be within screaming range. I *do* wish the storm would break."

A gust of cold, damp wind swirled into the room, causing the drapes to billow noisily. It was almost dark outside. Thunder still rumbled. A streak of lightning flashed with silver-blue fury, and the trees hurled violent black shadows over the ground. Mandy stood in front of the window, peering out, the wind blowing her long, tawny gold locks. She turned back around, framed by billowing yellow velvet drapes, a wry smile on her lips.

"Just one question," she said.

"Yes?"

"What's a nice girl like me doing in a place like this?"

"Mandy, if you want to—"

"I think it's enchanting, pet. Really. Bela Lugosi would have loved it. Shall we go back down? Your friend Bartholomew has probably brought our things in by now, and I want to get into fresh clothes before the charming sergeant comes. You could use a change yourself. That dress is definitely past its prime."

Our luggage was piled in the middle of the hall as we came downstairs, food basket, bag of oranges, and file boxes beside it. Bartholomew Cooper was coming through the door with the typewriter.

"Where does this go?" he inquired.

"In here," I said, preceding him through a curtained arch that led into the library. "On the desk." I pointed.

The room was filled with the musty odor of dust and glue, old leather and yellowing paper. I turned on one of the tall floor lamps as he set the typewriter in the center of the vast oak desk that dominated one corner of the room. Bookshelves loomed from floor to ceiling, and the large gray marble fireplace was soot-streaked. There was a long brown leather sofa and a matching leather chair, several low tables, a gold and brown globe on a tall brass stand. Faded Oriental rugs were scattered over the dark parquet floor, and uncurtained French windows opened onto the veranda.

"Why the typewriter?" he asked.

"I happen to write," I said primly.

"Yeah, I've read a couple of your things. 'What Every Girl Should Know About Nylon.' A painful experience for me, but then, I suppose the shopgirls eat it up."

"Not that it's any of your business, but I've resigned from the Sunday Supplement. I'm doing a book."

He arched one of those unusual brows, quizzical.

"On the court of Louis the Fourteenth," I added,

"for Philip Ashton-Croft, but then, you probably wouldn't know who he is."

"Probably not," he agreed.

"I'll need my files in here, too. Those mottled gray boxes."

"At your service."

Making a mock bow, he nodded and left the room. He returned a minute later with all three boxes, one stacked on top of another, his head and shoulders invisible. He moved rapidly, blindly, and I let out a little cry, seeing what was going to happen before he even stepped on the edge of the rug. As he put his foot down, the rug slid out from under him and he stumbled. He didn't fall, but the boxes did. Meticulously filed papers, folders, and clippings spilled over the floor like giant confetti, scattering in all directions. He looked down at the litter with abject blue eyes, then at me.

I didn't say a word. I didn't trust myself to speak. Without so much as looking at him, I began to pick up the papers and stack them on the desk, my lips tightly compressed, and after a moment he began helping me. In five minutes we had everything gathered up, the three empty boxes stacked beside the desk. It had taken Mandy and me over a week to get the files in proper order. Now everything was hopelessly jumbled. I was very, very calm, my anger under tight control. Bartholomew Cooper lounged against the desk and picked up one of the folders, examining the contents idly.

"Lauzun," he said breezily. "Unfortunate chap, what? I always felt he got a rotten deal. All those years in prison, just because he happened to love the King's cousin. Must have been hellish for a lively fellow like him."

"What would *you* know about it?"

"Nothing much," he replied, tossing the folder back on the desk. "I remember Vita Sackville-West chatting about him. When I was thirteen or so, Dad dropped in to see Sir Harold at Sissinghurst Castle, took me along. She was writing her biography of La Grande Mademoiselle at the time, recommended a couple of books to me. Can't say I ever read them . . ."

Lightly, with total nonchalance, he had put me in my place, reminding me that he was, after all, an aristocrat. Born and raised at Cooper House, and probably able to trace his ancestors all the way back to Charlemagne, he had an immediate entree into realms I could never hope to inhabit, and could toss off great names with complete aplomb. He wasn't snobbish, but then, he didn't need to be. Social revolutions notwithstanding, an aura of glamor still clings to aristocracy, and Bartholomew Cooper was, by birth, one of the golden few, no matter how unimportant he might consider it.

"Anything else I can do?" He sounded exactly like a handyman eager to please his employer.

"You've done quite enough."

"Guess I could put the car in the garage for you. You left the keys in the ignition. That's quite a car, by the way. Vintage Rolls. It belongs to you?"

"It belongs to Brent Stevens. He lent it to us for the trip."

"Brent Stevens? The television actor? You mean he's actually a friend of yours? Hey, that's pretty impressive."

He was making fun of me, and I knew it. I *had* mentioned Brent's name to impress him, and it had backfired. He found it amusing. Shoulders hunched, humming under his breath, Bartholomew Cooper strolled out of the room. The room seemed desolate after he left, as though he had taken all life and vitality with him. He was definitely disturbing, as disturbing as he had been as a boy, and I couldn't quite understand my reactions. He was infuriating, of course, and yet there was something else, something that eluded me.

Mandy had already taken her bags upstairs. I carried the food basket and oranges down the narrow hall into the large, dark kitchen, setting them on the old zinc drainboard. Then I took my bags up to my bedroom. Outside the elements were raging, thunder crashing, streaks of lightning flashing continuously, yet the rain still hadn't come. The lights flickered, growing dimmer, brightening, dimming again. I hoped we wouldn't have an electrical failure. It had happened a number of times in the past, so a plentiful supply of candles was always in the hall chest. I unpacked my bags as Mandy bathed, and after she finished I took a quick bath myself, changing into a leaf-brown dress with a short, generously pleated skirt. As I sat brushing my hair, Mandy stepped into the room.

"I'm glad to see the plumbing works," she said, "although the pipes make a rather alarming gurgle. What's wrong with the lights?"

"The storm," I replied.

"Think they'll go out?"

"Possibly. It's happened before."

"Dandy. Just what we need. Incidentally, what was that crash in the library as I was coming up?"

"The files. He dropped them."

"Are they—"

"Hopelessly jumbled," I said, putting down the brush and standing up with a weary expression.

"Oh well, it'll give us something to do in our spare time," she said philosophically. "Are you ready to go down, luv? I'm starved. There should be plenty of food left in the basket."

I turned on the lights in the kitchen. It was a large room. The stove and icebox dated back to the thirties. The dark brown linoleum was cracked, copper pans gleamed against yellow wallpaper stained with moisture, and huge varnished oak cupboards filled one wall. There was a rough stone fireplace, too, and deep blue canisters lined up along the zinc drainboard, cabinets above it. The room smelled of spices and smoke and apples, and it was cozy despite the lightning and thunder outside.

We had just sat down at the round, scarred wooden table when a key began to rattle in the back door, startling both of us. Bartholomew Cooper stepped inside, closed the door behind him, and looked at us with an amused expression.

"Hope I didn't alarm you," he said airily.

"*What* are you doing here?"

"I have kitchen privileges. Didn't I tell you? There's only a fused-out hot plate in my flat. Daphne said I was welcome to make use of the kitchen any time I wanted. She gave me a key, and I keep a few provisions on hand. Don't let me bother you. I was just going to throw a sandwich together, although I must say that feast you have spread out there looks extremely tempting—"

"Won't you join us?" Mandy asked sweetly.

"Mandy!"

"There's plenty, Lynn."

"Don't mind if I do," he said.

He took a plate down from one of the cabinets, got silverware and napkin from a drawer, pulled up a chair, and began to help himself generously to the various gourmet items Mandy had taken out of the basket. I stared at him angrily as he appropriated half a cooked pheasant, piled slices of glazed ham onto his plate, and spread pâté over a chunk of French bread. Mandy was all charm, a guileless look in her velvety brown eyes.

"Have some caviar, too," she said. "It's divine."

"Believe I will," he replied, reaching for the tin.

Bartholomew Cooper was completely at ease, eating heartily. I merely toyed with my food, fuming, as irritated with Mandy as with him. Mandy had a dreamy, rather vague expression, and I knew she was planning something. Her invitation for him to join us had not been without purpose, I suspected, and my suspicion was confirmed when, twenty minutes later, basket emptied and every last bit of food devoured, she turned to him with her most dazzling smile.

"I *do* adore roughing it, don't you? Such fun. Incidentally, I understand you're the one who discovered the body."

"That's right," he replied, not for a minute taken in by her ploy.

"It must have been a perfectly *dreadful* experience."

"It was."

"Well, come *on,*" she urged, "tell us all about it. We're dying to hear, aren't we, Lynn?"

"Not especially," I said.

Folding his arms across his chest, Bartholomew Cooper tilted his chair back and observed us with thoughtful eyes. The first drops of rain began to fall, pattering gently at first, growing louder and more forceful. The overhead light flickered, dimming to a feeble yellow glow, and shadows began to gather in the corners of the large old kitchen. The windows rattled noisily.

"I'd been dining with my brother at Cooper House," he said. "We're not on the best of terms, but Janie—Lady Cooper—insisted I come. I couldn't refuse without causing a row. It was after twelve when I finally left, and as I was driving up my headlights illuminated the front of the house. I saw Colonel March come streaking out. He paused for a moment, startled by my car, I guess, then raced into the woods. The front door was standing open. I went inside and found Daphne at the foot of the stairs. I telephoned the police immediately."

"Was the blood still flowing?" Mandy asked casually.

"There were pools of it."

"Flowing?"

"I suppose. I didn't take notes."

"Did Colonel March have the knife in his hand when you saw him?"

"I didn't notice."

"Surely you would have?"

"He may have had it. I didn't see it. He could have thrust it into his belt."

"I suppose so," she said, frowning. "They'd been feuding, hadn't they?"

"So they say. I wouldn't know. I'd been away, you see. In fact, I'd just come back that morning, which is why I felt obligated to dine with my brother and sister-in-law. When I left Cooper's Green two and half months ago, Daphne and the Colonel were as thick as thieves, but a lot can happen in that length of time."

"You were gone for two and a half months?"

"I was in New York," he replied. "On business."

I interrupted before Mandy could ask another question. "We'd better do the dishes," I said hastily. "Sergeant Duncan will probably be here soon, and I still have to phone Lloyd."

"Lloyd?" Bartholomew Cooper inquired.

"My fiancé," I said stiffly, getting up.

He glanced at my hand and, seeing no ring, grinned slyly. Lloyd hadn't given me a ring yet, and I suppose our engagement wasn't really official, but it was more or less understood between the two of us. The ring, the announcement—those things weren't nearly as important as what we had together, But I had no intention of explaining all this to the impudent Mr. Cooper.

He stood up, stretching his muscular arms. He was a splendid male animal, no question about it, exuding virility and robust vitality that would have been quite overwhelming to a less sensible pair of women. Mandy was well aware of his magnetism, but she was too sophisticated to be all that impressed. I found him merely irritating with his cocky grin and improbable eyebrows.

"Well, good night, all," he said heartily. "Thanks for the meal. If you need anything—anything at all . . ." He lingered over the words, eyelids drooping sleepily.

"I feel quite certain we can cope, Mr. Cooper." My voice was crisp. "Good night."

" 'Night," Mandy said lazily, gathering up the dishes and not bothering to glance at him.

With a merry wave, Bartholomew Cooper opened the back door and dashed out into the sheets of rain. It gave me satisfaction to know that he would be soaked thoroughly before he reached the carriage house. I began stacking dishes on the drainboard, slamming them down noisily. Mandy watched me, one brow slightly arched.

"I've never seen you react this way before," she remarked.

"React? What on earth are you talking about?"

"You had a crush on him when you were a child, didn't you?"

"A crush! I loathed him. I still do."

"Indeed?"

"Don't be absurd, Mandy. The idea is laughable. Bart Cooper represents everything I despise in a man. He's arrogant and cocky and—and—and much too good-looking. I happen to be very much in love with Lloyd. I could never be attracted to a man like—"

I broke off. Mandy didn't say anything, but a faint smile lingered on her lips, and there was an amused, knowing look in her eyes. I felt like throwing something at her. Mandy was a dear, and I loved her very much, but sometimes she could be maddening. Sighing heavily, I turned to the dishes, and began to wash them with brisk efficiency as rain pounded on the rooftop with a most disconcerting racket.

6

SERGEANT DUNCAN arrived half an hour later, his long black mackintosh dripping puddles of water on the hall floor, his thick blond hair plastered in a wet mass over his head. As I closed the door, I noticed his bicycle leaning against the front steps. It would take quite an incentive to induce anyone to ride a bicycle all that way on a night like this, but, I reflected, Mandy was quite an incentive. He stood like a hulking schoolboy, dripping, gazing at her with enthralled blue eyes and trying at the same time to look the stern, capable public servant. The effort was remarkably unsuccessful. He glanced suspiciously around the hall, and began to peel off the slick mackintosh.

"You're drenched," Mandy said, taking the garment from him and hanging it on the coat rack. "Come on into the kitchen. I've lighted the fire in the fireplace, and there's a fresh pot of coffee. You look like you could use some."

"Much obliged, ma'am, but first things first. There're an awful lot of doors and windows in this place. I want to make sure they're all securely locked before I do anything else."

"How efficient you are, Sergeant."

"Person could step right in through one of those French windows," he continued. "I don't like the setup, I'll be frank. I don't much like the two of you staying here."

"We're not alone," Mandy reminded him. "Mr. Cooper is still occupying the carriage house."

"Yeah," Duncan muttered. His scowl made his opinion of Bartholomew Cooper all too evident. "We'd better start checking those locks. If you'd like to show me around—"

He was speaking to Mandy. I don't think he'd even noticed me. They were obviously looking forward to a prolonged tour of the dimly lighted house— alone. I told Mandy to go ahead, that I had to phone Lloyd. Slipping her arm through his, she led Sergeant Duncan away, looking positively frail beside his solid bulk. I imagined it would take them some time to check all the windows and doors.

There was a considerable delay before I reached Lloyd. His voice was husky with sleep when he answered.

"Did I wake you?" I inquired.

"I must have dropped off on the sofa. I was going over a set of papers and—"

"You work too hard," I interrupted. "You wear yourself out, Lloyd. Why can't you let some of the others—"

"It took you long enough to phone," he said briskly. "I was expecting your call hours ago."

"I should have phoned earlier, but . . . Anyway, everything's fine here. The drive down was pleasant, and—"

"What did you find out?"

"About the house? I suppose I'll sell it, but I haven't—"

"You saw the police, didn't you?" He sounded impatient.

"Oh, yes. I stopped by the station."

"Well?"

"Do we have to talk about that? The case is closed."

"What did they say?"

I repeated everything I had learned, and there was a grave silence on the other end of the line. I could visualize his face, jaw thrust out, lips pressed firmly together, a serious, preoccupied look in his dark brown eyes. He would be toying with the heavy black-rimmed glasses, and the fingers of one hand would be tapping impatiently on the table top. When I finished he sighed heavily, and I could imagine the deep frown creasing his brow.

"I don't like it, Lynn. I don't like your being there. This fellow Cooper—"

"He's perfectly all right," I assured him.

"There're too many questions unanswered. Those local policemen—"

"It's an open-and-shut case, Lloyd. I wish you wouldn't—"

"I can't help but worry about you, dammit. I wish I were there with you. I should never have let you go in the first place. Staying out there in that isolated house—"

"Don't be absurd."

"Something's wrong. I have an instinct about these things, Lynn. It just doesn't add up. The motive, for one thing. Why should a doddering old man who raises Pekineses—"

"You and Mandy," I said wearily.

"Look, Lynn, I don't want to alarm you, but . . . Hell, promise me you'll keep your eyes open. Promise me you'll be careful."

"I promise," I said, irritated by his attitude, but flattered as well. It was nice to know he worried about me. In London he took me for granted. I felt a warm glow as I held the receiver to my ear, longing to hear more.

"What are you wearing?" I asked.

"Huh? What a silly question. I'm wearing my pajamas and robe."

"The brown satin robe?"

"Yeah." I had the impression he had to check before answering.

"I'm glad," I said. I had given him the robe for his birthday, and although I'd never seen him wearing it, I knew it must look handsome with his copper hair.

"You're *glad?* What do you mean? I don't follow you."

He'd probably forgotten I'd given him the robe. There wasn't a sentimental bone in his body.

"Take care of yourself, Lloyd."

"*You* take care."

"I will."

I waited. The longed-for words didn't come.

"I think maybe I can get this case wound up in a day or so," he said brusquely. "If so, I intend to come down there. The murder aside, you need someone to look after your interests. I don't want you to sign *anything*, you understand?"

"I understand."

"Lynn . . ."

"Yes?" Hope stirred.

"I miss you."

The three words weren't the ones I'd hoped for, but they were enough. I said good-bye and hung up with a feeling of satisfaction. He missed me. He had said so. For Lloyd, that was a great concession. One of these days that stern, remote façade would crumble altogether, and all the warmth and feeling I knew he possessed would come bursting through. He loved me, I knew that, and if he wasn't demonstrative, that didn't make his love any the less valid.

Mandy and Sergeant Duncan were still checking the locks. I could hear them moving around upstairs. Feeling a little sad without knowing precisely why, I went into the library and turned on the lamp beside the desk. The jumbled files were still piled there in a precarious heap. Several folders had slipped to the floor. Sitting down behind the desk, I began to try to restore some order. The lamplight flickered, once or twice going out completely, blossoming back to life a few seconds later. Outside the rain still poured, though without its previous fury.

I don't know how long I worked, sorting articles and clippings, putting them in the proper folders, but when I looked up Mandy was standing in the doorway, one eyebrow arched in amusement.

"Deaf, dear?"

"I—I didn't hear you."

"I only called your name three times. Make any progress?"

I stacked the folders I had been working on in a neat pile and pushed them aside. "A little. It looks like a hopeless task."

"We've checked all the doors and windows and had a cozy chat by the fire in the kitchen. Doug is leaving now."

"Doug?"

"The sergeant," she said lightly. "You seem terribly distracted tonight."

"I suppose I'm just tired. All this mess—"

"You've done enough for one night. Come along and say good-bye."

I followed her into the hall, where Sergeant Duncan was pulling on his mackintosh. His cheeks were a bit flushed, and his thick blond hair was mussed. Mandy smiled at him. He scowled, very severe and official.

"Everything seems to be in order," he said in a husky voice. "I don't think you'll have any trouble, but . . . uh . . . you've got my telephone number. Don't hesitate to call if you need me."

"I won't," Mandy promised.

"I don't think anyone can get in. You be sure and lock the front door behind me."

Young Douglas nodded his head and opened the door. We followed him out onto the veranda. Although thunder still rumbled menacingly, the rain had stopped. Sergeant Duncan hesitated, obviously reluctant to leave.

"I wish you were at the inn," he said grimly.

"We'll be perfectly all right," Mandy assured him. "It was ever so thoughtful of you to come all the way out here and check up. We appreciate it *hugely*."

"We certainly do," I added.

"No trouble at all. Uh . . . you won't forget the rehearsal, will you?"

"Of course not."

"The group'll appreciate it, a real actress poppin' in. Maybe you can give us a few pointers."

"Maybe I can."

"Well . . . uh . . . I'd best be shoving off. Take care."

He moved down the steps, mounted his bicycle, and pedaled off into the darkness. Mandy was smiling pensively as we went back inside.

"You must have had quite a long chat," I remarked.

"We did. I promised to get to the theater and watch the dress rehearsal. I can hardly *wait* to see him in eighteenth-century breeches and satin jacket. Isn't he adorable? But so *proper*. I felt sure he'd make a pass as we were moving down all those dark halls, but no such luck."

"I thought you weren't interested. I seem to remember some remark about all these men being tiresome."

"Did I say that?"

I nodded.

"Well, Douglas is different. He has a quality—a fascinating combination of smoldering masculinity and little-boy shyness. He's a primitive, unspoiled. I'm *so* tired of worldly, sophisticated males—"

"You're hopeless, Mandy."

"What a *wicked* thing to say! Oh dear, there go

the lights again. We'd better turn these down here off and go on upstairs. Listen to the thunder. It sounds like someone's blowing up a bridge."

I locked the front door and pushed the brass bolt into place. We turned off the downstairs lights and started upstairs. The hall lights flickered alarmingly as we moved toward our bedrooms.

We stopped in front of Mandy's door. "Did Lloyd have anything interesting to report?" she asked.

"Not really. He—he seemed worried."

"Because we're here?"

"He isn't satisfied with the police report. He seems to think—well, let's just say . . ." I hesitated, frowning.

"He thinks the murderer might still be loose." Mandy finished the sentence for me.

"Something like that. Mandy, *you're* not nervous, are you?"

"Nervous? *Me?* Don't be silly." Her voice was light and reassuringly gay, but I noted a slight tremor.

"The house is so quiet—" I began.

"And all the doors and windows are securely locked," she said firmly, "and husky young Mr. Cooper is sleeping in the carriage house, a stone's throw away. There's not the slightest reason to be alarmed."

"Not the slightest," I agreed.

"Just the same, I wish I hadn't read so many bloody thrillers. That last Brad Carter—most upsetting. Tell you what, luv, let's leave the hall lights burning. Not that we *need* to, but . . ."

"Fine," I said, relieved.

" 'Night, luv. See you in the morning."

As I went into my bedroom, I told myself that I was simply tired, bone tired, that was all. If my nerves were acting up, it was only to be expected. The house *was* large, and dark, and Aunt Daphne had been murdered just a short time ago . . .

I began to prepare for bed, slipping into a pair of beige cotton pajamas and taking out my beige robe printed with tiny pink roses, draping it over a chair, setting out my slippers so that everything would be handy when I got up in the morning. When I finally climbed into bed, I felt much better, all apprehension firmly banished.

Darkness flooded the room when I turned off the lamp. Closing my eyes, I sank into the feathery mattress, willing myself to sleep.

I was a child, roaming through the woods, examining the lichen on tree trunks, climbing up to peer at bird nests, delighted with my rustling brown and green world, happy to be away from the house. As I passed the old mill ruin, he came charging out, shouting lustily, his eyes aglow with savage mischief. I screamed. I ran. He pursued me. Strong arms grabbed me, one wrapping around my throat, the other around my waist, and he was laughing that devilish laugh. I struggled. He whirled me around, clutching me against his chest, and I looked up into his eyes, and suddenly I was an adult, and he was an adult, too, and that mischief was still in his eyes. He was holding me tightly, and I was no longer struggling. His lips moved seductively, and he lowered his head . . . I opened my eyes and, for a second, seemed to be suspended. Then I saw the moonlight shining on the ceiling and knew I had been dreaming. Those arms, the sensual lips parting as he bent to kiss me . . . An absurd dream, but disturbing nonetheless.

I slept again, and later, much later, I seemed to be standing outside. I saw the veranda spread with shadows, a darker shadow moving stealthily toward one of the French windows. I watched, my throat dry, my heart pounding. Who was he? What was he doing there? I tried to cry out, but no sound would come. He stood in front of the window, peering in. He tapped against the glass. The noise was distinct, ringing sharp and clear. I heard a loud rattle, a crash . . . I sat up with a start; tense, completely awake.

For perhaps a moment I was utterly paralyzed, unable to move a muscle, fear gripping me like a tangible being. My throat was still dry, my heart still pounding. I listened, straining to hear. The noises came almost immediately: the floor downstairs creaking, footsteps, the sound of someone stumbling, then silence, total silence. Each second seemed to stretch out, prolonged. I reached for the lamp and pressed the switch, but the light failed to come on. I pressed again, in vain. Obviously, the lines were down. I remembered a deafening clap and blinding flash right before I dropped off to sleep. Lightning had probably struck one of the poles.

"Lovely," I said irritably.

Faintly, through the darkness, I could see the bulk of the wardrobe and a dull silver blur on top of it: the old candelabrum. There were still stubs of candles in the three holders, and if I was lucky the matches would still be hidden in the bottom drawer. Climbing out of bed, I crossed the room and fumbled in the drawer, feeling for the matches. A sharp smell of sulfur assailed the air as I struck one. A bright yellow flame flared, sizzling, going out almost immediately. I dropped it, struck another. By the time I finally had the candles burning, the floor was littered with half a dozen charred matchsticks.

The candles spluttered, and the flames leaped wildly. Holding the candelabrum aloft in one hand, I opened the bedroom door and stepped into the hall.

It was icy cold and pitch black, and although the candles made a wavering circle of light around me, they only heightened the darkness beyond. As I stood in front of the door, my calm and resolution vanished. I peered into the darkness, listening, and when I heard footsteps approaching I almost fainted.

"So it woke you up, too," Mandy said in a flat voice.

"Mandy! You—you startled me."

"I was just on my way to your room."

"I had a nightmare. It woke me up."

"It wasn't a nightmare, luv. Someone broke into the house. I think we'd better go rouse Bartholomew," she said.

Her voice was calm, her face expressionless. In a crisis Mandy was cool and level-headed, far better able to cope than I. She had proved this several times in the past. I felt panic stealing over me as I watched the shadows cascading down the walls, but Mandy was unmoved. She wore a short white nightgown and belted negligee that left her shapely legs bare and a pair of fluffy white mules.

"Shall we?" she said. "Neither of us is going to be able to sleep until we make sure no one's in the house. Right?"

"I suppose so," I said feebly.

"The lights, of course, are out."

"I think the lines are down. The lamp wouldn't—"

"Give me the candelabrum. Your hand's trembling."

She took it and, squaring her shoulders, started down the hall. I followed close behind. The candle flames danced and darted, spluttering loudly. We paused at the top of the stairs, peering down into the darkness. Although her face was still expressionless, I could tell that Mandy was as unenthusiastic about going down as I was.

She glanced at me, eyes level, then shrugged her shoulders and began to descend. It took us perhaps a minute to reach the hall and get to the front door. It was the longest, most terrifying sixty seconds I'd ever lived through.

While Mandy held the candelabrum up high, I fumbled with the bolt, my hands shaking violently.

"You might *hurry*, dear," Mandy suggested.

"I can't seem to—there! I was turning it the wrong way."

Finally, I pushed the bolt back and flung the door open. A violent gust of wind swept in, blowing out the candles. We hurried across the dark veranda, down the steps and out into the night. Although the moon had already gone down, a faint light bathed the walls of the carriage house, vaguely illuminating the stone steps leading to the rooms above. We hurried up them. I knocked on the door for at least a minute.

"I thought he was a light sleeper," I said bitterly.

"Pound, dear."

I pounded, banging my fist against the door until my knuckles hurt. There was a loud crash within, an even louder curse shouted lustily in the darkness. Then we heard him stumbling across the floor. He must have tripped. A heavy body thudded against the door, a string of highly colorful expletives following. Then the door opened halfway, and Bartholomew Cooper poked his head out.

"What in the *hell*—"

"Someone broke into the house," I said calmly.

"Huh?" His voice was thick and drowsy.

"Both of us heard it."

"Christ! Can't a man get—"

"Are you awake?" Mandy inquired.

"Some watchdog!" I snapped.

"Look, what's this all about!"

"We think someone broke into the house," Mandy told him.

"Well, why didn't you *say* so!"

"It's rather chilly out here, pet. Mind if we come in?"

"There's no light," he said, holding the door open.

We stepped into the darkened room. I promptly stumbled over a rug, and would have fallen had I not knocked against Bartholomew Cooper. He grunted in surprise and flung his arms around me, tottering backward. Both of us swayed until he managed to steady himself. Muttering, he released me, and I stepped away hastily.

"Have you got any matches?" Mandy asked.

"I have a box in my pocket," I said, glad I had thought to keep them with me.

I gave them to Mandy. She lighted the candles efficiently, and warm golden light illuminated a large, cluttered room. There was a studio bed with tangled blankets and sheets, a desk with an ancient typewriter, piles of books, and assorted furniture that had once been in the big house, most of it chipped and battered. One chair had been knocked over, and the bedside lamp was on the floor, the shade sadly crumpled.

Bartholomew Cooper wore a pair of rumpled tan silk pajamas that must have been at least two sizes too large. His face was still flushed with sleep, his hair wildly unruly. Shaking his head, he looked at us.

"Now, what's all this about someone breaking in?"

"It happened not more than ten minutes ago," Mandy said. "Lynn and I were both awakened."

"*I* didn't hear anything."

"I'm not surprised, luv. Judging from the time it took us to wake you up, you wouldn't have heard an elephant stampede."

"I suppose you want me to check the house out."

"That was the general idea."

He strode across the room on his bare feet, opened the closet door, and pulled out a rather disreputable brown woolen robe. He put it on over his pajamas and began to look around the room for his slippers, finally locating them under the edge of an overstuffed green chair. They were badly scuffed, the brown leather cracked. Sartorial elegance obviously meant very little to Mr. Cooper. Grunting irritably, he marched over to the desk, jerked open a drawer, and pulled out a long metal flashlight.

"Ready?" Mandy asked.

"Yeah . . . uh . . . just a minute."

We waited patiently while he returned to the closet and poked around among the clothes. A box tumbled down from the shelf, landing on his head. He let out another colorful expletive and, a second later, turned around, clutching a long wooden object.

"What's that, luv?"

"A cricket bat." His voice was grumpy. "If I'm going to go searching a dark house for intruders, I plan to be prepared."

"Perhaps we should phone Sergeant Duncan," I told Mandy. "He said we should if—"

"I can manage!" he thundered. "Come along!"

Switching on the flashlight, he stormed out the door, Mandy and I following with considerably less drama. He stopped at the front steps, flashing the light along the length of the veranda. "No one out here. I don't see any signs of an intruder."

"You think we made it up?" I asked acidly.

"Shut up!" he barked. "Shall we go in?"

"Let's," Mandy said.

I suggested we start upstairs and work down. Bart agreed. The flashlight made a pool of light on the stairs as he started up. Mandy and I weren't far behind, neither of us particularly eager to be left alone in the shadowy darkness of the hall. We went through room after room upstairs, Bart leading the way, cricket bat in one hand, flashlight in the other. He was very thorough, peering behind doors, looking in closets, even lifting the counterpanes to make certain no one was under any of the beds.

"No one up there." He sounded disappointed. "You *sure* you heard someone breaking in?"

"We heard *something*," Mandy informed him.

"Could have been the wind, or thunder."

"I suppose it could have been," she agreed. "Shall we go through the rooms downstairs?"

"Come on," he said irritably.

I remembered the supply of candles Aunt Daphne had kept on hand in the hall chest, and suggested we look for them. Scowling impatiently, Bart held the torch for us while Mandy and I opened the chest drawers, searching. We found a dozen candles and a stack of old pewter holders, and in five minutes we had all the candles burning, stationed in strategic points throughout the rooms downstairs. By now I was bored with the whole thing, and beginning to believe that Mandy and I had imagined the noise. Even if there had been an intruder, he wasn't likely to still be in the house. I was perfectly content to wait in the front parlor with Mandy while Bart searched the rest of the house.

Fifteen minutes elapsed before Bart came clumping loudly down the hall and flung himself into the room. He tossed the cricket bat down and glared at us. His belt had come undone, and the moth-eaten old brown bathrobe hung open. His vivid blue eyes were snapping, and those improbable eyebrows had never looked more comically slanted.

"Did you check the basement?" I asked, just to taunt him.

"I checked everywhere! Not a sign of anyone. All the doors and windows are still securely locked. No one broke into the house. You pulled me out of bed for nothing. Women! If you think it's amusing to be—"

"You're mistaken," Mandy said calmly.

"What do you mean?"

"Someone did break in," she said.

"I just told you—"

"Look at this latch, luv."

He walked over to the windows to examine the latch. I peered over his shoulder. The latch was completely broken, hanging loose on one nail. As we watched, a gust of wind swept across the veranda, and the windows swung halfway open.

"Well?" Mandy said.

"It's broken, all right," he admitted.

"All these windows were locked before we went to bed. Sergeant Duncan and I checked. Someone—someone heaved a shoulder against the windows and broke the latch. That's what we heard."

"Not necessarily. It could have been the wind."

"The wind?" I said impatiently. "Do you expect us to—"

"These latches are very old, very flimsy. They'd give way at the least little pressure."

"Are you trying to say—"

He gave me a weary look, sighing again. "Watch," he said. Opening the windows, he stepped onto the veranda, crossed over to the next set of windows, and stood peering at us through the panes. As we watched, he leaned his shoulder lightly against the center section, where the windows met. The latch, securely fastened, rattled, creaked, fell clattering to the floor. The windows flew open, and Bart, still leaning, lost his balance and came hurtling into the room.

"What's that supposed to prove?" I inquired icily.

"Just a practical demonstration," he said. "The wind was fierce last night. A particularly strong gust could easily have caused the latch to break. It's a wonder all these windows down here didn't fly open."

"So you don't believe there was an intruder?"

"Not for a minute. You didn't see anyone, did you? You didn't *hear* anyone. Nothing's missing. The silver service is still on the sideboard. The Meissen box is still on the coffee table. The—"

"All right!" I snapped.

"I'm only trying to be reasonable," he said, hurt.

Mandy studied the broken latch, a thoughtful look in her eyes. "I suppose a strong-enough burst of wind *could* have broken the latch," she conceded.

I was secretly inclined to agree with her, but I had no intention of letting Bartholomew Cooper know that. I didn't intend to give him that satisfaction. The open windows rattled noisily. I picked up the latch he had broken off with his impromptu nudging.

"Well, this one was certainly broken off," I said crisply. "It will have to be replaced."

"I'll buy a new one today! Hell, I'll buy new ones for *all* the windows, strong ones. I'll bring a hammer. I'll put them on myself."

"I'll hire someone to do it."

"Like hell you will!"

"Really, Mr. Cooper—"

"I think we could all use some coffee," Mandy said. "It's getting light out. We don't need the candles any more. I'll snuff them out and put them away. Lynn, why don't you go brew the coffee?"

Mandy blew out the candle in the parlor, took up the pewter holder, and left the room. I closed the windows, though I hadn't much hope they would stay closed as long as the wind was so brisk. Bartholomew Cooper pulled his robe more securely around him and retied the belt, striving to look a bit more dignified. Then he followed me into the kitchen. I filled the coffeepot with water and reached for the canister, deliberately ignoring him. He leaned against the door frame, those vivid blue eyes watching every move I made.

"I'm really a nice guy, you know," he said casually.

"Indeed? Perhaps some people think so."

"And what do you think?"

"You really don't want to know that, Mr. Cooper."

"Bart. How many times do I have to tell you? The name's Bart. You don't find me an engaging chap?"

"I find you insufferable."

"Not really. No—not really." He sauntered over

to the table and sat down, resting his elbows on the tabletop. "Look, I guess I ought to apologize for storming around like that. I'm not at my best when I'm pulled out of bed in the middle of the night."

I lighted the gas burner and set the coffeepot on it. "When *are* you at your best, Mr. Cooper?"

"When I'm alone with a beautiful woman." His voice was heavily seductive.

I smiled to myself, amused by his brashness. He had charm all right, I couldn't deny that, and he was almost indecently handsome, the tousled hair, the rumpled pajamas and old bathrobe only heightening his virile magnetism, but I was immune. Totally immune, I told myself, watching the coffeepot begin to boil. Charm might dazzle some, but it could never take the place of intelligence, authority, stability, the qualities a sensible woman looked for in a man. Lloyd was intelligent. He had authority. He was nothing if not stable, and . . . The coffeepot began to rattle violently, geysers of boiling liquid spewing over the stove.

"Damn!" I cried, turning off the burner.

Bartholomew Cooper chuckled. I wanted to slap him.

"Careless of you," he said.

"I can't cook, if you must know!"

"You mean you can't even make a pot of coffee?"

"I didn't say that! I—"

"I can't either," Mandy said, entering the room. "Cook, I mean. It's most distressing—"

"I expected a big breakfast," Bart said, surly. "I think I *deserve* one, don't you?"

"Definitely," Mandy replied.

"There are eggs in the fridge. Bacon, too."

Mandy and I exchanged glances.

"I have a marvelous idea," she began.

Grumbling angrily, slamming pots and pans around with reckless abandon, Bartholomew Cooper began to prepare breakfast as Mandy and I went upstairs to dress. The sun was shining brightly now. The house was filled with shimmering rays of early-morning sunlight. I had almost forgotten the nightmare that had awakened me, and I resolutely refused to think about the disturbing dream that had preceded it.

7

"I DON'T KNOW when I've had a better breakfast," Mandy said. "Bartholomew may be temperamental, but he's a marvelous çook."

"It was a delicious breakfast," I agreed.

"Sweet of him to offer to take us to the funeral. I'm surprised you agreed to let him."

"We need an escort. He'll have to do."

"He was quite charming at breakfast, don't you think? Trying to make up for his previous churlishness, I suppose. He's a fascinating man, a man of many moods."

"I really don't care to discuss him, Mandy."

Mandy didn't say anything, but her eyes betrayed amusement. She was convinced that I was attracted to him, that I had had a crush on him when I was a child, and nothing I could say would convince her otherwise. Reaching for a sheaf of neatly typed pages fastened together with a paper clip, she examined it idly.

"Here are your notes on the Duchess d'Orleans. Where's the folder? Poor Henriette. I wonder if the king's brother really did poison her? I wouldn't put it past him. There it is, luv. Hand it to me, will you?"

I gave Mandy the folder, glad she had changed the subject. I was in a bad mood, weary from the loss of sleep and nervous about the funeral that I had to face later in the afternoon.

I had taken a short walk after breakfast, wanting to be alone to sort my thoughts out. Mandy remained to help Bart wash the dishes, and they were engaged in an intense conversation when I returned. They broke off when I entered, and I had the curious impression they were hiding something from me. What had they been discussing? I wondered. Bart left, claiming he intended to take a long nap. Mandy said nothing about the conversation in the kitchen, and I was too stubborn to ask her what they'd been talking about.

Was it about last night? Had Bart discovered something he didn't want me to know about? Had his tempestuous conduct been merely a sham to cover up something else? He and Mandy had been almost like conspirators when I stepped into the kitchen, and Mandy had seemed worried . . .

We were in the library now. It was only ten, and since we had three hours until the funeral, we decided to begin refiling my scattered notes.

"You're slipping, luv. You just put Montespan in the folder reserved for Madame de Maintenon. Both ladies would turn over in their graves. You look a bit peaked, Lynn. Sure you don't want to go up and take a nap? You have time."

"I'm perfectly all right. Anyone can make a mistake."

"You're edgy, luv. Something wrong?"

"I keep thinking about last night."

"It'll make an amusing story when we get back to London," Mandy said lightly, reaching for another folder. "But I for one was petrified."

"Do you really think it was the wind?" I asked abruptly.

"It must have been, pet. There were no signs of an intruder, and we didn't actually hear anything after that first loud crash."

"I did. I heard footsteps. When I first woke up. I —I thought it was part of the nightmare."

"*I* didn't hear any. You must have imagined them. We were both tired, Lynn, both a bit nervous. It was an amusing little adventure, but . . . Let's forget about it. All right? Bart's going to buy new latches and put them on this afternoon."

" 'Bart'? You suddenly seem very chummy with him."

"Does that make me a traitor? Really, Lynn, he's an interesting man. Not my *type*, of course, but that doesn't mean I can't be friendly. I felt almost sorry for him, the way you were treating him."

"Yesterday you said you had your doubts about him. You said you'd seen his face before in connection with something vaguely sinister. You seemed suspicious."

"Did I? Well, I was wrong. Like you said, luv, anyone can make a mistake."

"Mandy—"

Both of us were startled by the loud, jangling clatter that suddenly filled the air, followed by a shrill, piercing quack like that of a wounded duck. Hurrying to the front window, we peered out to see a plump, middle-aged woman pedaling furiously up the drive on a battered bicycle, the roses on her black straw hat bobbing. She squeezed the rubber horn. There was another deafening quack. Alighting from the bicycle, she kicked the stand into place, pushed the hat from her brow, and turned to see us standing at the window. She smiled, waved merrily, and scooted up the front steps.

Mandy and I exchanged puzzled glances.

By now our visitor was pounding heartily on the front door. I opened it to find a pair of bright, vivacious brown eyes studying me with a lively curiosity.

"Lynn? It is Lynn, isn't it? You poor, poor child. You won't remember me, of course. Wouldn't expect you to. I've put on a few pounds since you saw me last. More than a few, actually. I *do* love my chocolates. Can't resist 'em. Never could. I'm Myrtle, ducky."

"Myrtle?"

"Myrtle Clarkson, your Auntie Daphne's oldest and dearest friend. We had our spats, Daphne and me, some rip-snortin' ones, I don't mind telling you, but we were like that." She crossed her fingers. "Like sisters, we were. Poor Daphne. I still get all choked up, just thinkin' of it . . ." Her eyes grew sad. "And you, you poor, dear child. Such a blow. Such a dreadful blow for one so young. I just had to pop by and express my sympathy before the funeral."

She took my hand in both her own and squeezed it tightly, as though to give me courage. I vaguely remembered her now. I had rarely paid any attention to my aunt's friends, being either out on my own or fast asleep when they called on her, yet I seemed to recall a thinner, less flamboyant Myrtle who had come now and then to play cards and gossip.

"Won't you come in?"

"I know how it is in time of grief, ducky. I really shouldn't intrude like this . . ."

Wild horses couldn't have kept her out, I thought, watching her bustle into the hall with astounding alacrity. The house was, after all, the scene of a brutal murder, and I knew for a fact that the police had kept curiosity seekers away. Bart had chased off several himself. Gripping her enormous black patent leather purse tightly, Myrtle peered up and down the hall until she spotted the bloodstains. Her eyes widened.

"Oh my! That's where it happened. The police wouldn't let anyone come in, ducky, not even me, and me Daphne's oldest and *dearest* friend. I gave that sergeant a piece of my mind, I did, gave him what for, but he wouldn't budge an inch. Brutes, these coppers. As soon hit you over the head as *look* at you."

She stepped over to take a closer look at the bloodstains. I gave Mandy an exasperated glance.

Mandy was wearing a benign expression. I could tell that she was planning something.

"Poor Daphne," Myrtle said, shaking her head. "I always *knew* she'd come to a bad end, but I never expected anything like this!"

She shuddered dramatically. Short, rotund, lively, she wore black patent leather pumps, a shapeless purple dress, and a voluminous gray cape lined with matching purple, the kind affected by Margaret Rutherford in the Miss Marple films. Her incredible hat perched jauntily atop equally incredible blond curls. I found the woman somewhat overwhelming with her bizarre clothes and clattering tongue, and I was at a loss. She was a jovial creature, strangely engaging, but I knew full well she had come to discuss the murder. I had no intentions of discussing it with her.

"It was kind of you to call, Mrs. Clarkson—"

"Myrtle, ducky. Call me Myrtle. Everyone does."

"I appreciate your thoughtfulness, but—"

"Aren't you going to introduce me, luv?" Mandy asked sweetly.

"Oh—forgive me. This is my friend Amanda Hunt. She drove down with me."

"Pleased to meet you, ducky."

"Won't you come into the parlor, Myrtle?" Mandy asked.

I gave her a protesting look, which she blithely ignored as she led the way into the parlor. Mandy was quite clearly just as eager to pump Myrtle as Myrtle was to pump us. Irritated, but unable to do anything about it without being openly discourteous, I followed them into the room.

"Many's the time Daphne and I sat right there on that settee, sipping our gi—sipping our tea and havin' a heart-to-heart. Like sisters we were, and that's a fact. Hard to get along with, Daphne, I'll not deny it. She might have a vicious temper, might like to shout and hurl dishes, but she was the *soul* of kindness. A dear, dear woman to those who really knew her."

"I suppose the murder has caused quite a lot of talk in the village," Mandy said, ever so artless.

"Biggest sensation since Jenny Waters gave birth to triplets!" Myrtle exclaimed, plopping down on the settee. "Appalling, just appalling. You can't imagine!" She shook her head and made a disapproving sound. "The whole village'll turn out for the funeral. Been lookin' foward to it for days."

"I can well believe it," I said dryly.

"Reggie's body has been shipped to London to his sister. Private services will be conducted. Shame, really. Lots of folks were hopin' for a double feature, so to speak, but it can't be helped."

Myrtle was in her element, and finding it difficult to contain her enthusiasm. She was undoubtedly the town gossip, and this was a real scoop. Settling back comfortably, adjusting the folds of her cape, she opened her purse, dug out a slightly crushed box of chocolates, and offered it to us. When we both refused, she unwrapped a chocolate and popped it into her mouth.

"Adore 'em. Can't get enough. I figure what the heck, at my age I'm not after any man so why not live a little, let it spread. Two husbands I had, both dead now, bless their souls. Bernie Claymore—he's the postmaster, such a de*press*ing man, dips snuff—he's been after me ever since poor Jimmy passed over, but I pay him no mind. If there's anything I don't need, it's another husband, particularly one who dips snuff! Bernie's nice enough, I suppose, but that *sister* of his—"

"Did you know Colonel March?" Mandy asked, casually running her finger over the mantle.

"Reggie? Known him all my life. A sweeter man never drew breath. He proposed to me once—oh, years ago—I was still a girl, and him the handsomest thing in his uniform, so dashin' and all. I turned him down, sad to say. Many's the day I regretted it. Stevie was already in the picture by then, you see—Stevie was my first, had the cutest mustache, also had a rovin' eye, the rat! Poor Reggie went back to his regiment, heart-broken. Never married, Reggie. I fancy I was to blame for that.''

''I thought he was courting Daphne,'' Mandy said.

''Bosh! Don't you believe a word of it! Courtin'? If he was going to court anyone it would've been me, not Daphne. Oh, they were *friends*, all right. He took her to a few socials, a couple of bingo games, but there was never anything *there*, if you follow me.''

''I understand they quarreled.''

''Daphne quarreled with everyone. It was her na-ture, poor dear. Kind as could be at heart, but never could control that temper. Red hair, you understand, though I must say it hadn't really been red for years. Miss Jane Birch at Wig Outlet could tell you a thing or two about *that*. Yes, Reggie and Daphne had a fallin' out. It's my belief he was comin' to make it up with her that night.''

''With a knife?'' I inquired.

Myrtle calmly unwrapped another chocolate, ex-amined it thoughtfully, and put it in her mouth. ''Reg-gie didn't kill her,'' she said a moment later. ''Reggie wouldn't harm a fly. You only had to see him with those dogs of his to realize that. Treated 'em like ba-bies, he did, gentle as could be. I don't care *what* the coppers say, he didn't do it.''

''He was seen leaving the house,'' Mandy re-minded her.

''So? That doesn't prove a thing.''

''He shot himself immediately afterward.''

''Maybe he did. Maybe he didn't. I reckon the sight of all that blood would cause anyone to go off his rocker, particularly anyone as sensitive as poor Reggie.

If he *did* shoot himself, mind you. I ain't sayin' he did. I have my own idea about that."

Popping a final chocolate into her mouth. Myrtle crammed the box back into her purse and looked up at us eagerly, ready to divulge her big news. Her black straw hat had slipped forward a bit, one of the pink roses dangling over her brow. She clamped her purse shut, waiting for encouragement. Mandy wasted no time in providing it.

"Who do *you* think did it?" she asked.

"That other man."

"Which man?"

"The one who kept hangin' around, pesterin' the life out of her. He showed up about two months ago, could've been longer ago than that. Daphne wouldn't talk about him, not even to me, not even after she'd had a couple of gins. 'I don't want to talk about it,' she told me. 'He's gone now. I told him I'd call the police if he ever showed up again.' Well, I happen to know he *did* show up again."

"Who was he?" I asked.

"No idea, ducky. He always called on her at nighttime, always on the sly. Poor Daphne was frightened half out of her wits, I can tell you that. She couldn't hide it, no matter how she tried. Nervous as a cat she was. Edgy. Drank more than ever. No one knew about him 'cept me, you see, and she flatly refused to discuss him. I *knew* something was wrong—"

"You saw him?" Mandy prompted.

"I decided to pay a surprise visit one night. It was latish, and my telly was broken, so I decided to go see Daphne and maybe have a couple—a couple of cups of tea, and chat for a while. My bike was in the shop, busted chain, so I walked. It was a dark night," she continued, getting into stride, "and as I was coming through the woods I noticed this strange car parked at the side of the road beneath the boughs of the trees, like someone didn't want it to be seen. Didn't pay much mind to it, thought it might be a couple of teen-agers sparkin'—real scandalous, the way they carry on. Some of the village girls, that Cassie Porter for example—I could tell a few tales about *her*—''

''You were walking through the woods,'' Mandy said patiently.

''Right, ducky, and just as I was nearing the house I saw the man coming down the front steps. Hulkin' brute, he was, huge shoulders, wearin' an overcoat and a hat with the brim pulled down, just like in one of those gangster movies on the telly. Gave me quite a fright, it did. He didn't see *me*—I was standing behind a tree—but I saw him all right. I stayed there behind the tree till he was clean out of sight. Heard a car startin' immediately afterward—''

''And you came on to the house?''

'' 'Deed I did. I was worried about Daphne. She was in quite a state, I can tell you for sure. Ragin', hurling things, carryin' on somethin' awful, but she was scared too, scared out of her wits, poor soul. When I told her I seen the man and asked who he was, she shut up tighter 'n a clam. Wouldn't talk about him, just said she'd threatened to call the police if he showed up again. She changed, Daphne did. After that she wasn't the same at all. Oh, she still raged about, had her quarrel with Reggie, but she was different. Pale, she was, and there were circles under her eyes like she wasn't gettin' enough sleep. Real jumpy, too, always gave a start if she heard someone comin'—''

Her voice was low and dramatic. It was quite clear that Myrtle was having the time of her life, enjoying every minute of this. I knew, of course, that anything Myrtle said had to be taken with several grains of salt. Perhaps she *had* seen a man leaving the house. He could have been anyone: a salesman, an insurance man, someone come to check out the drains. With her lively imagination, her thirst for gossip, Myrtle would naturally paint the incident with florid colors, particularly after my aunt met such a tragic end. I paid little heed to her tale, although Mandy seemed to be fascinated.

"Interesting," she said thoughtfully.

"Daphne was hiding something. She never was a good actress. I knew it had somethin' to do with that man. He had some kind of hold over her. It's my belief he was threatenin' her. She never mentioned him again—I think she was scared to, but, like I said, I happen to know he *did* show up again. I saw him with my very own eyes."

"When was this?"

"Just a day or so before it happened—" She paused, brown eyes widening. Looking at us, she gave a portentous nod and then continued in a low, hushed voice. "It was late afternoon, and I'd been with Daphne. She was in *such* a condition, quiet, pale, worried. She'd grown thinner, and her hands shook somethin' terrible. Her wig was all askew, and she was wearin' a shabby old brown dress. Looked like an old woman, a sick old woman. All the thunder and lightning gone out of 'er. Not the same Daphne at all. She just sat there, drinkin', starin' into space. Didn't even insult me when I tripped over one of the stools. I said to myself, I said, 'Somethin' awful's going to happen.' I could feel it in my bones. I'm a bit psychic, you know. When I left this house I knew something perfectly dreadful was going to happen soon—"

"You saw the man again as you were leaving?" I said wearily.

"I climbed on my bike and rode away. The sun was just going down, and shadows were beginning to spread over the lawns. I followed the road through the woods, dusk fallin' fast, growin' darker by the second. I was about half a mile up the road when I saw the car again, movin' real slow. I pedaled over to the side of the road and stopped as he drove past. I got a *good* look at him this time, saw his face plain as I see yours now. Broad it was, with flat cheekbones and a square jaw. His mouth was wide, his nose looked like it'd been broken, and his eyes were dark. I may not know much, but I know a killer when I see one—I watch *all* the crime shows on the telly. Murderous he looked, downright murderous, those enormous hands grippin' the steerin' wheel like it was someone's throat. He stared right at me, and I don't mind tellin' you I got a move on! Never knew my bike could *go* so fast!''

Her chubby hands were clutching the purse tightly. She looked down at them. "I intended to call on Daphne the very next day to see if everything was all right, but I was busy. Had to meet with the committee and help plan the jumble sale. I should have gone to see her, I know. I should have given her a ring on the phone, but I didn't. I'll always regret it. Two days later young Cooper found her body . . .'' She pulled a handkerchief out of her purse and dabbed at her eyes, although I could tell she was eager to have our reactions.

"Mr. Cooper had been gone all this time, hadn't he?'' I asked.

"Been gone for over two months. Just got back that morning. If he'd been here it might not have happened. It was his first night back, and he'd gone to have dinner with Lord and Lady Cooper. Poor Daphne was all alone, way off out here by herself—''

"So no one saw the man except you?''

"Not a soul,'' she said, almost proudly. "I don't know what his business with Daphne was, but whatever it was was a deep dark secret. No one else in the village even remembers the car.''

I glanced at Mandy. She seemed to be lost in thought. Surely she couldn't put any stock in this preposterous tale, I thought. Myrtle was indeed engaging —one couldn't help but like her—yet her story was obviously a highly colored elaboration. I didn't doubt she'd seen the man. He was probably some harried, disgruntled fellow who had perfectly legitimate business with my aunt. The rest, I felt sure, was 99 percent Myrtle's imaginative fancy.

"Did you inform the police about him?" I asked.

Myrtle drew herself up, all prim dignity. " 'Deed I didn't," she said crisply. "After the way that sergeant treated me, and me just wantin' to see Daphne one last time? I should think not. If them coppers are so smart, let 'em find out about him on their own. Me, I don't meddle."

I found it hard to repress a smile. Glancing at the clock on the mantel, Myrtle stood up, adjusted the folds of her cape and tilted her hat at a cocky angle over the shiny blond curls.

"It's gettin' on, ducky. I reckon I'd better go. There are several little errands I have to run before the funeral, and I want to be there in plenty of time to get a good seat. The church'll be packed to the rafters! Poor child, this has been so difficult on you—"

• "Thank you for coming, Mrs. Clarkson."

"Myrtle, ducky."

"It's been nice meeting you," Mandy said.

"You two girls staying here all by *yourselves?*" Myrtle inquired as we stepped into the hall. "You're gutsy, I'll hand you that. You wouldn't catch *me* stayin' here, not for a million."

"Mr. Cooper is in the carriage house," I replied.

"Hump! *Him,*" she said, sniffing disdainfully. "I wonder what kind of protection you think *he'd* be. A bad 'un if I ever saw one, so *cocky,* and his brother, Lord Cooper, so respectable and grand. There're some who wonder what he *does* out here, and all those mysterious trips—well, it's mighty peculiar. I'll say that much—"

Myrtle would undoubtedly have said much more had I not smiled politely and opened the front door, ushering her out onto the veranda. Myrtle brushed at her skirt and swept the folds of her cape over one shoulder.

"Oh dear!" she exclaimed. "I almost forgot."

"Yes?"

"Well, ducky, I hate to admit it, but I had an ulterior motive in calling on you. I mentioned the jumble sale, I think. Didn't I? Well, it's starting tomorrow at one o'clock, and we're rather short of help. Clarissa Jennings took sick, and then Peggy O'Reilley had to leave for Coventry to be with that sister-in-law of hers, pregnant again, poor thing, and then—well, we could use a hand. I think Nell Stevens's niece is going to take over the bake sale, but that still leaves the book stall vacant, and I thought maybe—"

"I'm terribly sorry," I interrupted. "I'd love to help out, but there are so many things I have to—"

"I know it's asking a lot in your time of distress, and ordinarily I wouldn't *dream* of making such a suggestion, but we *do* need help so desperately. It's all for charity, ducky. We're trying to raise enough to have a new roof put on the orphanage."

"I'm sure it's a worthy cause, but—"

"Leaks somethin' awful, it does. Those poor little mites, dashin' around with pans and buckets when it rains, trying to keep the floors from floodin'—makes your heart bleed. Some of them sick, and—" She broke off, brown eyes mournful and filled with entreaty.

I felt trapped.

"We'd only require your services for an hour or two," Myrtle continued in a persuasive voice. "I know you're bowed with grief, know how hard all this must be on you, but it would do you good to get out, keep busy, put on a brave front. It would mean so much to us—a real gesture, your helping out at a time like this. A real inspiration to others, seeing you there smiling through your tears, working for the good of those poor little orphans."

"Well—"

"There! I knew you'd say yes! One o'clock, ducky, in the basement of the church. I'd appreciate it mightily if you could come a little early. Mobs always show up, searchin' for bargains. We like to be ready for the onslaught."

"I'll be there." My voice was singularly unenthusiastic.

Myrtle beamed with satisfaction. "Oh, just one other thing, ducky. We're a bit short on items to sell. I know for a fact that Daphne's attic is *crammed* with junk—old dishes, clocks, bits and pieces you couldn't possibly want. If you could possibly find time to gather up a few things to bring along, we'd be ever so grateful. It's all for the sake of those poor little—"

"I'll try to find time."

"You're such a peach, ducky. So considerate, and you bowed down with grief—it's nothing short of noble. Does my poor heart good to know there are still some decent young people in the world. Well, I'd best be getting a move on." She swirled her purple-lined cape, adjusted her hat again, and tripped nimbly down the stairs. "Ta ta!" she cried gaily. "See you at the funeral!"

Myrtle mounted her bike, shifted her plump body around on the seat, and kicked the stand free. Giving a loud blast on the horn, she waved merrily and pedaled down the drive. I watched with a sense of dismay, unable to believe I had committed myself to help at the jumble sale. I turned to Mandy, a sour expression on my face.

"You were a lot of help, I must say!"

"Don't look so unhappy, luv. It'll do you good to get out, keep busy, put on a brave front. Think of those poor little orphans."

I gave her a venomous look and went back inside. Mandy followed me into the library. It was barely eleven. We had at least an hour before we had to dress for the funeral, and we continued to work on the files. Mandy was unusually silent, that preoccupied look back in her eyes. I could tell she was thinking about the murder, thinking about Myrtle's story of the man in the overcoat.

"You didn't actually believe her?" I said.

"What? I'm afraid I wasn't listening—"

"Myrtle. Her story about the man. It was absurd. She may have seen a man, but the rest of it is preposterous. He was probably a salesman or—or some kind of repair man."

"Probably was," she murmured.

"Mandy, you don't think there's anything to it?"

"Of course not. Hand me that folder, will you? I think I've got all these notes about Ninon in order. Is there an extra paper clip? This really isn't taking as long as I thought it would."

I didn't press the issue. I saw that it would be futile. Mandy might change the subject, but she couldn't hide the truth. She wasn't that good an actress. She had listened to Myrtle's tale with intense interest, and I realized with some alarm that she had believed every word.

8

I WAS TENSE and nervous, dreading the ordeal of the funeral. Sensing this, neither Bart nor Mandy said anything as we drove to the village. Mandy wore a subdued royal-blue dress, her tawny gold hair in a French roll. Bart was impeccable in dark suit and tie, shoes polished to a sheen, his dark locks neatly combed. I was amazed at the change in him. The breezy, irreverent fellow of this morning was gone, in his place a quiet, sober man who seemed a tower of strength. During the drive he seemed unaware of our company, a remote expression on his face, mouth set in a grim line. I wondered what he was thinking about.

A place had been reserved for us in front of the church. I tensed even more when I saw the swarms of people congregated on either side of the walk, eagerly awaiting our arrival. It seemed that the whole village had indeed shown up, and the mood was far more festive than solemn. There was a great stir as the car pulled up. I saw Myrtle, surrounded by her cronies, all of them gabbling excitedly. Sergeant Duncan stood by the door, arms folded, a disapproving look on his face.

Mandy arched her brow as Bart got out and came around to open the door for us.

"It's a sell-out," she said wryly. "S.R.O. Chin up, luv."

"I'm all right."

"I detest funerals. Always did think they were barbaric. It'll all be over in a little while. Lord, that mob! I feel just like Marie Antoinette on her way to the block.''

Bart helped us out of the car and took my arm. The crowd grew hushed. With Bart on one side and Mandy on the other, I made my way up the walk and into the church. A buzz filled the air. As we walked down the aisle to the front pew, there was a clamor behind us as people rushed in to grab their seats. Hundreds of avidly curious eyes watched as we sat down, and I knew they were taking in every detail of our dress and demeanor. Solemn organ music began to play. Mandy reached over and took my hand, squeezing it tightly.

The music rose and swelled. I saw the banks of gladioli and chrysanthemums, bright, florid, orange and blue, and I saw the closed bronze casket on its stand. Clive Hampton had made all the arrangements, following Aunt Daphne's instructions. I had caught a glimpse of him as we came in, his face sober yet avaricious. I knew he had expected me to call as soon as I arrived, but I was going to avoid him if possible. I didn't trust the man.

A door opened, and the vicar stepped to the pulpit. Vicar Peckinpah was a small, worried-looking little man with flushed cheeks and a too-tight collar. Reality seemed to fade. I seemed to be far off, observing everything with curious detachment.

The music died away. There was a prayer. The vicar began to speak in a strained, tremulous voice. I thought of my childhood, remembering my aunt as she was then, wishing I had been able to love her, wishing she had been the plump, rosy-cheeked, loving aunt of fiction with an apron around her waist and cookies baking in the kitchen. As I grew older, I had grown fond of her, in my way, but I had been glad so much distance separated us. She was gone now. I wished I could cry. My head ached. There was another prayer, then a stir in the crowd as six pallbearers marched to the casket and removed it from its stand, carrying it out the side door.

That feeling of detachment was still with me as Bart led me out to the graveyard in back of the church. We stood under a striped marquee. I saw the old tombstones under the spreading boughs of the oak trees. I was acutely aware of Bart's firm hand gripping my elbow as they lowered the casket into the ground, and then he was leading me away through the crowd. Several people spoke to me, expressing sympathy, and I think I must have answered them. Clive Hampton tried to stop me, but Bart shook his head at Hampton and led me past him.

And then we were standing in front of the church again, four of us now, Sergeant Duncan beside Mandy. People leaving watched us with open curiosity, but no one came near. The ordeal was over. Mandy was saying something to me, her voice low.

"I asked how you feel."

"Much better." The sense of remoteness evaporated. "I—I could use a drink, if you want to know the truth."

Sergeant Duncan looked shocked. Mandy smiled.

"I imagine you could, luv."

"The pub serves terrific stingers," Bart remarked, some of his solemnity vanishing.

"A stinger would be divine."

Mandy took Sergeant Duncan's arm. "Look, why don't you two go on. Douglas will drive me back to the house in the police car, won't you, Doug?"

"I'm not sure I ought to, ma'am. It's an official vehicle and—"

"Oh, come on, Sergeant. Bend a little."

Duncan looked extremely dubious, but nevertheless he let Mandy lead him away. I turned to Bart. He stood with hands in his pockets, his neatly groomed hair beginning to wave a little, its natural unruliness gradually triumphing over brush and comb.

"People are going to talk," he said lightly.

"Are they?"

"Going to the pub immediately after the services, particularly with an acknowledged rogue like me—they're going to say you're totally unfeeling. Sure you want to go?"

"Quite sure," I replied. "I'm not at all concerned with what people might say. Let them think the worst."

"Oh, they will. No doubt about it."

He opened the car door and helped me in, gallant, extremely handsome in his dark suit. I was surprised at myself, glad that Mandy had gone on with Sergeant Duncan, that we were alone. Bart had been stern and protective at the funeral, genuinely concerned for me, and I appreciated that. Perhaps I hadn't been fair to him, I thought.

Bart started the motor and pulled away from the curb. He made no attempt at conversation, driving slowly, that remote expression in his eyes again. As on our drive from the house, he seemed unaware of my presence, and once again I wondered what he was thinking about. He was a total enigma, volatile one moment, thoughtful the next, and there was so much about him I didn't understand. What did he do for a living? Did his brother give him an allowance? Why had he gone to New York? He had mentioned a flat in London. If he could afford that, if he could afford the trip to New York, why did he maintain the rooms over the carriage house, so far away from all the activities and interests that were certain to appeal to a man of his nature?

"*Are* you a rogue?" I asked suddenly.

"Huh—oh, of course I am. If you don't believe it, just ask any of the local gossips. I live a life of total dissipation. I seduce young maidens. I perform mysterious experiments in my rooms over the carriage house. I roam the woods in the wee, small hours of the night—"

"Can't you be serious for a minute?"

"My brother's the serious one in the family. Edgar takes his position *very* seriously. He's staunch and steadfast and oh so aware of all the commitments and duties being a Lord entails. He's charitable. He's fair. He's *involved.* Gives blue ribbons at the livestock shows, awards prizes at all the school exercises, makes a speech at the drop of a hat. A dull fellow, Edgar, but much admired."

"You resent him, don't you?"

"Resent Edgar? Whatever for?"

"Well, he did inherit Cooper House, and—"

"You couldn't pay me to live in that drafty pile of stone. No, I'm delighted to be the second son. I'd make a wretched Lord, entirely unsuited for the role."

There were many things I longed to ask him, yet I sensed his replies would be equally frivolous and evasive. I couldn't help wondering if Bartholomew Cooper were as carefree as he pretended to be. I had sensed strength in him earlier, and I kept remembering that stern look in his eye when he put Clive Hampton off. There was, I decided, much more to him than what appeared on the surface.

Bart parked the car across the street from the pub. People stared at us openly as he helped me out of the car. I suppose it *was* outrageous, going to the pub right after the funeral, but I really didn't care what people might think. Bart seemed to find their stares amusing. He was obviously used to flouting convention.

"It'll be all over town in fifteen minutes," he said amiably. "Mrs. Buchanan is peering out of the grocery-store window. She's almost as bad as Myrtle Clarkson, though not quite."

"Myrtle came to see me this morning."

"I know," he said. "Amanda told me all about it while we were waiting for you to come downstairs."

Taking my arm in his, he led me across the square. As we approached the pub, the doors opened and a young girl came out, none too steady on her feet. She wore black high heels and a remarkable crimson dress, much too tight, the neckline cut extremely low to emphasize a bosom that clearly needed no emphasis. She tottered in the doorway for a moment, blinking. Her brassy blond hair was worn in short, bouncy curls, and there were deep shadows about her dark blue eyes. She couldn't have been much more than nineteen, I thought. She would have been rather pretty had it not been for the bizarre outfit and somewhat amateurish make-up job. There was something strangely vulnerable about the girl, despite the scent of dime-store perfume and cheap golden earrings. As we drew near, she gave a start and hurried on down the street, high heels tapping noisily on the pavement. It was almost as though the sight of us had frightened her in some way.

"Cassandra Porter," Bart said, staring after her. "I wonder what's wrong with her this afternoon. Took off like she'd seen a ghost."

"You know her?"

"Everybody knows Cassie. Poor girl's had a rough go of it lately. Her mother died four or five years ago, just when a girl needs a mother most, and her father gave her little or no supervision. The boys came around in packs, whistling, serenading under her window. Her father was usually too drunk to notice. He drank himself to death, finally, and Cassie was left with the cottage and very little else. She went to secretarial school for a couple of months, but that didn't pan out. I'm afraid poor Cassie took the easiest way. The boys still hang around. Cassie has lots of new stockings but no visible means of support."

"How sad," I said, curiously moved.

"Every village has its Cassie," Bart replied, pushing open the pub doors. "She's a good girl at heart, but, alas, the flesh is weak. How well I know . . ."

The pub smelled of old wood, leather, and beer, a not unpleasant mixture. The interior was cozy, with a low-beamed ceiling and oak-paneled walls. A much-punctured dart board hung in the back, with several darts sticking to it. I was relieved to see that we were the only customers. Bart led me past the leather-covered bar to a table in the corner. Checked cloths were spread over each table, and there was an ancient juke-box dating back to the thirties, glowing with color but blessedly silent. Helping me into my chair, Bart called his order to the stocky, pugnacious-looking man behind the bar and sat down across from me.

"You held up pretty well back there," he said quietly. "I was afraid you might break down."

"Were you?"

"It was rough on you, I know."

"It was rough," I agreed, "but I don't break down easily. I wouldn't give them that satisfaction."

He smiled wryly. "They were expecting a show, all right. I'm afraid you disappointed them in that respect. Peckinpah did himself proud. I didn't even recognize the kind, saintly woman he kept referring to."

"My aunt was many things, but she was hardly saintly."

"No, Daphne would have laughed raucously and called him a bloody hypocrite. You two weren't close, were you?"

"Not at all. I—I was fond of her in my fashion, but Aunt Daphne and I never got along well. I was merely a bother to her when I was a child, an irritant to her when I was older."

"The old girl was proud of you, you know. Oh, she'd never have let *you* think that, but she was constantly thrusting dog-eared articles into my hands and talking about her brilliant niece, the successful news-paper woman."

"I find that hard to believe."

"Oh, she raved about your short skirts and lipstick. She was firmly convinced you were heading for damnation with the wild company you kept, but she believed the love of a good man would have a steadying influence. I suspect she had matchmaking plans in mind."

"Indeed?"

"Indeed. She kept insisting I should look you up the next time I went to London." He grinned, eyes dancing with amusement. "When I told her I was a confirmed bachelor, she said I was as bad as you were and we could both go hurtling straight to hell for all she cared. Then she poured another drink and launched into a vicious tirade about youth in general."

"You seem to have been on quite intimate terms with my aunt."

"I frequently popped over to chat," he said. "I found Daphne amusing, and I think she rather enjoyed having me around the place. She was always irritable when I told her I had to leave for a few days, always pleased to see me when I got back."

"I—I can't understand why you'd want to stay out there. It seems so unconventional—"

"I'm a very unconventional chap. Haven't you noticed? Ah, here's Bob with our drinks."

The bartender approached our table, wielding a tray with two drinks and a dish of salted nuts. He placed the drinks in front of us and set the dish in the middle of the table, looking extremely bad-tempered. He was an ugly fellow with broad features, a broken nose, and dark, glowering eyes. Thickset, muscular, he was definitely someone you wouldn't care to meet in a dark alley.

"Don't mind Bob," Bart said, observing my reactions. "He's always been a dour fellow, downright menacing to look at, but as gentle as a lamb underneath that gruff exterior. Angelic disposition. Right, Bob?"

"None of your lip, Mr. Bart," he growled, "and might I remind you you owe me four pounds ten."

"Four pounds ten?" Bart looked incredulous. "Well, be a good chap and put these on the bill. I'll settle with you later."

"Later meanin' before you step foot outside this pub," Bob warned in a threatening voice.

"Certainly, my good fellow, certainly. He fairly dotes on me, Bob does. Been serving me drinks ever since I was old enough to lift a mug. I fancy his affection for me is darn near paternal."

Bob looked as menacing as ever, but I thought I saw a half smile curl those wide lips.

"By the way, Robert, what was the matter with Cassie? She seemed unusually nervous when she came out. You make a grab at her?"

"That ain't funny. I'm a married man, I am, and well you know it. I wouldn't mess with a piece of goods like her, not on your life. She came in early, lookin' terribly upset. Sat at the bar, downin' one drink right after th' other, her face all pale and drawn-like. Something was worryin' her, worryin' her bad, but me, I don't ask questions. I just tend to my own business. When I saw she was about to fall off the stool, I made 'er pay up and get out. She didn't argue, just slapped her money down on the bar and took off."

"Most peculiar," Bart said thoughtfully. "I suppose the poor girl has a bad time of it—"

Bob made a disapproving noise, picked up the tray, and went back behind the bar. Taking up a dry cloth, he began to polish glasses, totally disinterested in us. Bart ate a few nuts and lifted his glass to me.

"Cheers," he said.

The drink was very strong, but it seemed to have no effect whatsoever. I tried to relax, tried to forget the funeral, those eager stares and the sight of the casket being lowered into the ground. Some of the tension was still inside, and Bart seemed to sense this.

"Why don't you tell me about the book?" he suggested.

"The book?"

"The one you're writing for Ashton-Croft. I've always been interested in the court of Louis the Fourteenth."

"You're just being polite."

"I'm not, I assure you. I find the period fascinating, really. All that grandeur, all those tumultuous passions concealed behind flawless etiquette. When did you first decide to write a book about it?"

"I didn't actually decide. I did a series of articles in my spare time and Mr. Ashton-Croft happened to see them. He said—"

And so I talked about the book, telling him about my research, describing some of the fascinating characters and unusual anecdotes I'd uncovered in the process. I spoke with some vivacity, unable to contain my enthusiasm for the subject, and he seemed deeply interested, listening intently, frequently asking surprisingly well-informed questions. I discovered with amazement that Bartholomew Cooper shared my love of history, was, in fact, something of an authority on the affair of the poisons. Crime, he claimed, had always intrigued him.

"Perhaps because I'm such a mild-mannered chap myself," he added with a grin.

"You weren't very mild last night."

"I wasn't, was I? Well, we all have lapses."

"I suppose we do."

He grinned again, looking particularly appealing with his curling mouth and one dark, silky brow absurdly crooked. He *could* be charming, I thought, extremely conscious of his magnetism, enchanted by that errant lock of hair that fell over his forehead like a large comma. I felt much, much better, all tension vanished, and I realized that he had deliberately had me talk about the book so that I would forget the funeral. It was transparent, but it was thoughtful nevertheless.

"Another drink?" he inquired.

"I've had two already. I'd better not. I . . . Thank you, Bart. You've been very considerate."

"That surprise you?"

"Frankly, yes."

"Oh? I may have been a rough, nasty little boy, chasing you through the woods, tying you up against a tree, but that doesn't necessarily mean I'm a rough, nasty man. I have my good points."

"I'm beginning to realize that."

"Ah—things bode well for the future . . ."

There was a husky catch in his voice, and he looked at me with a lazy gaze that was most disconcerting. For some reason I thought of the dream I had had, and I felt a vague uneasiness begin to stir inside. I had an insane impulse to reach up and rest my palm against that lean cheek. I was appalled. It was the liquor, of course. I should never have had that second drink. Bart watched me closely. I had the uncomfortable feeling he could read my mind.

"Something bothering you?" he asked.

"Don't overdo it," I said. "You may have seductive eyes, but I've no intention of becoming another of your conquests."

"You think I have seduction in mind?"

"I know darn well you do."

"Being seduced by me could be quite an experience."

"I'll bet."

"I could provide references if you're really interested."

"You're beginning to irritate me again."

"A little harmless flirting throws you?"

"I—I don't flirt. I'm engaged to be married."

"Not officially."

"How do you know?"

"Amanda told me all about your Lloyd."

"Amanda should be shot."

"He sounds like a stuffy fellow, not at all your cup of tea. You want someone with more spirit."

"Like you, you mean?"

"Yeah, come to think of it."

"I think we'd better go now," I said frostily.

"There, you see, we're fighting again. It seems every time we're together we end up fighting. I enjoy a good scrap, I won't deny it, but I'd much rather be friends."

"I really don't think there's much likelihood of that, Mr. Cooper!"

"It was Bart a minute ago."

"I must have been mad, thinking you could be halfway—I've only myself to blame. I should never have come with you!"

"You find me devastatingly attractive. Why don't you admit it? Think of all the time we're wasting with this eternal squabbling. We could be having a rich, rewarding—"

"I'd hate to slap your face in public."

"I'd probably slap you back," he said chattily.

I stood up abruptly and with such energy that the chair almost toppled over behind me. I had to grab hold of it to keep it from falling. His eyes twinkled merrily.

"You're ready to leave, I take it?"

"*Quite* ready."

Bart stood up lazily. "Oh well, you'll come 'round in time. I'll just have to be patient."

I bit back the scathing retort on the tip of my tongue, as he moved over to the bar to settle his bill. Grabbing my purse, I went outside, my cheeks a bit flushed, the anger still seething inside, but when he joined me a few minutes later I was completely com-

posed, my manner icily polite. Bart thrust his hands
into his pockets, not the least bit perturbed.

"I want to run over to the hardware store and buy
those latches before we go back to the house. Want to
come with me, or would you prefer to wait in the car?"

"I'll wait in the car, thank you."

"Right. Shouldn't take me a minute."

He sauntered off, hands still in his pockets, head
cocked to one side. He wasn't whistling, but he might
as well have been. Furious with myself, I was half
tempted to phone for a taxi to take me back to the
house, but I wouldn't give him the satisfaction. No, I
would be very cool and utterly dignified on the drive
back, and after that I intended to avoid him like the
plague.

Lost in thought, I started toward the car parked
across the square. Passing the large clump of shrubbery
near the old cannon, I heard a hoarse whisper. It
sounded like someone beckoning to me. I stopped, and
then I saw the girl standing in the curve of greenery,
almost concealed by the leaves and shadows. I recognized her at once. One couldn't mistake the bright
crimson dress, the brassy blond curls. She signaled for
me to come nearer and, puzzled, I obeyed, wondering
what on earth she could want.

"I've been waitin' ever so long," she said in a low,
whiskey-soused voice. "I waited, just on the chance
you might be alone, just on the chance I might be able
to speak to you." Taking my arm, she drew me into
the dim recess afforded by the shrubs. We were almost
totally hidden from view. "God, I hope no one saw
me. I waited until the square was empty and no one
was around before dashin' into these shrubs—"

"You—you wanted to speak to me?"

She nodded, her deep violet-blue eyes filled with
anguish. The girl was frightened, so frightened she
could hardly speak. There was a sense of urgency
about her every gesture, and I noticed again that

strange vulnerability. Cassie was a pathetic creature. Misguided she might be, and weak, yet she was little more than a child. There was a peculiar innocence about her, a quality only stressed by the cheap perfume and crudely applied make-up. She lowered a leafy branch and peered anxiously around the square before speaking again.

"I'm Cassie Porter, ma'am," she began, her voice barely audible. "Maybe—maybe you'd rather not talk to me. They say I'm wicked and ought to be run out of town, but a girl has to—I couldn't—I *wanted* to be respectable, and I tried hard. I tried to learn all them shorthand symbols, tried to learn to type, but—"

"Never mind, Cassie. I understand."

"I thought you might. I saw you—I didn't dare go to the funeral, but I was watchin'. I saw you goin' in. I said, 'She's not like them others. Maybe she'd listen to me. Maybe she'd understand why I couldn't—' I have to talk to someone, you see. I've gotta *tell* someone." She peered through the shrubs again, watching the few people who moved along the pavements in front of the shops. "I'm scared," she said, turning back to me. "I'm scared somethin' *awful*. If he knew—"

"Try to calm down, Cassie," I said in what I hoped was a comforting voice. "Just relax. What is it you want to tell me?"

The girl made a valiant effort. She took a deep breath, trying to summon some measure of composure, trying to overcome her fear, but when she spoke again the tremor was still in her voice.

"I live in a cottage on the other side of the woods from your aunt's house, 'bout a mile away, the woods between. There's four cottages, all located near each other. Colonel March, his cottage is the closest one to mine. Some people—they think I'm terrible, they don't want to have anything to do with me, but *he* wasn't like that. He was kind. He knew me ever since I was a little girl, knew my pa used to beat me, and he was always so nice to me, used to let me play with the puppies. After I dropped out of secretarial school—it didn't make no difference. He gave me one of the pups to keep, said he knew I'd take good care of Puggie . . ." She paused, on the verge of tears.

There was a moment of silence while Cassie fought back the tears. She pulled a tattered lace handkerchief out of her bag and dabbed at her eyes. But as she replaced the handkerchief, a change came over her. Her features tightened. There was a hard, defiant look in her eyes.

"What they say about him—it ain't true. Colonel March was the kindest man who ever lived. He was sweet. He was understandin'. Miss Morgan, he never killed your aunt. He never shot himself. I *know*."

"How—how do you know, Cassie?" There was a tremor in my own voice now, and I felt a chill, anticipating her words.

"I didn't dare go to the police. I was scared—so scared I couldn't even think straight. They wouldn't't've believed me anyway. That Constable Plimpton, he's all right, I guess, but Sergeant Duncan —he said he had his *eye* on me, said I'd better watch my step. Just because a girl entertains 'er friends, just because they give me presents now and then—"

I waited patiently, knowing it would be unwise to pressure her.

"That night, the night it happened—I was comin' home. Jerry Flemming took me to the pub that evenin'. We danced and had a few drinks, and then I saw it was almost midnight and told 'im I'd better be gettin' home. You'd think he'd've offered to walk me back, but no, not him! So I was by myself. I was a little tipsy, I admit, but—"

We both heard the footsteps. Cassie gave a start, her face turning pale. She peered through the shrubbery again, and over her shoulder I could see Bart crossing the street, a parcel under one arm.

"I don't want him to know I was talkin' to you," Cassie said quickly, urgently. "I don't want anyone to know. You'd better go now. Hurry, before he spots us—"

"Cassie, you've got to *tell* me—"

"I'll meet you," she said, frantic. "The—the old mill, there in the woods by the river bank. You know where it is? I'll meet you there at—at six o'clock—"

Cassie stepped farther back into the shrubbery. I hurried away, heart pounding. I reached the car perhaps a minute before Bart did. When he got in I was gazing calmly out the window. He tossed his parcel onto the back seat and started the motor. As we drove away from the square I saw no sign of Cassie. I supposed she was still hiding in the clump of shrubbery. Bart chattered amiably as we left the village. I ignored him, maintaining a stony silence, and finally, disgusted, he grew silent too.

It seemed to take us forever to reach the house.

9

When I told Amanda in no uncertain terms what I thought about her treachery, she wore an air of injured innocence and claimed she had had no idea that discussing Lloyd with Bart constituted high treason. He had asked, and she had told him merely that Lloyd was a lawyer, very stable, rather solemn, and divinely good-looking even if he was a bit dull. Having established her total lack of guile, she proceeded to bombard me with questions about our trip to the pub.

"I mean, something must have happened. Bart slammed out of the car in a rage, looking like he wanted to blow up the world, and you, luv, would have made the Snow Queen look positively cozy."

I refused to discuss it with her, and went upstairs to change clothes. Loosening my hair, I put on a dark gold turtleneck sweater and a short pleated skirt of brown and gold checked tweed. It was not yet four, and I wondered how I was going to contain myself until time to meet Cassie in the woods. I would simply have to put it out of my mind, go on about my business until five forty or so. I hadn't told Mandy about my encounter with the girl, and I had no intentions of doing so—not just yet. Stepping over to the window, I stared out at the shabby, sun-drenched herb gardens and the vivid green treetops beyond.

I couldn't shake the vague feeling of uneasiness that was beginning to mount inside. Yesterday I had been totally prepared to accept the police account of my aunt's murder. I had scoffed at Mandy's improbable theories, her stubborn conviction that all was not as it seemed, that too many questions remained unanswered. I had laid it all to her addiction to thrillers and paid very little attention, but too much had happened since then for me to be quite so sure about everything.

The wind was probably responsible for the broken latch. Myrtle was undoubtedly a clattering gossip, ready to make something of nothing. Cassie had been drunk this afternoon, and she had admitted to being drunk the night of the murder. Even if she had seen something, she could hardly be considered a reliable witness.

Each incident could be rationalized, but taken together they were beginning to form a most alarming picture.

Lloyd wasn't at all satisfied, either. He wasn't happy about our being here in the house. He had been extremely worried when I spoke to him on the phone last night. "I have an instinct about these things, Lynn. It just doesn't add up. The motive, for one thing." But then Lloyd was so easily worried. I remembered how alarmed he had been over those prank telephone calls. He had asked me endless questions about my father, almost as though he believed Daddy might still be alive. Later, when I told him about the murder, he felt there might be some connection. But what connection could there possibly be? Lloyd was a worrier by nature. Still . . . I straightened up and brushed a lock of chestnut hair from my forehead, determined to remain calm and levelheaded.

I would meet Cassie by the old mill at six o'clock. I would listen to her story very carefully, and if I thought there was anything to it I would go straight to the police. Probably it would be as insubstantial and fanciful as Myrtle's had been. Downstairs, the clock struck four. I turned away from the window, sighing.

What to do for the next two hours? I really should

phone Clive Hampton and make some effort to see about disposing of the house. There were all sorts of details to attend to, but I knew I was going to procrastinate as long as possible. Besides, Lloyd didn't want me to sign anything until he got here. I was bound to make a hopeless muddle of any business I undertook to transact on my own. It would be much easier to just put everything in his capable hands and spare myself the bother. He'd know exactly what to do, what to sell, to whom, and at what price. Clive Hampton could wait.

I supposed I might as well go back downstairs and do some more work on the files. Aunt Daphne's death had caused quite a setback, but then, that was understandable. As soon as all this was settled, I would hole myself up somewhere peaceful where I could work in earnest, without interruption, staying with it until the book was completely finished. I was eager to get back to my routine, eager to put all this behind me.

I was on my way downstairs when the front door opened and Bartholomew Cooper came into the hall. Dressed in a loose gray sweatshirt with the sleeves shoved up over his forearms and a pair of very tight, faded blue-jeans, he gripped a hammer in one hand, the parcel of latches under his arm. Seeking me on the stairs, he paused, grinned, and made a mocking little bow.

"General handyman at your service, ma'am. Where would you like me to begin?"

"I couldn't care less."

"Come on, now. You're not still angry, are you? Look at me. I took a cold shower and I'm a new man. Friends?"

He looked engagingly boyish. I almost smiled. I caught myself just in time. I knew full well the dangers of that disarming charm, and I wasn't about to succumb to it a second time in one day.

"Why don't you start in the parlor," I suggested, only a trifle less chilly.

"Want to come watch?"

"No, thank you."

I came on down the stairs and moved past him, in what I hoped was a poised, dignified manner. He shrugged his shoulders and went on into the parlor, whence, in a moment or so, loud, clattering bangs sounded. Mandy was curled up on the brown leather sofa in the library, a pencil in one hand, a crossword-puzzle book in the other, consternation in her eyes. She was wearing a fetching green and beige striped knit dress.

"Oh—there you are, pet. Smashing outfit."

"Your dress is nice, too. Expecting company?"

"Doug might come by later. I believe in being prepared. I need a word that means to emboss metal by hammering on the reverse side. It starts with a p. Six letters."

"Pound?"

"I tried that. Only five. The first three letters match. P, o, u, blank, blank, e."

"Pounce," I said, moving over to the desk.

"*Pounce?* I thought that meant to—oh well, I won't quibble." She leaned forward, industriously filling in squares. "There. It fits! You're amazing, luv. I suppose it's your literary background."

She tossed the book aside and sat up straight, stretching like a contented, well-fed cat. Mandy always looked gloriously languorous and sleek when there was a new man on the scene, and Douglas Duncan was very much on the scene. He was quite different from her usual enthusiasms, and I wondered if she might actually fall in love with him. That would be a novelty.

"Speaking of pounding," she said, "what on earth is that noise?"

"Your chum Bartholomew. He's putting on the new latches."

"Does he have to bang so loud?"

"I think he hopes to get on my nerves. Want to work on the files for a while?"

"I guess so," she replied, unenthusiastic. "Doug was so cute when we got to the house. He walked me to the door and then he just stood there, looking stern and manly." She perched on a chair, gathering up a handful of papers. "I could tell he wanted to kiss me, but he just couldn't work up enough nerve. I patted him on the cheek and came on in. He takes these things so seriously. I suppose it has something to do with being a policeman."

"You'd better be careful," I told her.

"Whatever do you mean?"

"I mean Sergeant Duncan isn't like the others. He doesn't play by the rules of the game. I doubt if he even knows them. You might, just might, find yourself out of your depth."

"Really, Lynn, how perceptive of you."

I had to smile at my own naiveté. My giving Mandy advice about men was like a rank amateur telling Bobby Fischer how to play chess.

We worked for forty-five minutes, making remarkable progress. One file box was completely filled, each folder in order, and I saw that the job wasn't going to take nearly as long as I had first thought. Mandy was in a rather indolent mood, sighing frequently, a pensive look in her eyes, no doubt thinking about her tall, strapping sergeant. The constant banging of the hammer was getting on my nerves, and when, shortly before five, Bart came sauntering into the room, I found it difficult to control my irritation.

"All done in there," he said breezily. "I'll have to start work on these windows in here now. Uh . . . don't let me bother you. Go right on about your business."

That was impossible, of course. With the claw end of the hammer he began to pull the old latches off, letting them drop to the floor with a jangling clatter. I looked at Mandy. Mandy looked at me. Without saying a word, we put the files aside and stood up. Bart arched one crooked brow, but continued his work. If he had laughed, I would have hurled a lamp at him.

As we stepped into the hall, I thought I heard a peculiar tapping noise, but I paid it no mind. There was a loud, clanging racket from the library as yet another latch fell to the floor. Mandy shrugged her shoulders.

"I'm wondering about dinner," she said thoughtfully. "I wouldn't dare attempt anything on that stove, but I think I could slice some ham for sandwiches without severing a main artery. There is plenty of bread and cheese. You hungry, pet?"

Before I could answer, there was a great banging on the front door. We were both startled. I opened it to find a short, slender, extremely perturbed little man studying his knuckles with some concern. He wore a once-dapper, now near-shabby brown suit, matching vest, brick-red tie, and, incredibly, spats. His sandy-gray hair was thinning, his face was the color of old parchment, and his watery blue eyes, behind gold-rimmed spectacles, were definitely worried.

"I knocked and knocked," he said timidly, "but no one heard me. That noise—"

"The handyman is putting new latches on the window," I said, taking great satisfaction in referring to Bartholomew Cooper as such.

"Are you Miss Lynn Morgan?"

I nodded. I noticed that he was carrying a worn leather briefcase. In front of the house, I could see a small, ancient black car, sadly in need of a new paint job. Bart's racket had drowned out any sounds of its approach.

"I . . . uh . . . my name is Mortimer Brumley," he began in a mild, hesitant voice.

"Mortimer?" Mandy inquired.

"This is my friend Amanda Hunt, Mr. Mort—Mr. Brumley," I said quickly, giving Mandy a severe look. "Did you wish to see me about something?"

"Y—yes. I'm afraid there's been a shocking mis—uh . . . I'm a lawyer, Miss Morgan. I have my practice in the next village. I—there's something we need to discuss."

"Won't you come in?"

His manner was meek and apologetic. Nervously gripping his briefcase, he followed me into the parlor. Mandy, not about to be left out, was right behind him. Her eyes were filled with amusement as she looked at the spats again, and I gave her another silent reprimand as Mortimer Brumley set the briefcase beside a chair and ran his finger about his tight collar, looking thoroughly uncomfortable. The noise from the library had diminished considerably. I supposed Mr. Cooper had realized just how far he could go.

"Please sit down, Mr. Brumley."

He sat down, and Mandy and I did likewise. Mandy was showing quite a lot of leg, the sight of which seemed to disconcert our guest even more. He cleared his throat and looked in the other direction.

"You wished to discuss something with me?" I prompted.

"Yes. There's . . . uh . . . there's been a most unfortunate misunderstanding, Miss Morgan. Most unfortunate. I don't suppose anyone's to *blame,* under the circumstances, but there are bound to be . . . uh . . . shall we say, bad feelings? Hampton can't be held responsible, of course. He was working under a perfectly natural assumption that the will—I assumed, naturally, that your aunt had informed him of the change. Evidently she hadn't."

Mandy was suddenly very alert.

"This has something to do with the will?" she asked.

Mortimer Brumley nodded miserably. "I didn't *know*, you see. My sister was taken ill suddenly. Mumps. At her age. Poor girl was embarrassed as could be. I had to go down to Cornwall and take care of her, watch after the kiddies. She's got four, and rowdy youngsters they are, too. That George—most unsettling experience. Gussie's a widow, you understand, and there was no one else she could call on." He shook his head, blanching a bit at the memory of the four children.

"Please continue, Mr. Brumley. What does all this have to do with my aunt's will?"

"Before it was all over with, George caught them, too. Mumps." His eyes suddenly twinkled, and there was a faint smile on his thin lips. "Did my soul good to see the little bas—uh . . . anyway, I was gone for over three weeks and was totally out of touch during that time. My practice is a humble one, Miss Morgan, and I don't have a secretary. If I had, she would have informed me of your aunt's death."

"You're trying to tell me my aunt made a new will?"

He nodded. "I didn't learn of her death until this morning, you see. I got back only last night, and as I was having my toast and marmalade this morning I happened to see the funeral notice in the paper. It was quite a shock, I don't mind telling you, and when I read that you, Miss Morgan, were her sole heir—well, I was taken aback. I knew immediately there'd been a dreadful mix-up."

"A mix-up?" I said lightly.

Mortimer Brumley looked pained, shifting uneasily in his chair. "Your aunt came to see me about three and a half months ago, Miss Morgan. She was in . . . uh . . . quite a state. Seems she'd had a violent argument with her regular lawyer. She swept into my office like a thunderstorm and for fifteen minutes did nothing but vilify Clive Hampton, said he was a scoundrel, a total incompetent, a—well, she said quite a few other things I needn't mention. Your aunt had a rather impressive vocabulary. At first I thought she intended to sue him and wanted me to prepare the case, but she finally calmed down enough to inform me that she was taking her legal business elsewhere and had chosen me as the elsewhere. I mean . . ." He hesitated, knitting his brows. "She said she'd have Hampton transfer all her papers to my office, and in the meantime she wanted to make a new will. I agreed to help her with it."

"And the will was made?"

"Yes indeed. I have it right here in my briefcase. I didn't ever hear from Hampton. I assumed he would get in touch with me, but he didn't. I kept intending to phone his office and check with him, but then Gussie took sick and I had to go lend a hand and—this is *very* distressing, Miss Morgan."

"I'm sure it must be."

It was so typical of Aunt Daphne, I thought. She was always quarreling with people. Since he had handled all her legal affairs and had to see that her taxes were paid, Clive Hampton would have been a prime target for her wrath. Probably they had had some minor disagreement, and Aunt Daphne had gone to Brumley to spite him. Then, after a few gins, she had forgotten all about it, greeting Clive Hampton the next time he called as though nothing had ever happened.

"I'll have to contact Hampton, of course," Brumley continued. "We'll have to work this thing out. I thought . . . uh . . . I felt it would be better if I came to see you first, though. Soften the blow, that sort of thing. I hope you understand my position."

"I understand perfectly, Mr. Brumley. Might I see the will?"

Looking more pained than ever, he pulled the

briefcase into his lap and began fumbling with the strap. He dug nervously among the papers, finally finding what he wanted and extracting it. He handed it to me, avoiding my eyes. It wasn't a long document, but I could see at a glance that it was flawlessly executed, signed, sealed, tied up in a neat legal bow. Mortimer Brumley might have an absurd name, and he might look like a timorous, inept little man, but he was obviously a good lawyer. It took me only a minute to read the will, and then I gave it back to him.

"It seems quite satisfactory," I said calmly.

"Oh yes," he replied, putting it back into the briefcase. "This is her legitimate will. No question about it, legally. It supersedes any previous document."

Mandy could hardly contain herself. "Come *on*, Lynn. What did it *say?*"

"It said," I replied, "that the Hon. Bartholomew Cooper is my aunt's sole heir."

"What!" he roared.

I don't know how long he'd been standing there in the doorway, hammer in hand, but he made his presence known now, a look of utter amazement on his face. Mortimer Brumley turned pale, gripping the arms of the chair in mortal terror as the stalwart fellow in sweatshirt and jeans came charging into the room, waving the hammer like a madman. Bart's cheeks were flushed a bright pink. His blue eyes were snapping with anger. Tangled raven locks spilled over his brow.

"This is outrageous!" he cried. "I had no idea—"

"I'll just bet you didn't," I said icily.

"Listen, I didn't have anything to do with this! She must have been off her rocker. Sure, she liked me —I liked her, too—but she had no right to do something like *this!*"

"She had every right. It was her property."

"You think I—"

"Your performance is excellent. You really should be on television."

"Now listen here—"

Mortimer Brumley took a deep breath. His hands were shaking visibly. Bart turned on him, eyes fierce, the hammer still gripped firmly in his hand. Brumley flattened himself against the chair.

"What—who—" he stammered.

"The Hon. Bartholomew Cooper," I said acidly.

"There's been a mistake!" Bart exclaimed. "Where's that will? I want to see it." He took the will and read with a hard, determined look in his eyes.

When Bart finally handed the will back to him, Brumley put the papers in his briefcase, fastened it, and stood up on shaky legs.

"I . . . uh . . . I'll contact Hampton, Miss Morgan. I'm sure we can work this all out."

"There's nothing to work out," I replied. "The will is quite clear. Mr. Cooper inherits everything."

"Now, just a minute," Bart began, brows lowered, "if you think for one minute I'm going to accept one lousy penny of that inheritance, you've got another think coming!"

"Oh?"

"Listen, Lynn, you've got to be reasonable about this."

"I've had my say, Mr. Cooper. I never expected anything from my aunt. I never wanted anything from her. It's clear you put in quite a bit of time and effort to get her to make that will, and you're welcome to the lot. It's not a large amount, but after you sell the property you should have a nice little stake. I suggest you go to the Riviera. I understand there are a number of lonely old ladies there, far richer than Aunt Daphne ever hoped to be."

"You're asking for it—"

"Come on, luv," Mandy said lightly, taking Brumley's arm. "I'll walk you to the car."

Brumley didn't hesitate. Still shaken, he was more than eager to get out of what he obviously considered a madhouse. They left, and Bartholomew Cooper and I stood facing each other. Most of his anger seemed to have left him, and he looked like a confused and slightly belligerent little boy.

"I know it looks bad, Lynn, but, dammit, you know what a quixotic, eccentric old dame she was. She did things on the spur of the moment, crazy things. I *did* help her with little jobs around the place. I did listen to her talk sometimes. I liked her. I found her amusing. She took a fancy to me—I couldn't help that. It was wicked and unpardonable for her to change her will like that, but it'll be quite simple to remedy. We won't have much trouble proving she was unstable when she made it. Hell, she was dotty! We both know that."

I stood in front of the settee, looking at him. In a strange kind of way, I was enjoying myself. He was miserable, a beseeching look in his eyes. I almost felt sorry for him.

"Lynn, listen to me—"

"I've heard quite enough."

"Don't be like this!"

"You expect me to pat you on the back?"

"You actually think I chiseled you out of your inheritance? You actually think I'm a—an *adventurer?*"

"That's precisely what I think."

"Christ! I don't believe it. I just don't believe it. Next thing you know you'll be saying I murdered her!"

"Did you?" I asked calmly.

He looked stunned. For a moment he stood absolutely still, blue eyes filled with incredulity, and then he curled his fists into tight balls, the rage mounting again, far more fearsome than it had been before. Two bright spots of color burned on his cheeks, and his nostrils were flaring. My heart began to pound rapidly. I took a step backward, realizing I had gone much too far.

"I—I'm sorry," I whispered. "I really didn't mean that."

He reached me in one long, athletic bound, seizing my arms in a tight, painful grip. He shook me, and when he threw his arm around the back of my neck I actually thought he intended to strangle me. He wrapped his other arm around my waist and jerked me up against him with such force that the breath was almost knocked out of me. Before I could cry out, his mouth was over mine and all that savage anger was going into the kiss. He swung me around in his arms, and I clung to his shoulders, afraid we were both going to fall. His mouth continued to punish and probe, and my head whirled as I struggled, and then, when I ceased, when I was totally limp, he released me, giving me a shove that sent me reeling back onto the settee with a resounding thud.

"You're an absolute bloody idiot!" he cried. "I love you, you bloody fool, and you're without question the most obstinate, the blindest, the most infuriating creature I've ever met!"

He stormed out of the room. The front door slammed with a violent bang that caused the windows to rattle. A moment or so later another door slammed, the door to the rooms over the carriage house. Mandy came inside. She had the tact to tiptoe past the parlor and go on upstairs. I sat there on the settee for a long, long time.

10

I HAD ALMOST forgotten about meeting Cassie. Bart's emotional pyrotechnics had driven everything else out of my mind. It was ten minutes till six, and I was still on the settee, filled with a heavy sadness, wanting to cry but unable to do so. I felt lost, like a little girl who has broken her only toy, and I couldn't understand the feeling. Those last words of his kept repeating themselves over and over again in my mind, and I knew I had been grossly unfair to him. I had taunted him, all the while knowing he spoke the truth.

He wasn't an adventurer. I couldn't really believe that. I didn't know why he had chosen to take the rooms over the carriage house, but I knew it wasn't because he'd hoped to bilk Aunt Daphne of her money. She didn't have that much, for one thing, and —and he just wasn't that kind of person. Why, then, had I been so unyielding? Why had I pretended to think the worst of him? Sitting there as the fading rays of sunlight spilled in through the windows and stained the floor with dark gold, I came close to some truths about myself. I fought with Bartholomew Cooper because I was afraid, not of him but of myself.

The moment I first saw him, moving so confidently into the front hall, an old, long-dormant feeling had stirred inside of me, bewildering me, and I had resisted it by striking out at him. Mandy had hit the nail right on the head. I had had a violent childhood crush on that rough, ebullient boy with his wooden sword and lusty shouts, and the emotion had never quite left me. We were adults now, but it had taken only the sight of him to bring that old feeling back to life.

It was just as well I realized it. I could cope with it much better now. He was thoroughly impossible, and I was in love with Lloyd, but at least I could be polite and friendly to him in the future. I had been stiff, prickly, constantly on guard, and now that I knew the reason I could laugh at myself and treat him like I would treat anyone else. I wasn't querulous by nature. Bart had brought out all the worst qualities in me, and I finally understood why. I would apologize to him as soon as I had the opportunity.

I stood up wearily. My mouth felt bruised, and the backs of my legs were sore where they had hit the settee. Glancing at the clock, I saw that I was going to be late meeting Cassie. I went outside, moving down the steps and following one of the gray flagstone paths that wound through the gardens. I passed the untidy beds of bluebells and walked under one of the old white wicker trellises weighted down with honey-suckle, still thinking about that scene in the parlor. "I love you, you bloody fool." That was nonsense, of course. He just said that for effect. I was attractive, and he was very male. He wanted to go to bed with me. He wasn't the first man who felt that way and, God willing, he wouldn't be the last. Love had absolutely nothing to do with it.

I couldn't blame Bart for the will. It was so like Aunt Daphne to do something like that. She was hasty, impulsive, unthinking. He had probably performed some little service for her—mending a lamp, perhaps, or putting new hinges on a door, or maybe he had just listened to her talk, making her feel important—and on the spur of the moment she had decided to reward him. Not openly. Aunt Daphne deplored sentiment. She would leave him all her property and,

at the same time, show me just what she thought of
my conduct in London. Perhaps she had deliberately
quarreled with Hampton, knowing he might question
the wisdom of such a will, leaving her free to go to
Brumley. Once the will was made, there was no reason
to maintain the feud with Hampton. It was illogical,
but then, Aunt Daphne had never done anything like
anyone else. Wildly eccentric, she had gone her own
way, thumbing her nose at logic and convention. Bart
had been incredulous. If anything, he had been even
more surprised than I was.

Reaching the low gray stone wall, I scrambled
over, exactly as I had done so many hundreds of times
in the past. In the woods, surrounded by trees and
shrubbery, I followed the narrow, well-worn path I
knew so well. These woods had been my sanctuary
when I was a child, my hiding place from the world,
my secret kingdom which had been so cruelly invaded
by the tan, slender boy who felt they were *his* domain,
his pirate's nest, his Indian haunts, his Tarzan jungle.
I knew every tree, every shrub. In the distance I could
hear the rushing sound of the river, but the noise was
drowned out by the stiff crackle of twigs, the scurrying
of small creatures, the wind sweeping through the
treetops.

I stopped abruptly, listening.

Something was wrong. I could feel it, sense it in
the atmosphere. I was completely attuned to these
woods, thoroughly familiar with every sound, every
smell. I knew instinctively that something was not as
it should have been. The noise. There had been something . . . footsteps. Someone else was here. Someone was following me. As I stood there, tense, every
nerve alert, I could feel someone watching me. The
sensation was almost tangible, like touch. I peered
down the dim, green and brown pathways between
tree trunks, so thick with shadow, but I could see no
one. Still, the aura was there, as real as scent, and as

impossible to define. My knees seemed to go weak. My throat was dry.

Unreasonably, I kept thinking of Myrtle's tale of the mysterious man with brutish features and large hands. If . . . if Colonel March *had* been innocent, as so many believed, then my aunt's murderer was still free. He might still be in the vicinity. He might have broken into the house last night, looking for something. He might . . . I forced myself to put these thoughts aside, knowing it was pure folly to indulge in them. I mustn't think such things—not now, not here.

A twig snapped loudly. Down one of the pathways a clump of shrubbery trembled, leaves rustling with a noisy crackle. There was the faint, almost inaudible sound of stealthy footsteps creeping away, then silence. I stood very, very still, my heart beating rapidly. Overhead, a bird called out with shrill vibrato, a normal, reassuring sound. A small animal scurried through the brush. I managed to get hold of myself. I had been nervous, keyed up, and my imagination had played tricks on me. No one had been watching me. No one had followed me into the woods. My own alarm had created the sinister atmosphere. I took a deep breath, relaxing, scolding myself, yet as I continued on my way to the mill I still felt a vague uneasiness. Once or twice I thought I heard footsteps behind me, but I realized it was nothing but an echo of my own footsteps, curiously distorted here in the thickness of trees and underbrush. Nevertheless, I wished Cassie had chosen someplace else for our meeting. The woods were no longer a friendly haven—perhaps because I was no longer a child.

Following the riverbank now, I stepped over wet roots and large, mossy stones. I might have been in a primeval forest, completely away from civilization, and that feeling did little to reassure me. I paused now and then, glancing over my shoulder. I wasn't really apprehensive, but I had had a fright, and the uneasiness persisted. I was relieved to see the old mill up ahead.

It sat on the other side of the river, almost completely surrounded by trees, reached by an old stone bridge that arched over the water. It was a total ruin. The wheel was rotten, several paddles fallen away, and one whole brown stone wall had crumbled. The roof, though still intact, sagged dangerously, half the slate shingles missing. When I was a child it had been one of my favorite places, endowed with romance, my own private castle, but it didn't look romantic now. It looked forbidding, with piles of debris and dark, paneless windows. Hesitantly I crossed the bridge, stepping over rubble and standing there in the weed-infested yard.

"Cassie?" I called.

There was no answer. For a moment I thought she hadn't shown up, and then I heard someone moving inside. She appeared at one of the windows, her face drawn and pale. Without saying a word, she motioned for me to come inside. I stepped through the dark, gaping doorway, the door long since missing, and almost stumbled on the rough, buckled wooden flooring.

"I thought you weren't comin'," Cassie said in a low voice. "I've been here for almost half an hour."

"I'm sorry, Cassie."

"Did you tell anyone?"

I shook my head. "Of course not."

"Did—did anyone see you leave—follow you?"

"I don't think so."

"You're not *sure?*"

"I—I thought I heard someone in the woods, but it must have been my imagination. I couldn't see anyone."

Cassie stepped over to one of the windows and peered out, watching the bridge for several minutes. Silhouetted against the light, she looked even younger and extremely frail. Most of the make-up was gone now, and she wore a short blue skirt and blue and brown striped blouse, scuffed loafers taking the place of the tottering high heels. Although the cheap perfume still clung to her, there was no smell of liquor now. She was quite sober, her eyes deep and solemn.

"No one followed me, Cassie," I said quietly. "I was—rather upset over something that happened earlier. I imagined the noise."

"He might be out there," she said, peering through the window, her back to me.

"Who?"

"The man who murdered Colonel March."

Her voice was flat, unemotional. She turned around to face me. It was extremely dim here inside the mill, but I could see her clearly, see the hard expression on her young face. Behind me the branches rustled, and the sound of the river was very loud. Cassie came closer, leaving the window. She didn't seem frightened now, merely resigned.

"I was drunk this afternoon," she said. "I—I shouldn't have called you over like that, not in my condition, but I had to speak to you, Miss Morgan. I can't keep this to myself any longer. I guess—I guess I was pretty incoherent there in the square. I was terrified someone might see us together. If—if I hadn't been drunk I wouldn't have had the nerve—"

"Tell me what you know, Cassie." My own voice was surprisingly unemotional as well. I wondered why I should be so calm.

"That night, the night your aunt was murdered, I was coming home from the pub and I saw him clearly. He—earlier on I saw this car parked at the side of the road, under some trees. I wouldn't have noticed it, only I stumbled and dropped my bag. When I bent down to pick it up I saw the moonlight shining on the fender. I thought it was funny, that car parked way off out there where no one could see it. I peeked inside. It

was empty. I went on down the road—the back road
that leads to the cottages . . ."

"Go on, Cassie."

"I want to be sure I get everything right. I want to
be sure I don't forget any of the details. The—maybe
the police'll believe you. They'd think I was lyin',
tryin' to stir up trouble. I couldn't talk to them. He—
he might have found out about it. When they questioned me, I lied. They questioned everybody in the
cottages after they found his body that night, but I
didn't tell them anything. I was afraid he might—"

With great effort, she controlled the tremor in her
voice. Stepping over to the fallen wall, she stared at
the dusty, crumbling stones. One of the pale rays of
sunlight slanted across the place where she stood, like
a dim, hazy spotlight picking her out. Her figure didn't
appear nearly so voluptuous in the plain skirt and
blouse. She looked perhaps fourteen, her shoulders
hunched, her arms folded about her waist.

"I heard the shot," she continued, calm now. "I
thought how peculiar it was—it was after midnight,
you see. Why should anyone be huntin' that late at
night? I was walkin' on the side of the road, in the
shadows, and I was just a few yards from Colonel
March's cottage when I saw that man come out the
front door. Quick-like, I darted behind a tree. I
watched him open the gate. He passed right by me, not
more than three feet away. My heart was beatin' somethin' awful. I thought I was goin' to faint."

"What did he look like, Cassie?"

"Big. He was wearin' an overcoat, dark and heavy,
and a hat with the brim pulled down, but I saw his
face in the moonlight. It was ugly—all battered-
lookin'. He walked on down the road, keepin' to the
shadows, and I sobbed—he might have heard me. He
turned around. He might have seen me, I don't know
—I ran."

I should have been weak, filled with a sense of

horror, but I had no reaction at all. Perhaps I was just numb. I stared at the girl, at the damp, mildewed walls of the mill, at the warped floor with its litter of rusty cans and wrappers left by someone long ago. I smelled the rotting wood, the damp stones, the acrid odor of bat droppings, and I heard a bird cry out with a shrill, scolding note. None of it seemed quite real.

"I ran home as fast as I could. I locked all the doors. Puggie was upset. He was restless, whinin', like he knew somethin' was wrong. Later on I heard cars and the excited voices. They'd found his body. The police knocked on my door. They came in, asked me a lot of questions, asked me if I'd seen anything or heard any noises. Constable Plimpton was polite, I guess, but that Sergeant Duncan kept prowlin' around the room. He picked up my things, examinin' them with a look of disapproval. He opened up the closet door, snoopin', all the time Constable Plimpton was questionin' me. I should have told 'em then, but—I was so frightened."

"I understand, Cassie."

"Finally, Constable Plimpton told Sergeant Duncan it was obvious Colonel March had killed himself and it was obvious why he'd done it. They left. The next mornin' I got all the details from one of my friends. He said Colonel March had stabbed your aunt to death and then came home and shot himself. The knife he'd done it with was at his side when they found him. I—I knew it wasn't so."

The peculiar sense of numbness remained. It was rather like the sensation I had experienced at the funeral: a remoteness, a sense of being apart and viewing all this with objectivity. I had every cause to believe Cassie's story. Her terror was quite genuine, and there was no earthly reason why she should have made any of this up. She wasn't a gossip, like Myrtle, and Myrtle's story corroborated Cassie's narrative. Both had described the same man. Both had mentioned a car half hidden under trees. There was no longer any doubt in my mind. Colonel March was innocent of my aunt's murder. He had been murdered himself.

"Would you recognize the man if you saw him again?" I asked quietly.

Cassie nodded, her short golden curls bouncing. "I'll never be able to forget that face."

"I'll have to tell the police, Cassie. You realize that?"

"I know. I—I'll probably get into trouble for not sayin' anything before. I—I was just—"

Both of us heard the noise at the same time. Cassie gave a start, her face turning even paler. It had sounded like someone stumbling over the rubble outside. Quickly, without thinking, I ran to the door. The yard was empty, but a clump of shrubbery nearby was trembling violently, as though someone had just brushed past it. The wind caught my hair, whipping it about my face, and I saw that all the shrubbery was trembling. A brisk wind had suddenly sprung up. It had probably blown one of the rusty cans across the yard, and that was what we had heard.

Cassie was standing in the doorway, holding on to the frame.

"There's no one here," I said.

My voice was firm, but I wasn't entirely convinced. Someone could have crossed the bridge quite easily without our hearing the footsteps over the sound of the river. Someone could have been standing near one of the windows, listening . . . I saw that Cassie was thinking the same thing. I tried to give her a reassuring smile.

"You mustn't worry," I told her. "Everything will be all right. The police will find him."

"If he saw me that night he'll try to—"

"He didn't see you," I interrupted. "If he had . . ."

"If he had he'd already have tried to kill me.

That's what you were goin' to say, isn't it? Maybe he's just bidin' his time. He must have known I didn't tell the police anything, but now—"

She broke off, suddenly wary.

"I shouldn't have come," she said. "I shouldn't have told anyone. I'd better go back home now, Miss Morgan."

"I'll go with you," I replied.

"No. I—I wouldn't want anyone to see us together."

"I could stay with you, or you could come back to the house with me."

"I'll be all right," she assured me. "Ralph Burton's coming over to the cottage. I—imagine he'll spend the night." She glanced at the watch on her wrist. "He should be arriving any time now. You go on, Miss Morgan. Do . . ." She hesitated. "Do what you think is best. I'll talk to the police if I have to."

"Cassie, I wish you'd—"

"Ralph'll be with me, Miss Morgan."

I knew that the girl was frightened, and I was reluctant to leave her, but she insisted I go. Crossing the bridge, I looked back and saw her still standing there in front of the ruined mill. She lifted her hand in a weary, defeated little gesture and, turning, vanished into the woods behind the mill. I went on down the riverbank to the path that would take me back to the house.

It was growing late now. The shadows were thicker than ever, spreading darkly over the path. I don't know why I wasn't afraid. I walked quickly, but not once did I look behind me, not once did I feel the least twinge of alarm. Some of the numbness was still there, and I felt calm, incredibly calm. It took me only a few minutes to reach the garden wall. I climbed over and hurried toward the house, intending to call the police immediately.

The phone rang just as I opened the front door. I

noticed that my hand shook as I picked up the receiver. My voice sounded strangely distant when I spoke. Perhaps I wasn't so calm after all.

"Lynn? Is that you? You sound—"

"Lloyd," I whispered. "Thank God."

"What is it? What's wrong?"

"I—I was just going to phone the police."

"The police! Lynn, what's happened?"

I suppose it was delayed reaction. My hand was shaking violently now, and nervous tremors seemed to shoot through my body. I sat down on the old Jacobean chair beside the phone, gripping the receiver tightly. I took a deep breath. I tried to summon control and finally succeeded, but there was still a nervous tremor in my voice as I repeated what Cassie had told me at the mill.

There was a long silence at the other end of the line.

"Christ," he said finally. "I knew something was wrong. Right from the start."

"I have to phone the police. They'll know what to—"

"No," he said firmly. "I'll handle everything." His voice was sober, deliberate. "Those local cops can't be worth a damn, Lynn. They made a muddle of it the first time, they're bound to again. I know a couple of very efficient men at Scotland Yard—"

"You don't understand. Cassie might be—"

"Don't interrupt me. Listen. I'll contact Scotland Yard as soon as I hang up. Hunter and Jamison will know exactly what to do. This thing is too big, too important to leave to the locals."

"Lloyd, I feel I should—"

"Trust me, Lynn."

"I do. You know I do, but—"

"You're upset. It's perfectly understandable—Christ! If only I were *there!*"

I wished fervently that he was. At the moment

there was nothing in the world I wanted more than to see his handsome, solid face. I wanted to lean on him and feel his strong arms holding me tightly.

"I'll be there," he told me. "I'll leave first thing in the morning. I'm due in court, but I'll have Stevenson take over for me. I should be arriving sometime tomorrow afternoon, latish."

"I'll be so glad to see you—so glad."

"In the meantime, I don't want you to say a word about this to anyone. Not a word. I'll phone Scotland Yard immediately, as soon as I hang up. They'll get on it right away."

"Sergeant Duncan may be coming to see Mandy tonight. I—I'll have to tell him. I couldn't—"

"I don't want *anyone* to know." His voice was sharp. "I want Hunter and Jamison to have a clear field, without any interference. They can contact the local police themselves."

"I—all right, Lloyd."

He said good-bye, and I hung up, feeling much better, certain he would take care of everything. I looked up, startled to see Mandy standing on the stairs, a worried expression on her face.

"I've been eavesdropping, luv. When the phone rang, I started downstairs to answer it and saw you coming in. I heard everything, Lynn."

"Mandy—"

"Let's don't talk about it right now. While you were gone I made sandwiches and brewed a pot of coffee without a single mishap. Let's eat. I'm famished. Incidentally, the electricity is working again. They must have repaired the lines sometime this morning."

I didn't think I would be able to eat, and was surprised to find myself with such a hearty appetite. The sandwiches were delicious, the coffee rich and strong. Outside a blue haze was thickening into night, but the kitchen was cozy with the light pouring over the cracked brown linoleum and scarred wooden table.

The copper pans gleamed. Mandy chattered away, trying to take my mind off things. Sergeant Duncan had
come by while I was gone, earlier than expected because he had to attend a rehearsal tonight. I was rather
relieved, for I couldn't be sure Mandy wouldn't say
anything to him, even though I had explained about
Scotland Yard. I found myself listening for a key in the
back door, half expecting Bart to barge in on us as he
had the night before.

"Not a sound from him," Mandy said, reading my
mind. "I suppose he's in his room."

"That was quite a scene this afternoon. I was—
horrible to him. He had a right to explode like that."

"I shouldn't worry about it, luv."

"So much has happened. There's so much to discuss—"

"I know, but not tonight. It's been a very long
day. You look absolutely exhausted, and I feel totally
done in. I think we should both get to bed early."

I agreed with her, although I doubted that I
would be able to sleep. After clearing up in the
kitchen, we made a tour of the house, checking to see
that the doors and windows were locked. The new
latches Bart had put on looked strong and secure. We
left a light burning in the hall downstairs, as well as
one upstairs. Mandy said she was going to read for a
while, so I took my bath first, reveling in the hot,
sudsy water. It wasn't quite nine o'clock when I
climbed into bed and turned off the lamp. I expected
to stay awake for hours, reliving the events of the day
in my mind. It seemed incredible that we had been
here for little more than twenty-four hours. Was it
only yesterday morning that we had set off in Brent's
ancient, battered Rolls?

I must have gone to sleep almost immediately.
The room was beginning to fill with light and the
clock showed five when I awoke abruptly. Something
had awakened me with a start. There was a sharp,

piercing clamor. I realized it was the telephone ringing.

I hurried into the hall. Mandy was just stepping
out of her room.

"Who in the world—"

"I have no idea. We'd better hurry."

I moved quickly downstairs, Mandy right behind
me. The telephone continued to ring, shrill, insistent.
I picked up the receiver, rather breathless from the
race downstairs.

"Hello."

There was no answer, only heavy silence.

"Hello?" I repeated.

"Lynn—" It was a low, hoarse whisper. "Baby,
this is Daddy—"

The shock must have registered on my face.
Mandy grew suddenly tense, knowing who it was
without my saying a word.

"You've come home, Baby."

"How—how did you—" I began.

"Wherever you go, I'll be there. You've come
home, Baby. At last you've come home—"

11

OUR POSITIONS were curiously reversed. In London, I had been unconcerned about the phone calls, convinced they were made by a prankster, while Mandy had been vastly upset. Now I was alarmed and Mandy was almost nonchalant, telling me there was nothing to worry about. Someone was obviously playing a rather nasty joke, she assured me, and it would be foolish to dwell on it.

"I mean, everyone knew where we were going," she said, "all of our crowd. It would have been easy enough for any one of them to get the number."

"No one we know would do such a thing."

"You think not? You don't really know some of those people. It's probably one of your rejected suitors —you turned down so many invitations, pet. I could name ten men you refused to dine with. One of them just decided to get back at you. Wounded ego, that sort of thing. Don't worry about it, Lynn."

"It—I was so shocked."

"Naturally. That's what he wanted. Lynn, let's get dressed and cook breakfast. Between the two of us, we should be able to manage. I couldn't possibly go back to sleep now. Neither could you."

Listlessly I slipped into a full-gathered brown skirt and white knit sweater, putting a pair of sandals on my feet. I stood in front of the mirror, brushing my hair, and I saw the faint shadows about my eyes. The skin seemed to be stretched tautly over my high cheekbones, and I was extremely pale. I went downstairs, to find Mandy already in the kitchen, looking radiant in dark gold slacks with matching sleeveless tunic. Cheeks flushed, velvety brown eyes determined, she was surrounded by pots and pans, dark blue bowls, a dish of unbroken eggs, a hunk of raw sausage, various jams and jellies, bread. A skillet of grease was popping fiercely on the stove.

"I feel terribly ambitious," she said brightly. "You break the eggs, I'll slice the sausage. Does that toaster work?"

"It must. We had toast yesterday."

"Right. That grease is awfully hot. Should I just drop the sausage in or do I do something else first?"

Needless to say, breakfast was a total disaster. The sausage was the consistency of charred leather. The eggs were inedible. We ended up drinking several cups of coffee apiece and spreading strawberry preserves over toast only slightly burned. Mandy made it all seem rather festive, and I felt much better as we lingered at the table, early-morning sunlight streaming through the windows.

"Lynn." Mandy's voice was thoughtful, rather hesitant.

"Hmmm?"

"Do you remember what he looked like?"

"Only vaguely," I replied. "I was so young when he left for Australia, barely six years old."

"Do you remember what he looked like?"

"He was large—he seemed frightfully large to me, but I guess that's because I was so small myself. He had a big face, rather gruff-looking, and dark black hair. He—he used to toss me up in the air and catch me in his arms, laughing, and then he'd hug me tightly and call me his little girl. I—I think he loved me very much."

"Does it bother you to talk about it?"

"Not in the least. You're not going to suggest—"

"That he might still be alive and handy with the telephone? Not at all. The idea's absurd. I was just curious. It seems so strange, his going off like that, leaving you with your aunt."

"I was heartbroken," I said, remembering quite sharply the pain I had felt when Daphne told me he was gone. "He never said good-bye. I—I suppose he wanted to avoid an emotional scene."

"It must have been quite traumatic for you."

"It was. I cried for weeks. I never could understand exactly why he left, but I think it must have had something to do with some sort of business venture. He wasn't a successful man—that's why we came to live with Aunt Daphne in the first place, because there wasn't any money. I think he must have gone to Australia in hopes of making a new start. I suppose he planned to come back for me."

"Did your aunt ever talk about him much?"

"Never. She tore up his photographs, too. I remember that distinctly. I think she was angry with him for going off like that, leaving her with the responsibility for me. She resented me, all the years I was here. She made that quite obvious."

"Didn't your father write?"

"Oh yes. Once a month, regular as clockwork. At least she let me have the letters—most of them. Of course, she opened them and read them before giving them to me. I could read quite well by that time."

"I know, luv, you were a regular little prodigy, whipping through the complete works of Balzac at ten. Staggering."

"Sometimes he sent presents," I continued, finding it strangely comforting to be talking about him. "I remember a doll, obviously handmade, with a stuffed rag body and brightly painted face. I loved that doll, kept it for years—Lord knows what eventually became of it. I seem to remember a little red box, too, quite pretty. I kept trinkets in it. I suppose Aunt Daphne threw it out years ago.''

I sighed, looking down at the empty blue coffee cup. "He died when I was thirteen. My mother, of course, had died before we ever came to Devon. It—it wasn't a bad childhood, really. I had all the books I wanted to read, a whole library full of them, and I had the woods to roam in. Aunt Daphne let me do pretty much as I pleased so long as I kept out of her way and didn't associate with any of the village children. I was lonely, but I had never known anything else.''

Mandy stood up. "You're depressing me, luv. I wish I'd never brought it up. Look at this mess! Did *we* do that? I've never seen so many pots and pans in my life. They must have multiplied while our backs were turned.''

"I'll help. It won't take us long to clean up.''

"No, you run along. You're still a bit pale. A walk in the gardens will do you good. I'll attend to this. I may not be able to cook, but I'm terrific with dirty dishes.''

I protested, but Mandy was quite firm, and I could see that it would be futile to argue with her. Shooing me out of the kitchen, she began banging the pots and pans around quite happily, probably reminiscing about her days as a waitress. I took her advice and strolled out into the gardens, feeling rather melancholy, still a bit worried about the phone call. I was puzzled by Mandy's about-face, too. In London she had been near hysterical about the calls. Why, then, did she pass this one off so lightly? Was it because she had seen how upset I was?

It was a splendid morning. The air was fresh and clean, inebriating, the kind of air one never encountered in London. Colors were sharp and vividly defined: leaves green, jade green, dark green, brown, bluebells a bright blue, hollyhocks a vivid purple and red against the mellow gray wall. Tiny silver snail trails glistened on the flagstones, and the earth was a rich, loamy brown. Even the house looked better this morning, large and sprawling, leafy shadows playing on the sun-washed walls, the multi-level roof gleaming a dull bronze spread with chimney shadows.

It was hard not to be cheerful on such a morning, and I could feel my melancholy slipping away, feel strength returning. Everything was going to be all right, I told myself. Lloyd would be here this afternoon, and the men from Scotland Yard were already at work. The phone call had upset me, but it would be foolish to brood about it. The sun was warm on my cheeks, and the air was like a fine wine, reviving me, driving away the worries that plagued me.

Following the path around the side of the house, I came upon Bart's car parked in front of the carriage house, the back seat filled with a jumble of books and boxes, tennis racquets, shoes. The trunk was open, his ancient typewriter set beside a heap of clothes, the familiar cricket bat sticking out. There was a peculiar sinking sensation in the pit of my stomach as I realized what it meant. The door upstairs slammed, and I turned to see him coming down the stairs, arms laden with more clothes. He saw me, nodded, and moved past me to pile the clothes haphazardly on top of the others.

"You're leaving?" I asked.

"That's pretty obvious, isn't it?"

His voice was polite, his manner amiable enough, but there was an invisible wall around him. He stood there in the sunlight wearing brown loafers, tight denim trousers bleached the color of bone, and an exquisite bulky-knit crew-neck sweater of oatmeal tan, speckled with brown and rust. He had never looked more appealing, and he had never been so distant. Feathery black locks tumbled over his brow. He smiled, but there was no warmth. His vivid blue eyes regarded me with cool objectivity. There was so much

I wanted to say, but the words seemed to stick in my throat. He didn't make it any easier. He rested his hands on his thighs, looking slightly impatient.

"You—you don't have to leave," I finally said.

"I think it's best this way, don't you?"

"I—yes, I suppose so."

"I've already talked to Hampton over the phone. There'll be no trouble about the second will. You'll get everything."

"I don't want it," I replied, sounding childish.

"Neither do I. I don't intend to argue with you, Lynn. I think we pretty well covered everything yesterday."

"I guess we did."

There was a long silence. He tapped his fingers restlessly against his thighs, waiting, definitely impatient to be rid of me. I looked into his eyes, and I knew I had deceived myself. I had, finally, lost. I had loved him for years without even knowing it, and now that I knew it was too late.

"Well?" he said.

"I'm sorry about yesterday, Bart."

"Are you?"

"I shouldn't have made those insinuations. I know—I realize how unfair I was."

"Forget it."

"Where will you go?"

"To the inn, right now. I'll stay there a couple of days or so, then after this thing about the wills is settled I'll move on to London. I have the flat there."

"I—see."

He was stiff, unyielding. He saw how uncomfortable I was, and made no effort to help. He didn't care. I was simply one he'd missed, one he had failed to seduce.

"Look, I've got several more loads to pack up. If there isn't anything else—"

"The latches. I haven't paid you for them. I'll—"

"Don't bother. Consider them a gift."

I wanted to plead with him, beg him to stay, but my pride prevented it. I looked at him, and I could feel my cheeks coloring, feel the anger begin to mount—blessed anger, preventing the other emotions from taking hold. There was no reason for him to be so cold, so bloody unyielding. I had apologized, and if he wanted to sulk, if he . . . Thank God he was leaving before I made an even greater fool of myself.

"I insist on paying you," I said crisply. "I don't want to be under any obligation to you."

"I'll not take your money."

"How much did they cost?"

"Listen, I don't want to fight. Okay? I'm liable to lose my temper again and do something foolish, say something foolish."

"Like you did yesterday."

"Like I did yesterday."

I stared at him, longing to say something that would demolish him but unable to think of it. Bart smiled a crooked smile, one eyebrow slanting up at the corner.

"Too bad we couldn't hit it off," he said. "Believe me, the loss is all yours. Maybe one of these days you'll realize that."

"Your conceit knows no bounds."

"Yeah, I know. I'm insufferable. No argument. You're lucky to be getting rid of me."

"For once we're in complete accord."

He started to say something else but thought better of it. He shrugged his shoulders, shook his head good-naturedly, and went back up the stairs, leaving me standing there with burning cheeks. I wanted to scream. I walked quickly around to the front of the house and hurried up the steps. Then I stopped, as I felt the tears run down my cheeks. I wiped them away angrily, furious with myself. He had deliberately humiliated me, made me feel shabby, and I was glad he was leaving—genuinely, sincerely glad.

I don't know how long I stood on the veranda, holding on to one of the peeling white posts, a prey to conflicting emotions that swept over me in waves. I heard him loading the car and, some time later, heard the motor starting and watched him drive away. He stared straight ahead, not once looking back, and the car disappeared around a curve between the tall leafy trees, and then there was only sunlight and shadow on the drive, making patterns as the wind caused branches to sway.

I was in a wretched, irritable mood when I went back inside. Mandy met me in the hall, a puzzled crease between her brows.

"Bart knocked on the back door while I was still in the kitchen," she said. She held up a set of keys. "He gave me these."

"He's gone," I explained. "He drove away a few minutes ago."

"Just like that?"

"*Just* like that."

"You needn't snap my head off!"

"I—I'm sorry, Mandy. I went for a walk, as you suggested, and I felt revived, felt so much better, and then I ran into Bart and—and he managed to spoil everything, just like he always does. He's gone now, and I'm *glad.*"

"Did he say where he was going?"

"He's going to the inn. He'll stay there for two or three days, then he's going on to London."

"Oh well." She lifted one shoulder in an actressy shrug and sighed. "I'd rather hoped he'd be around to cook dinner tonight, but I suppose we can order something in the village and bring it back. I wonder if Cooper's Green has a Wimpey's."

Neither of us mentioned Bart's name again. I wandered around restlessly, and Mandy made a couple of telephone calls, speaking low as though she was afraid I might be listening. One, no doubt, was to Sergeant Duncan, and the other was probably to her agent in London, who, I knew, had asked her to check with him. I was sitting on the leather couch in the library and looking moodily at the wall of books when she came in. There was a purposeful expression on her face.

"Lynn, it's after ten. I guess we'd better get on up to the attic and start sorting through the junk."

"Whatever for?"

"Don't tell me you've forgotten about the jumble sale?"

"Oh Lord!" I groaned.

"You also told Myrtle you'd try to find time to gather up a few things to bring with you. Remember?"

"Unfortunately."

"Come on, don't look so glum. It'll be fun to prowl around in the attic. There's no telling what we might find."

Reluctantly I followed Mandy upstairs and down the hall. We climbed up the narrow attic stairs, opened the door, and stepped into a vast, musty, crumbling world of old barrels and piles of dust-covered books, magazines dating back to the turn of the century, trunks, old dress forms, antique lamps, and broken, discarded furniture. Rays of sunlight stirring with dust motes slanted in through the high dormer windows. The bare wooden floorboards creaked noisily as we moved across them. In spite of myself, I felt some of the old fascination for the place coming back.

Staring around at the accumulation of several generations, I felt an overwhelming sense of the past, and there was a touch of nostalgia as well. I remembered by-gone days when, with the oil lamp shedding a warm yellow light and rain pounding on the roof overhead and lashing against the windows, I had amused myself for hours exploring the treasures to be found in the old trunks smelling of camphor and dry silk and lilac. Curled up on the faded rose sofa with broken springs and lumpy cushions, I had studied the pictures in the yellowing magazines and imagined myself living in those days of horse-drawn carriages and velvet furbelows. In the old viewer with its wooden handle and foggy lenses, I had looked at the stiff cardboard scenes of Rome and Venice, faded a pinkish-brown.

"An antiques dealer would go out of his mind!" Mandy exclaimed, interrupting my reverie. "What a fabulous old Victorian lamp! Look at this glass, Lynn. Tiffany? I wouldn't be surprised."

Mandy's enthusiasm was boundless. Far more knowledgeable about such things than I, she kept pointing out treasures that would fetch a good sum on the antiques market. Oblivious to dust and cobwebs, face smudged and gold slack suit getting deplorably soiled, she threw herself into the job with that vital energy I had always admired. Between the two of us we managed to fill a sturdy cardboard box with less-valuable items: brass candlesticks, ivory fans, costume jewelry, a pretty lamp, various old but still usable items of clothing. After the box was filled, Mandy sat down on the floor, leaned her back against the wall, and began leafing through a book of fashion plates we had come across earlier. I was rummaging through the old oak cabinet on the other side of the room.

"Fantastic!" she called. "Lynn, these should be framed. They date back to the eighteen eighties! Bustles, parasols, fur muffs . . ."

I was examining a dust-covered but lovely set of gold-rimmed bone china with delicate blue flowers and not really paying attention to her. I rubbed the dust off the teapot, marveling at the beauty of the piece and wondering why the set had been relegated to up here. Kneeling down, I looked to see what was on the other shelves: a collection of glass dogs, a heap of dress patterns, a dusty velvet pin cushion, a hundred or so old *Punch* magazines, a small red lacquered box . . . I picked up the box, startled to see it. I had mentioned it only this morning.

"Imagine finding this," I said.

"Hmmm? What, luv?"

"The little red box I was telling you about, the one my father sent to me from Australia." I opened the lid. The box was filled with yellowing sheets covered with bold, rather crude handwriting. "His letters are here, too."

"His letters?"

Mandy wasted no time in joining me in front of the cabinet, fashion plates forgotten.

"I wonder why Aunt Daphne kept them. I guess she thought I might want them when I grew up. There are no envelopes."

"No return address, either," Mandy remarked, taking out one of the letters.

"What an unusual little box. I've never seen one like it before. The lacquer's not quite smooth, rather grainy. The lid's a bit crooked. It's obviously handmade, like the doll was. He must have made it himself."

"What are we waiting for, luv? Let's *read* them!"

Mandy clearly expected the letters to reveal a great deal about my father. She was doomed to disappointment. We sat down on the old sofa with the box between us. It didn't take us long to read them. There weren't more than twenty or so. Short, ungrammatical, they were filled with platitudes, a father telling his daughter how to conduct herself, inquiring about her schoolwork, her health, and so on. There were no personal references, no references to his work, nor did he ever mention Australia. Duller, less-revealing letters would be hard to imagine. Legs propped under her, elbow leaning on the arm of the sofa, Mandy frowned.

"Are you *sure* he was in Australia?"

"Positive. I—I think it was Sydney."

"Strange he never mentioned it. Strange, too, that none of them has a return address, just the date each letter was written. If we had the envelopes there would be postmarks, but they're missing. Doesn't it strike you as odd, Lynn?"

"Not particularly."

"These letters could have been mailed from anywhere. It's almost as though he were trying to hide something."

"Nonsense. Letter writing doesn't come naturally to some people. He obviously found it difficult to express himself—that's why there are so many platitudes. You must bear in mind, too, that he was writing to a child. I find nothing at all mysterious about them. They're simply dull."

"Maybe so," she replied, unconvinced. "Still, I wish there were some way of knowing."

"I have no reason to doubt he was in Australia."

"Your aunt—when she gave you the letters, they were already opened?"

"Yes. I told you, she read them all herself first."

"Were they still in their envelopes?"

"Mandy, I don't see why you keep harping on—"

"Try to remember, Lynn. Indulge me."

I sighed wearily. Casting back in memory, I saw Aunt Daphne coming into my bedroom, red curls tumbled, a sour, disapproving look on her face. She was wearing a purple dress printed with red flowers, and she smelled of gin. "Here's another letter from your father." I saw myself, small, in pigtails, reaching for it. I pressed my brows together, concentrating. Had there been an envelope? I saw her already gnarled hand, nails chipped, a large, loose garnet ring on one finger. It was holding a sheet of paper—a single sheet, no envelope. I told Mandy.

"But that doesn't prove anything," I protested.

"Perhaps not."

"I think you're being absurd. Just because of those telephone calls—"

"It has nothing to do with them," she said quickly—too quickly. "I suppose I was just disappointed they didn't tell us more about him. Anyway, it's not worth pursuing."

She got to her feet and stretched languidly, affecting an indifference that wasn't at all convincing. I knew her too well to be taken in by this sudden reversal. Slightly annoyed, I gathered up the letters, stacking them together. As I was starting to put them back in the box, I noticed the card.

It was large, wedged face down in the bottom of the box. I pulled it out. Once white, it was now a dingy gray, and the black ink had faded to violet. The message was written in the same crude handwriting as the letters: *I hope you will follow the right path. Love, Daddy.* The platitude was typical of those most of the letters had ended with: *I hope you eat all your spinach, I hope you study real hard, I hope you mind your Aunt Daphne,* and so forth.

"What's that?" Mandy inquired.

"A card. He must have sent it when he mailed me the box. One corner was stuck in the seams at the bottom."

"Let's see."

I handed it to her. Mandy read it, shrugged, and gave it back to me, still affecting that disinterest that didn't fool me a minute. I put letters and card back into the box and closed the lid, noticing again that the fit wasn't quite right—the lid buckled slightly.

"Well, I guess we'd better hurry. Both of us will have to bathe, and you promised Myrtle you'd get there early. I'll drive you there, pick you up when it's over."

"I thought you were going to come with me—"

"To a jumble sale?" Mandy looked horrified. "Friendship extends just so far, luv. I'm sure you'll manage nicely, but personally, I'd rather be shot."

12

A FIRING SQUAD really might have been preferable after all, I reflected as Mandy drove the Rolls around the square toward the vast brown church where the jumble sale was to be held. Set far back from the street, copper spire rising nobly above the huge oaks that surrounded it, the church was protected by a walled courtyard with high iron gates. At twenty after twelve, a horde of chattering women was already milling about impatiently in front of the gates. Armed with umbrellas, shopping bags, and great heavy purses, they cast angry glances at the church, eyed each other suspiciously, shoved closer to the gates. They looked more like plump, red-cheeked Amazon warriors in print dresses than genteel matrons.

"My God, they're going to storm the place," Mandy said, pulling up at the curb. "The mob in front of the Bastille must have looked just like this."

"Mandy, you can't desert me now."

"I have things to do," she said firmly. "I'll pick you up at three."

"Where are you going?"

"Here and there. I want to see Douglas about something, and then I'm going to drive over to Merrymead. I understand they have a large library. There's something I want to check up on."

"Can't it wait?"

"Stiff upper lip, luv," she replied, ignoring my question. "You'll have fun managing the bookstall. If

you happen to see any early Peter Cheyney or James
Hadley Chase thrillers, put them aside for me. Look,
here comes Myrtle."

Flanked by three hefty dames who were built like
soccer stars, Myrtle came down the steps of the church
and marched briskly across the courtyard. The crowd
rushed forward as she approached the firmly pad-
locked gates. There was a great uproar, violent pushing
and shoving, bags swinging viciously, umbrellas pok-
ing. Shrill voices rose as she began to unlock the gates,
but Myrtle's strident sergeant-major bellow easily
soared above the rest of the noise. "Back!" she roared.
"We open at *one!*" Leaving two of her co-workers to
guard the gates, she shoved her way through the constantly swelling throng and approached the Rolls, extremely self-important. She looked preposterous in a
green crepe dress and matching hat. A tacky gray fox
furpiece hung around her neck. Her plump cheeks
were flushed, her merry eyes alight with excitement,
as she leaned through the window of the car.

"Here you are at last, ducky! I was beginning to
worry, then I saw you driving up. Thought I'd better
come out and provide a bodyguard. You'd never make
it through that mob! Aren't they something? Our jumble sales are always popular!"

"So it would seem," I said, heart sinking.

"We always have such terrific bargains. The girls
can hardly *contain* themselves! They come from miles
around, hoping to snap up treasures. Oh, I see you
brought some more loot! We can use every scrap. The
box is there in the back seat, Fenella. Get it!"

Fenella had steel-gray hair and belligerent black
eyes. She must have weighed over two hundred
pounds, a formidable figure who would have made the
fiercest professional wrestler back against the ropes in
terror. Without a word, she opened the door, scooped
up the heavy box in one mighty heave, and hoisted it
out and up on one shoulder as though it contained

feathers. Myrtle gave her an approving smile and opened the front door for me. I climbed out, casting a pleading look at Mandy, who blew me a kiss and drove away, leaving me at the mercy of Myrtle and her crew.

"Out of the way!" Myrtle cried lustily, thrusting her way back through the throng and dragging me with her. "Step aside! Gates open at one and not a minute before! Back! Don't wave that umbrella at *me*, Alice Hendricks! You'll wait out here just like the rest of 'em!"

Fenella bringing up the rear with the box balanced on her shoulder, we reached the gates without being pulled apart, although I did get slammed on the back with a bulky purse. Once through, Myrtle clanged the gates shut and re-locked the padlock. Feeling myself trapped in a world of P. G. Wodehouse characters gone berserk, I followed Myrtle and the others into the dim foyer and down a flight of stone steps to the basement, where the level of chaos was, if anything, even more frenzied.

"Your stall's over here, ducky," Myrtle said, leading me past tables stacked with dishes, bric-a-brac, clocks, tea cozies, and crocheted doilies. "Lovely of you to help out like this. You were just splendid at the funeral, ducky, so noble. I meant to call on you again and bring a casserole, but every minute's been taken up here. Someone has to take charge or they'd botch the whole show. Mmm, heavenly smell." This as we passed the cake stall, lovely cakes of every description arranged in tiers. "Bertha Clemmons won first prize for her angelfood, though everyone knows she used a mix! Over here, ducks. I thought you'd be more at ease with the books."

Like all the others, the bookstall was homemade, painted white, with a slightly tilted roof. The long, flat counter in front was laden with hundreds of books, half of them neatly upended with the titles showing and the rest heaped in wildly disordered stacks. Myrtle opened the gate at one side and led me in. The shelves under the counter were crammed full of more books.

"We're in quite a dilemma," Myrtle explained. "All the books haven't been priced yet, just those neatly arranged there. You'll have to mark them yourself, ducky. It's quite simple—those with dust jackets fifteen pence, those without ten. The really battered ones and all the paperbacks are five pence each. After you've marked them, put them in front with the others. The idea is to keep replenishing the stock as they take them away. None of those under there has been priced yet. I'd help, ducky, but I've got to attend to things—"

"I think I can manage."

"You're a peach, a regular peach. You don't have to worry about collecting the money. Everything's paid for at the cash register. We have half an hour yet. You oughta be able to price most of these before the mob arrives. Here's a pencil. Well, ta ta for now."

Myrtle adjusted the gray fox around her neck, straightened the brim of her hat and, throwing me a merry smile, hurried away to referee an argument that was raging on the other side of the room. As opening time approached, the din rose, the activity increasing to a point of near hysteria. Ignoring it through sheer willpower, I began marking the books, quickly. I discovered three Peter Cheyneys and two early James Hadley Chase epics and, quite shamelessly, marked them at five pence each and stuck them on the bottom shelf for Mandy. I had the books on top of the counter marked in twenty minutes or so, then I began arranging them in neat rows. The huge clock on the wall showed ten minutes till one, seven till, five, then both hands pointed to one and there was a thundering noise overhead and wild shrieks as if from a tribe of attacking savages. The invasion had begun.

An hour passed. An hour and a half. The basement was warm and stuffy. The walls were denuded of pictures, only the grimmest-faced ancestors and the tackiest prints remaining. The tables and stalls were thoroughly ransacked, the best bargains long since carted off. The first violent wave of humanity had come and gone, and although the basement was still crowded, people were browsing now, fingering articles doubtfully and passing them by to search for better buys. The woman at the cash register mopped her brow with a linen handkerchief. Fenella fanned herself with a palmetto fan.

As I stood at my stall, idly watching the crowd, a feeling of uneasiness came over me. I had no idea why, but I suddenly felt uncomfortable. The feeling had come upon me suddenly. One moment I had been relaxed, slightly amused, eager to finish up here and be gone, and the next I was ill at ease, my nerves on edge. I was receiving vibrations, responding to some intangible force that hadn't been here before. Looking up, I saw Myrtle hurrying toward me.

The green hat was crushed. The gray fur hung limply around her neck. She stopped in front of the counter, an excited look on her plump, rosy face.

"Don't look now, ducky," she whispered dramatically, "but he's *here!*"

"Who? What are you—"

"That man—the brute who kept pesterin' poor Daphne. He's here. I saw him with my own *eyes!*"

"Are—are you sure?"

Nodding emphatically, she glanced over her shoulder like a conspirator and then nodded again, leaning toward me.

"Over there, by the dress racks. It's him, ducky. I'm positive. He keeps *staring* at you."

That explained it. I could feel his eyes on me, and, remembering Cassie's story, I felt my skin prickle. Trying to seem casual, I glanced toward the dress racks. A large man in an overcoat was standing against the wall, partially hidden by one of the racks. The smile vanished from my lips. His face was broad, features blunt, his eyes glowing like dark coals. For perhaps half a minute I stared directly into those eyes, hypnotized by them, and then he stepped behind the rack.

"Are you all right, ducky?"

I nodded, passing a hand over my forehead.

"I like to have dropped my teeth, seein' him there. I was chattin' with Stella Dickerson, admirin' the beads she'd bought, when I happened to look up and there he *was,* big as life." Myrtle pulled out a bag of chocolates and popped one into her mouth. Her brown eyes were full of excitement. "I recognized him immediately. Isn't likely I'd forget a mug like his, is it? He just stood there against the wall, starin' at you with that menacing look in his eyes—"

"He—you're certain he was the man you saw that night?"

"Positive, ducky, absolutely positive. I wonder what he was doin' here? He wasn't buyin' anything. He just stood there, starin' at you—you look a bit pale, ducky. I think you need—"

"I'm perfectly all right."

"—a glass of lemonade, with ice. That'll fix you up. They're sellin' it at the snack stall. You just sit down on that stool there, ducky. I'll fetch it right away."

Myrtle scurried off. There was a stool behind me, but I didn't sit down. I rearranged the remaining books, trying to gain control of myself. The sight of him had given me a shock. My nerves were still on edge. The man had gone. I knew that without even looking up. It was as though some evil force had departed, taking the vibrations away. I kept thinking about Cassie, about the sounds we had heard outside the mill. Had he followed me through the woods? Had he been lurking by one of the windows, listening to our conversation? As I had stared into those dark, hypnotic eyes I had felt a definite threat. He hadn't even tried to disguise it.

My hands had stopped trembling. I took a deep breath, wondering what I should do. He had murdered my aunt. I was certain of that. He had murdered Colonel March, too. Should I phone the police? Lloyd would be here soon, sometime this afternoon. The men from Scotland Yard already knew everything, Lloyd had told them, and they were probably in Cooper's Green now, investigating. Lloyd . . . Thank God he was coming. He would take charge of everything. I must pull myself together. I must remain calm, particularly around Myrtle. I mustn't let her suspect anything.

By the time she came bustling back with the lemonade, I was completely composed.

"Here you are, ducky. Drink this."

"Thank you," I said, smiling. "I—I was just feeling a bit tired."

She wasn't about to be diverted. "Do you know who he is?" she asked in a low, eager voice.

"I haven't the vaguest notion."

"I wonder what he wants. The way he was lookin' at you—it gave me the creeps."

I took a sip of the iced lemonade, stalling, knowing I had to be very careful.

"I shouldn't worry about it," I said lightly. "He's probably just some tourist who heard about the sale and stopped in. Listen, it's almost three. I haven't had a customer for quite some time. I wonder if you could find someone to relieve me? I have ever so many things to do, and—"

"I know, ducky," she said, immediately sympathetic. "You're still broken up over the funeral. Well, all the cakes've been sold. I'll get Nell's niece to take over for you. This has all been such a shock for you . . ."

The Rolls was parked in front of the church,

Mandy sitting behind the wheel. She seemed distracted, a thoughtful look in her eyes. She gave me a vague, absent-minded smile as I climbed in beside her.

"I found several books," I told her, tossing the parcel into the back seat. "Three Chases, three Cheyneys."

"Marvelous, luv. How was it? Dreadful?"

"Dreadful," I replied.

Her mind was definitely elsewhere. She started the car and pulled away from the curb, circling the square, heading for the outskirts of the village.

"What did you do this afternoon?" I asked.

"Oh—nothing much," she said evasively. "I solved the problem about dinner, though. There was a charming little delicatessen in Merrymead. I bought some wonderful goodies—a baked chicken, ham slices, potato salad. It's all there in the box in the back seat."

"Did you go to the library?"

"Mmm-hmmm," she murmured. "I'll tell you about it later, when we get home."

"Mandy," I said hesitantly. "Something happened at the jumble sale. That man—the one Myrtle saw—he was there."

"Oh?"

She didn't seem at all surprised. I described him to her, described my reactions, told her how he had been staring. I expected her to bombard me with questions, but she merely swerved to avoid a deep rut and drove on down the road. I was disappointed, and mystified as well.

"Did you phone the police?" she asked casually.

I shook my head, staring through the dusty windshield at the low-hanging branches that almost scraped the top of the car.

"Lloyd asked me not to tell the police anything yet. I'll be so glad when this is all over."

"It soon will be," Mandy said. Her voice sounded

strange. She hesitated for a moment. "Lynn—everything is going to work out fine. I promise."

It was an enigmatic statement, and Mandy was acting most peculiarly, almost as though she were part of some conspiracy I knew nothing about. I remembered that mysterious conversation she and Bart had had in the kitchen, their worried looks, and I remembered her telephone calls this morning. She had taken care to speak low so that I wouldn't overhear anything. Why? We had no secrets from each other. I was still puzzling over this as we turned up the drive and approached the house.

Mandy parked in the garage, and as I got out I noticed the large empty space where Bart's car had been. I closed my mind to that. I wouldn't think about Bart, not now. He was gone. I told myself I was glad, but the sense of loss remained. We went inside, carrying the parcels with us. The house seemed larger than ever, emptier. I was acutely aware of the deserted rooms, the peculiar silence. The atmosphere was different. I had a feeling that the house itself was waiting for something to happen, but Mandy didn't seem to notice anything. She closed the door and, seeing my expression, asked me what was wrong. I couldn't explain.

"It's just—don't you feel a difference?"

"Difference? I don't know what you're talking about."

"There's—something in the air. I can sense it."

"You're tired, pet, and seeing that man upset you. You're imagining things."

Mandy went on down the hall to the kitchen to put the food away, and I stepped into the parlor, unable to shake the feeling that something was amiss. The room was a dim, shadowy blue until I opened the draperies to let in the sunlight. Wavering rays slanted through the French windows like pale yellow fingers touching the edge of the carpet. I sat down, and the house seemed to settle around me. I knew I was tired, and I *had* been upset, but this peculiar feeling had nothing to do with that. The very silence seemed ominous. I stared at the red lacquer box sitting on the table. I had brought it down from the attic this morning, but I didn't remember placing it there. Surely I had left it in my bedroom.

Mandy came into the room, looking sensational in her melon pink slack suit with the wide brown belt. She looked bothered, too. Something was preying on her mind.

"Mandy, I—I'm certain I left this box in my bedroom. Did you bring it down here?"

"The box? Oh, yes. I brought it down while you were in the bath. I wanted to glance at the letters again."

"You're still not satisfied with them, are you?"

She didn't reply. She stepped over to the window and looked out, her back to me. She wasn't herself at all. She finally turned around, and her velvety brown eyes were grave.

"There's something I have to tell you, Lynn. I—I don't know whether I should or not. Maybe it would be—"

"What is it?" My voice was strained. "It's about the letters, isn't it?"

"Yes, luv," she said. She sat down on the large, overstuffed chair, and I could see that she was still debating whether or not she should tell me what she had discovered.

"You found out something about my father," I said.

Mandy looked into my eyes, nodding slowly.

"Something unpleasant," I added.

"Lynn," she began, "when we stopped by the police station to talk to Constable Plimpton, he said he thought he remembered you. You told him you stayed on with your aunt after your father left for Australia. I don't know if you noticed or not, but when you said that he looked—puzzled. He covered up quickly, changing the subject, but I could tell that something had momentarily thrown him.''

"I remember that. I didn't pay any attention to it at the time.''

"When I saw the letters—well, they bothered me. Something wasn't right, I knew that immediately, and then I remembered Constable Plimpton's reaction. I drove to the police station after I let you out at the church. Constable Plimpton was extremely evasive when I asked about your father. He didn't want to discuss it. 'Some things are best left alone,' he said. 'The girl believes her father went to Australia. What good would it do for her to learn the truth now?' I finally convinced him it was important, and he gave me the basic facts. He wasn't in office when it happened. I had to go to Merrymead for the details. They have a large library there, with all the back issues of the London papers on file.''

"He didn't go to Australia," I said calmly.

"No, luv, he didn't. Your aunt told you that to protect you. She told all her friends the same thing. Evidently she had some influence with the local newspaper editors, because the story never appeared in any of them. It was hushed up completely. Only the local police knew what happened, and they kept quiet out of respect for your aunt. The London papers, however, carried full reports. Are—are you sure you want to hear this?''

"Quite sure.''

"Your father already had a police record when he brought you to Devon. Nothing really serious, but—he was known to the police. Perhaps he came here to get away from his criminal associates, start a new life, and raise you in a different atmosphere. It didn't work out that way. Perhaps he was disillusioned with country life and realized his sister wasn't the genteel old maid he'd imagined and was unsuitable to look after a young niece. Perhaps he thought he could pull one last job and realize enough to completely break away —that's all supposition. Five months after bringing you here, he and one Herb Sheppard robbed a London jeweler, killing a clerk and fleeing with a fortune in uncut gems. The police eventually tracked them down to this house. Both men were captured."

"What part did Aunt Daphne play in all this?"

"She apparently knew nothing about the robbery until the police showed up. Her brother had told her he was bringing a friend to stay with them for a few days. She was horrified when she learned the truth. Both men were tried, convicted, and sent to prison."

"Then—he isn't dead?"

"He died of a heart attack in his cell thirteen years ago," Mandy said quietly.

"I—I see."

I looked at the pretty, poorly constructed red lacquer box on the coffee table. He must have made it in one of the prison workshops. He must have made the doll, too, the one I had been so fond of. My father may have been many things, but he had loved me. I knew that in my heart. It was my one consolation now.

"I—I'm glad you told me, Mandy. Somehow it makes it easier to know he didn't willingly go off and leave me."

"I thought you might feel that way. That's why I decided to tell you."

"What happened to the jewels? Did they find them?"

Mandy shook her head. "They were never recovered. Sheppard claimed he didn't know what had become of them, and your father refused to reveal anything. The police searched this house from top to bottom. They searched Sheppard's flat in the city. They found no trace of the jewels, none whatsoever.

They eventually decided your father had turned them over to some third party. He—he died with his secret."

We were silent for several minutes. The rays of sunlight reached farther into the room, and the clock ticked loudly, monotonously. When I finally spoke, my voice was surprisingly calm.

"All this has some connection with Aunt Daphne's murder, doesn't it?"

"I suspect it does, luv."

"And the phone calls—they have some connection, too."

"They might. I—don't know."

I stood up, amazed at my own calm. I refused to be upset. I refused to give way to the panic that was building up inside. It would accomplish nothing. I had to hold on. I had to.

"Lloyd will be here soon," I said, and there was only a very slight tremor in my voice. "He—he'll know what to make of this. He'll know what to do. I'm not going to worry about it. I'm going upstairs to freshen up for him. Everything is going to work out fine. You said so yourself."

"I know. I just hope . . ."

"Yes?"

"Nothing, luv. Pay no attention to me. You run on upstairs and put on something smashing for Lloyd. I'll just sit here for a while. There are some things I need to think about."

I hesitated, looking at her closely. She tried to appear casual, but it didn't quite come off. There was something else, something she still hadn't told me. I didn't question her. Mandy might be competent enough on stage and on television, but she could never hide anything from me. She was extremely worried. I wondered why. I had likened the various incidents to pieces of a giant jigsaw puzzle that were fitting together to make an alarming picture. I had a feeling the last piece would soon fit into place.

13

IT WAS SHORTLY after four when I came back downstairs. I was wearing a soft blue silk dress sprigged
with tiny lilacs. My hair was brushed to a shiny gloss.
I had applied just enough make-up to emphasize my
natural coloring, and I knew that I was looking my
best. It had a therapeutic effect. Lloyd would be here
soon, and he would take everything in his strong, capable hands, and there was absolutely no reason to
worry. I felt almost lighthearted as I stepped into the
hall.

"It's out of the question," Mandy was saying,
holding the telephone receiver to her ear. "I know,
luv, I appreciate that. I know you went to a lot of
trouble setting it up—" She looked up at me, frowning. "No, it isn't that. I'd love to play one of Charles
the Second's mistresses. Really. I'm tired of Maisie.
Yes, it would be a real break. BBC is—I would be there
if I could, but something has—" She broke off, listening, her eyes full of patient resignation. "Yes, yes, of
course. He saw me as Maisie and he thinks I'd be perfect. It's a chance of a lifetime, I grant that—" She
sighed. "I know, luv, it *is* important. Ordinarily I'd
leave an iron lung to audition for the part, but—" She
paused again, making a face, and I could hear an ur-
gent voice on the other end of the line. "All right,
Herbie. I'll try. I promise. If I'm not there they'll just
have to use someone else. What? Yes, I understand
your position. Hmmm? Okay. Sure. Good-bye."

"Your agent?" I inquired.

She nodded. "Himself. Talk about irony. BBC is starting a series on Charles the Second, and the producer saw one of my commercials. He thinks I'd make a terrific Nell Gwynn and wants me to audition for the role, but the auditions are tomorrow morning at ten. I tried to explain to Herbie why I couldn't be there but he wouldn't listen. I'd love to do that part, but—"

"Why can't you be there?"

"I couldn't possibly go off and leave you alone here. It would be unthinkable—"

"I wouldn't be alone. Lloyd will be here."

"I know, but—"

"Don't be absurd," I said firmly. "You can get a train and be in London tonight. Opportunities like this don't turn up every day. There's absolutely no reason why you should pass it up."

Mandy protested vigorously. She was torn by indecision. I could see that she desperately wanted to make the audition, but she was worried about leaving me. I assured her that I would be perfectly all right, that Lloyd would certainly arrive before dark, and that I wouldn't dream of letting her miss such a spectacular opportunity. When she continued to protest, I simply picked up the telephone, called the train station, and made a reservation for her on the five-thirty train for London. I hung up and told her we'd better get upstairs to start packing.

"You're marvelous, Lynn, just marvelous! You're certain you won't mind? I'll phone tomorrow after the audition, and I'll take the train back tomorrow afternoon. I mean, I know Lloyd will be here, but I don't want to miss anything. Nell Gwynn! I would be perfect in the part. I do a smashing Cockney accent, and—"

Now that the matter was settled, Mandy could hardly contain her excitement. She continued to chatter vivaciously as we packed her things, and I was delighted to see the old Mandy back in full swing again.

The train station was a Victorian monstrosity on the other side of the village, all gingerbread woodwork, faded red tiles, and cupolas. Mandy got out to pick up her ticket while I parked. We met a few minutes later on the old wooden platform. The train made only a brief stop at Cooper's Green. Few passengers were waiting to board. A stout woman in a brown coat sat on the green bench with two restless children, the girl clutching a doll, the little boy licking a large lollipop and casting malicious glances at us. A workman in a gray shirt and thin leather apron was stacking crates at the other end of the platform. A weary-looking porter in a wrinkled dark-blue uniform and leather-brimmed hat leaned against a post with his arms folded.

"It may be late," I said, peering down the tracks.

"Look, Lynn, you've been a dear. I know you're eager to get back to the house to meet Lloyd. Why don't you go on? There's no need for you to wait."

"Well, I would like to be there when he arrives—"

"Of course you would! You run along. I'll phone you first thing after the audition. Wish me luck."

"I'm sure you'll get the part."

"Herbie says it's a cinch. I'm going to charm that producer right out of his mind."

The train came chugging in as I left the parking lot. I drove slowly back through the village, and as I passed the inn I saw Bart's car parked in front. I felt a twinge of guilt, remembering how badly I'd treated him. I chewed my lower lip, frowning as I drove on past. He was out of my life, and I was lucky. I realized that deep down inside. I wondered if he had gone to see Clive Hampton yet. That was something else I wouldn't have to bother with. Lloyd would take care of it.

I half expected to see Lloyd's car parked in front of the house, but he hadn't arrived yet. I left the Rolls in the garage and walked around to the front steps. The veranda was shrouded in shadows, the old porch rocker barely visible, the hanging pots dripping with ferns. I was reluctant to go inside, and although I knew it was absurd, I couldn't shake the feeling that the house was watching me, waiting for my return. Now that I was completely alone, it seemed even more sinister. With Mandy at my side, with Bart in the carriage house, I had been able to ignore any reservations I might have had about staying here. It was different now. I was alone, isolated, surrounded by woods.

Standing on the steps, I hesitated.

The day had been bright and sunny, but masses of clouds were building up now, and the sky was gray. The lawns and gardens were drained of all color. A brisk wind caused the treetops to bend and wave. The ferns hanging on the veranda swayed, rustling with a noise like whispers. Something seemed to be warning me not to go inside. I sensed it in the air, all around me, a curious, inaudible warning, an unheard voice urging me to turn back, beware, beware.

I almost lost my nerve. I almost got back into the Rolls to drive to the village, and then I realized how foolish I was being. My nerves were on edge, and the house was hardly welcoming, but there was no reason to feel like a skittish, apprehensive young girl. I was a sensible adult, and I must act like one. Squaring my shoulders, I went inside.

The peculiar atmosphere I had noticed earlier when Mandy and I had returned from the village was even stronger than it had been before. The hall was dim and gloomy, and I stood there for a moment, trying not to look at that spot at the foot of the stairs where the bloodstains still showed. The air seemed to be stirring with ominous undercurrents. I had the distinct impression that I wasn't alone. Someone seemed to be hovering just out of sight, listening to me, watching me, and I glanced uneasily at the stairs. Something stirred there on the landing above, a dark form barely visible. A floorboard creaked. I moved quickly to the foot of the stairs and switched on the light.

There was no one there. It had been my imagination.

More floorboards creaked upstairs, and although it sounded like stealthy footsteps creeping away down the upper hall, I had the sense to realize the noise was perfectly normal. As the wind blew against them, the windows rattled in their frames, and there were low moaning noises as wind whirled down the chimney flues. Standing still, straining to hear, I listened to all the creaks and moans and rustles typical of an old house when there was a high wind. Ordinarily I would have been oblivious to them. Now each noise seemed to be strangely distorted, magnified.

Through sheer willpower I ignored the ominous aura that seemed to hang like an invisible pall over the house. It was growing darker outside. There was a distant rumble of thunder. I turned on the lamps in the hall, the library, the front parlor, and although the light diminished the gloom, it did nothing to alleviate the sinister atmosphere that clung to the walls, stirred in the air. Try though I might, I couldn't rid myself of the sensation that I wasn't alone, that someone else was lurking in the dark halls upstairs, listening to my every movement. Common sense told me it was all in my mind, but that was little comfort.

I knew I had to keep busy, keep my mind occupied. It would do no good to brood about things. Stepping into the library, I sat down at the desk and began to work on the files again, wondering just how much time Mandy and I had spent on them since Bart had so clumsily demolished weeks of labor in one fell swoop. I remembered the foolish grin on his face when he surveyed the mess. I remembered my own cool anger.

It seemed such a long time ago. I worked, but although I managed to get several folders back in order, it was difficult to concentrate. Thunder continued to rumble in the distance, and the light outside was fading fast. Glancing at the clock, I was surprised to see it was twenty till seven. What was keeping Lloyd? Had I given him proper directions for reaching the house? Had he taken a wrong turn and gotten lost?

I was growing hungry, and, remembering the food Mandy had brought from the delicatessen, I pushed the files aside and started down the hall to the kitchen. I had almost reached it when I heard someone coming down the back stairs. The footsteps weren't loud. They were cautious, stealthy, as though whoever was coming down paused every step or so to listen. I froze, certain it wasn't my imagination. I hadn't turned on the lights in the back hall, and it was half in darkness. The rear part of the house, where the back stairs were, was totally shrouded with black. I stood very still, my heart beating rapidly, and I watched the shadows stir, heard a curious rustle, saw something moving quickly through the dark.

"Who's there?" I called. My voice was hoarse.

There was no reply. I had expected none. I stumbled forward groping for the light switch on the wall near the kitchen door. I found it, pressed on it. Shadows vanished as light streamed down. There was no one in sight. I stepped to the back stairs and peered up. The stairs were enclosed, tattered blue wallpaper covering the walls. They were quite empty, but as I stood there I had a strong feeling that someone had just left, the air retaining the impressions of his body. There was no place he could have gone unless he had ducked into one of the back rooms, and surely I would have heard him. A window rattled nearby. Thunder rumbled. The incident had unnerved me, and I felt weak, in no mood to linger back here. I returned to the front of the house, food forgotten, wondering what to do.

Then I heard a car pull up in front of the house. Filled with relief, I hurried to the front door and opened it, a joyous smile on my lips. The smile faded when I saw Myrtle Clarkson getting out of an ancient beige Ford.

"Hello, ducky!" she exclaimed, coming up the steps. She was jovial as ever, but she seemed tense, worried. "A storm's brewin' up, sure as shootin'. I borrowed my neighbor's car. Wouldn't want to be out on my bike on a night like this."

Her words hardly registered, so deep was my disappointment. I led her inside and closed the door and took her into the parlor. Myrtle plopped down on the settee, her eyes alight with excitement. She wore a tan dress, and a fringed multi-colored Spanish shawl that two women had been fighting over at the bazaar was wrapped around her arms and shoulders. For once, her blond curls were uncovered and, I noticed, slightly lopsided. She looked around the room as though expecting to see someone else.

"Where's your friend, ducky?"

"Mandy? She had to return to London. I drove her to the station earlier this afternoon."

Myrtle's eyes widened with alarm.

"And young Cooper at the inn! Oh, everyone knows you threw him out, ducky. You—you mean you're *alone* out here?"

"Yes, but—"

"Thank goodness I decided to come! You can't stay out here alone, not now, not with a homicidal maniac on the loose! You'll come straight home with me."

I gave her a puzzled look.

"I thought you might not've heard. That's why I decided to drive out here, to see if everything was all right. I could've called, but I thought the two of you might want to come home with me, under the circumstances. I have somethin' dreadful to tell you, just dreadful."

"Indeed?" My voice was calm.

"Lord, ducky, it gives me the trembles just thinkin' about it. My nerves are frazzled, just frazzled. Let me get a chocolate . . ." She dug into her purse, pulled out a paper sack full of chocolate drops, and popped one into her mouth, her eyes wider than ever. "There's been *another* murder, ducky! The whole village is in an uproar. I don't mind tellin' you, I'm keepin' my shotgun handy tonight!"

I stepped over to the windows and peered through the glass panes. Beyond the veranda railing, the lawn was dark gray, spread with heavy black shadows. As I watched, silver fingers of lightning ripped at the sky. An explosion sounded in the woods. I wondered if a tree had been struck. The lamp flickered behind me, and I could hear Myrtle rattling the paper sack. I knew what she was going to tell me. I was very calm, waiting for the inevitable.

"I've never *been* so upset, I declare. I came home, ducky, absolutely exhausted from the jumble sale—it was a rip-roarin' success, incident'ly. We made more money than we ever have, and there'll be a special sale tomorrow on the items that weren't sold today. Anyway, I came in, my feet killin' me, my whole body bone tired, and I switched on the radio, thinkin' I'd listen to some soothin' music while I made my dinner. Well, when the newscaster broke in with the special report—"

"It was Cassie, wasn't it?" I said quietly, still staring out through the panes.

"How did you know? They found her body this afternoon, while we were just gettin' started with the jumble sale. The report didn't reveal much, didn't give any of the juicy details, but I have other means of gettin' my information. Didn't take me long to find out all the particulars. The poor girl had been dead for hours when they finally found her. Brutally strangled, she was, her throat covered with horrible black bruises. The police think it must've happened last night. Ralph Burton—he's one of the local lads, a real hell-raiser, always after the girls, always in trouble—he went to see her last night and the cottage was all dark and she didn't come to the door when he knocked. Her dog was barkin' somethin' awful . . ."

The sack rattled again as she dug for another chocolate. I turned away from the windows and went over to one of the chairs. I sat down, my head spinning. I saw the room, lights flickering, saw Myrtle with her vividly hued shawl, but everything seemed to be covered by a shimmering haze. Edges blurred, details went out of focus, colors melted. The spinning stopped. I looked down at the hands in my lap. They might have belonged to someone else.

"Ralph thought she'd stood 'im up, thought she was out with some other fellow." Her voice seemed to be coming from a great distance. "He didn't think too much about it. The dog barked all night long, barked all morning, and the neighbors finally decided somethin' might be wrong. They called the police, and Sergeant Duncan drove out. He found her. Horrible it was. She'd put up quite a struggle. The room was a shambles, furniture knocked over, lamps broken, poor Cassie there on the floor—"

She chattered on, making vivid gestures, her voice growing more and more excited, and I hardly heard her. He had been there. He had been listening. He knew that she could identify him, knew he had to kill her. I remembered the weary, resigned expression on her face when I last saw her. I remembered that limp, defeated gesture she had made. I wanted to cry, but no tears would come. I was numb, unable to feel anything. Myrtle chattered on and on, providing details, describing the horror, but her words were merely background noise.

"—him. I have instincts. I felt it was my duty. Constable Plimpton listened to me, but he seemed distracted. I could tell he thought I was a crackpot, a busybody, but I didn't let that bother me. I told him everything—how that man had pestered poor Daphne, how afraid she was of him, my seein' him come out of the house that night. *They* think Cassie was murdered by one of her boyfriends—she was a scandalous creature, truth to tell, shockin' conduct, all those boys, all those presents. Like I said, I have instincts, and I *know* there's some connection. Cassie must've seen something. Her cottage is right near Reggie's and—"

My numbness vanished. I looked up. "You went to the police?"

"I felt it was my duty. I should have told 'em about that man as soon as Daphne was murdered, but I didn't. Now there's been another murder, and I had to speak up. When I think of the way he came to the jumble sale, bold as brass—the way he stared at you. I told 'em about that, too, but they didn't pay any attention. 'We're extremely busy, Mrs. Clarkson,' he told me, just like I was wastin' his time! There was a whole mob of coppers at the station. It was a regular beehive, radios blarin', phones ringin', people runnin' in and out. They had poor Ralph Burton there, questionin' him. The lad was sweatin' somethin' awful, kept sayin' he wanted to see a lawyer. I told 'em, I said, 'You've got the wrong man.' Then that Sergeant Duncan took hold of my arm and drug me outside. Talk about police brutality! I'm going to file a complaint! No copper's gonna shove *me* around—"

"They think the boy did it?" I interrupted.

"They think *one* of 'em did. Ralph claims he came right back, but they think he hung around, waited for her to return, followed her inside. Talk about dolts! There I was, tryin' my best to help—"

She talked on and on, describing her outrage, expressing her opinion of policemen in general. I stood up, not even hearing her, and Myrtle was so startled by my abruptness that she finally shut up. Looking at me with deep concern, she said, "You're so pale, ducky. I know what you're thinkin'. You're afraid he'll come after *you* next. That's the first thing I thought of, soon as I left the police station. Lynn, I thought. That poor girl might be in danger. The way he was starin' at—"

"Nonsense," I said crisply.

"You can't stay here alone, ducky. You must realize that. I don't know what it is, but he's after something. First he murdered poor Daphne, and now—"

She broke off. She was genuinely concerned about me. I could tell that. She might be a gossipy old busybody, but her intentions were good. Stuffing the bag of chocolates back into her enormous purse, she climbed to her feet.

"He may come after *you*," she said in a hushed voice. "You must come home with me. I couldn't go off and leave you here by yourself. If something happened I'd never be—"

I took her arm, leading her to the door. I'd never felt calmer in my life. My one desire was to get rid of her. I had to think. I had to compose my thoughts before Lloyd arrived.

"I won't be alone for long," I said gently, firmly. "My fiancé will be here soon. He's driving up from London. I expect him any minute now. I appreciate your concern, Myrtle, but there's no need to worry."

"Your fiancé?" she said, curious, eager for details. "I didn't know you were engaged, ducky."

"Yes. He's a lawyer. I—I'll tell you all about it. Later. We'll have a nice long chat. I'll call you."

"You're sure you'll be—"

"I'll be all right."

I opened the front door. We stepped onto the veranda. As we stood there, another flash of lightning streaked down, exploding with silver-blue fury. Myrtle shuddered, wrapping the shawl closer about her. She was still reluctant to leave, but I was firm, insisting there was no need for her to stay.

Myrtle climbed into the old car and drove away. My relief was great as I watched the bright red taillights grow smaller and smaller, finally becoming tiny red blurs that disappeared into the night. My calmness and clarity of mind were astounding. Shock, horror, fear, all emotional reactions had been firmly put aside for the time being, and I was able to see things with a cool, lucid objectivity, almost as though I were in no way involved. I was amazed at my own composure.

I should have been afraid. Myrtle, in her garbled, excited way, had hit upon a truth. The man was after something. What? It was something extremely important to him, something he had been willing to kill for. He had thought Aunt Daphne could help him find it. When she had failed to cooperate, he had murdered her, just as he had murdered Colonel March and Cassie. He was coldblooded. Human life meant nothing to him. He was not going to give up until he had what he wanted, and somehow I was involved. I had the key. He had been watching me, watching the house. He had followed me through the woods. He had followed me to the jumble sale. He had broken into the house the night before last. I was convinced of that now. Bart and Mandy had tried to conceal it from me, but I knew.

As I thought, I began to see—vaguely at first, then more and more clearly, as though clouds of fog were gradually evaporating.

The last cloud lifted, disappeared.

I saw. I knew. I understood.

It was an intricate pattern. It had begun with the telephone calls. What had seemed a cruel, senseless prank had meaning. When Aunt Daphne had called me that night, she had been drunk and hysterical, but there had been an urgency in her garbled message:

"—here now. I have to talk to you. I have to tell you about—" In my mind, I finished the sentence for her. I knew what she had meant to tell me before we were disconnected. I visualized her terror as he ripped the phone out of her hand and slammed it down. He must have pulled out the knife then, and she must have run toward the stairs. When I called back, the phone in the hall must have rung repeatedly as he stabbed her and left her to die.

I understood it all now. I knew who he was and what he wanted, and I knew where to find it. It was so clear, so simple—so simple I hadn't been able to see what was right there before my eyes.

I had been standing on the veranda, lost in thought, for several minutes, and every piece of the puzzle was in place now, the picture complete. It was horrifying, and I realized my own danger, but I knew I had to keep calm, hold back the panic that threatened to overcome me. Lloyd would be here any minute, and I would be able to give him all the answers. He would tell the men from Scotland Yard, and they would capture the man who had murdered three people, who would murder again to get what he wanted.

I went back inside and locked the door, testing it to make sure that it was secure. The lights flickered in the hall, dimming, and I prayed there wouldn't be another power failure. I had the uncanny feeling that someone had just been here in the hall, watching me as I stood outside. I took a deep breath, trying to steady myself. It would be so easy to snap, to give way, to be reduced to a mass of trembling fear, but I couldn't allow that. Not now. I leaned against the door, summoning control. There was another crash of thunder, deafening. The whole earth seemed to shake, and then everything grew still, silent, the silence so total I could hear my own breathing.

I ran into the library, searching for some small object that would serve my purpose. There was a thin letter opener on the desk. It would do nicely. I picked it up, and as I stepped back through the hall on my way to the parlor I paused, listening. In the dense silence I thought I heard a car motor, far away, approaching. Relief swept over me. I rushed to the door, unlocked it, threw it open, expecting to see headlights sweeping up the drive. There were none in sight. The sound had died away.

What was keeping him? He should have been here long before now. Latish, he had said. Perhaps something had held him up. Wearily, I closed the door and re-locked it.

Lloyd would be here soon. I must be patient. I would have much to tell him. I would have something to show him as well. I was sure of that. *I hope you will follow the right path*, my father had written on the card, and the lid of the box wouldn't close properly.

I went into the parlor. The red lacquer box was on the table. I picked it up and examined it carefully, certain my theory was right. Sitting down on the settee, I emptied the letters and card onto the table and pulled back the lid. Yes, the thin sliver of wood on the inside bulged out as though warped. Hardly thicker than a piece of paper, it splintered and tore away as I applied the letter opener against the edge. The folded sheet of yellowing tablet paper dropped out. I knew what it was even before I unfolded it. The map was crudely drawn, but it was simple enough to understand. There was the river, there the old mill, there the clearing with the oak stump and, beside the stump, a heavily marked X. *I hope you will follow the right path*, he had written. However dubious it might be, my father had left me a legacy.

I was still looking at the map when I heard the heavy footsteps coming up the front steps. Someone pounded on the door, continued to pound, and I knew it wasn't Lloyd. My body seemed to turn to ice. There had been a car after all, but it had stopped in the woods, out of sight. There was a dull thud . . . another. He was trying to break the door down.

14

THE DOOR was strong, solid oak. I hoped it wouldn't give. There was another great thud, a loud grunt, then the sound of heavy breathing. He stood in front of the door for a moment, and then he began to walk around the veranda. I didn't scream. The terror was so complete that it had a numbing effect. My body was frozen, and I seemed to be drugged, my mind far away, suspended, and none of this was real. The sheer, stark horror was part of a nightmare, and I would awaken. Surely it would vanish. It couldn't be real. It couldn't be happening. The floorboards of the veranda groaned noisily as he came around the corner and walked along the side of the house. I managed to stand, still clutching the map, everything unreal: the room, the noise, my own pounding heartbeats.

He stopped in front of the French windows. I could see him clearly through the panes. He was huge, at least six feet tall. The heavy overcoat made his shoulders seem even wider, and his face was brutal, the wide mouth pressed tight, the broken nose humped, the dark eyes burning. He stared at me, and I stared back, paralyzed, powerless like a small bird mesmerized by a snake. He wore a pair of black leather gloves, and he raised a hand and curled it into a tight fist. I watched as he rammed the fist through the glass. The pane shattered, sending a hundred pieces of glass clattering to the floor. He reached in, found the latch, unlocked it, and pulled the door open.

Slowly, deliberately, he stepped into the room.

He stopped, standing several yards away, and took a deep breath. His overcoat was coarsely woven and bulky. The leather gloves were new, shiny black. His complexion was grainy and pitted, pale, and there was a jagged white scar from left temple to jaw. His hair was black, streaked with gray, and his dark eyes were glowing with pleasure. He was enjoying himself, enjoying my terror. The wide lips spread in a sadistic smile, curling up at the corners, and he chuckled.

"Hello, Lynn baby," he said.

The dark, glowing eyes, burning with satanic glee, mocked me. Leather-gloved hands clenched and unclenched at his sides, as though they had separate life and were eager to coil and crush and kill. He exuded evil like a heavy musk. I stared at him. This man had murdered three people in cold blood, and he had enjoyed it. Probably there were other victims I knew nothing about. He looked at me, and he seemed to be reading my mind. He chuckled again, taking great pleasure in his power to frighten and intimidate.

"I've had my eye on you for some time," he said huskily. "We've got something to settle, then you're going to die."

I hardly heard the words. That numbing terror had worn off, and now I was fully conscious in every fiber of my being of the danger. Panic rose, mounting, nerve ends taut, jangling. I was faint, dark clouds pressing around the corners of my mind, total blackness threatening to overcome me. I could feel my knees weaken, and I started to sway. Yet somehow my mind was still able to function, and I knew I couldn't give up, couldn't give in to the panic shrieking inside. I had to fight. Not physically—that would be futile. My only hope was to outwit him. If only I could stall him, keep him at bay until Lloyd arrived . . . Through sheer willpower I managed to speak, and to my own surprise my voice was perfectly level.

"You're Herb Sheppard," I said.

"Yeah, you guessed it."

"They released you from prison after all these years."

"Released? Fat chance of that! No, baby, they didn't release me. I arranged my own release, know what I mean? I had to kill a couple of guards in the process. Jenson I stabbed. I brought Barlow out with me, used him as a shield, made a hostage out of him. He wasn't any use to me after I got to my hideout, so I killed him too. Slow. Real slow."

"The police must be—"

"They've been lookin' for me for damn near three months—haven't found me yet. I got help, see. Real expert help. Soon as I collect the jewels, I'm going to cut out. They'll never find me."

He looked around the room and spied the heap of letters and the broken box. "So that's it," he said as he saw the map, still in my hand. "Damned clever of 'im," he muttered, "damned clever. I'll take that, please."

I threw the map toward him. It dropped at his feet. Herb Sheppard bent down and picked it up, examined it for a moment, finally crammed it into the pocket of his overcoat.

"I've been very patient," he said thoughtfully. "It's finally paid off, just like the lad promised me it would. No one knew where the jewels were, you see. They never showed up on the market. None of the fences ever laid eyes on 'em. I knew they had to be around somewhere."

"You thought Aunt Daphne had them."

"At first, yeah. I soon realized the old bitch didn't know anything about 'em. The lad told me, he said, 'There's only one person who can lead us to 'em,' and that person was you. He was right. I got real impatient. Every copper in the country lookin' for me and the jewels still missin', but he said we had to wait, had to play the game. I wanted to kill the old bitch right at the beginning, but he said that would be a mistake. He worked everything out, showed me exactly how we'd go about finding the jewels, and it was clever, real clever. I finally agreed to play along."

"Aunt Daphne—"

"I made sure she wouldn't talk. I told her if she breathed a word I'd come back and kill her, and she said she didn't care, she'd go to the police anyway. Then I told her I'd kill *you* first, and that shut her up. She was terrified. I knew she'd keep her mouth shut."

"Then why—"

"The last time I came to see her she got panicky. The lad told me we'd have to be patient. Everything was working out just as he told me it would. We couldn't rush things, he said. You didn't know anything about the robbery, see, thought your old man had gone to Australia, but the phone calls were jugglin' your memory. Sooner or later you'd remember something. Anyway, I wasn't satisfied just sittin' around, twiddlin' my thumbs, so I came back here to search the house again, and she got panicky. I heard her usin' the phone. She called that Colonel fellow, told him to come over as fast as he could, and then she called you. I cut her off before she gave everything away. I saw she was hysterical, saw she wasn't going to keep her mouth shut, so I killed her. Then I went outside to wait for her friend to arrive—"

It was working. He wanted to talk about it. He wanted to relive each moment. Talking about what he had done made him feel powerful. I realized that, and I knew I had to play upon it. I was alone, helpless, and he had the map now, but there was no hurry. He could take his time, enjoy his triumph to the full.

"You killed Colonel March, too," I whispered.

"Yeah, that was a clever stroke, a real clever stroke. I was hidin' in the woods, waitin', and the bastard got into the house without me seein' him. He

knew somethin' was wrong, see, and he'd come on
foot, sneakin' up quietly. I heard him shout, and then
I heard a car comin' up the drive. He came streakin'
out of the house right in front of the headlights and
went tearin' into the woods. I didn't know who was in
the car, but I knew they'd think he'd murdered the
old bitch. I still had the knife with me, see, I hadn't
even wiped it off. So I followed him home. He heard
me and took his gun out—" He paused, chuckling,
dark eyes alight with satisfaction as he recalled his
cleverness.

"So you shot him," I said.

"He was blusterin' like a real military hero,
makin' threats, wavin' the gun in my face. I took it
away from him—it was like takin' a toy away from a
child. He passed out. I think it must've been shock.
The rest was easy. I was wearin' gloves, see, no danger
of leavin' fingerprints, so I wrapped his hand around
the knife and left his prints on it and placed it at his
side. Then I wrapped his fingers around the gun,
aimed it, made him shoot himself. It was simple." He
nodded, a wide grin curling his heavy lips. "Everyone
thought it was a murder and a suicide, just like I
planned."

"Not quite everyone," I told him.

"You're talkin' about the whore, aren't you? I
thought I heard someone when I was leavin' the cottage that night, but I couldn't be sure. I forgot all
about it. I have you to thank for leadin' me to her. If
that little tramp had talked, if she'd given out my description, every cop in the country would've swarmed
into the area."

"You followed me into the woods."

He nodded, still grinning. "When you left London I was right behind you. Someone had to keep an
eye on you, in case you discovered something. I've
been hangin' around, watchin' the house, keepin' my
eye on you. When you headed into the woods yester-

day, I was sure you'd found somethin' or you were going after the jewels. I was disappointed, I don't mind admittin', but when I heard that girl blabbin' I realized it was a lucky break. If she'd talked . . ." He frowned, and then he looked down at his hands, flexing the fingers, admiring them. "You should've seen the fight she put up. Even when I had her down on her knees, chokin' the life out of her, she fought."

He stared at his leather-gloved hands. I felt my nerves stretch, jangle. The black clouds were forming again, and I knew I couldn't hold on much longer. The panic was fighting to break free, and I was screaming inside. Sheppard looked up at me, rubbed his hands along his thighs, the smile broadening. His eyes burned with anticipation.

"You gonna fight?" he asked.

"My—my father tricked you," I said quickly. "He took the jewels and buried them. You didn't—didn't know where they were. He was the only one, and—and he wouldn't talk."

I had sidetracked him, anger temporarily taking the place of anticipation, my own murder forestalled, if only for moments. Moments were priceless. They could mean the difference between life and death. I had to keep him talking . . . It was my only hope.

"He double-crossed me, the bastard. The cops thought he'd handed 'em over to someone else, but I knew better. They belonged to me. I planned everything. I needed a second man. I called him in at the last minute. It was my idea, my plan. I did all the work. I killed that clerk. Morgan stole into my room while I was asleep and took the jewels, so when the cops came, the jewels were gone. They never found 'em, but I knew I'd find 'em once I got out. It's taken me all this time—"

"He never told anyone where they were," I said, the words catching in my throat. "He—he must have known he had a heart condition. He must have known he was going to die. He made the box in the craft shop, put the map inside the lid, wrote a cryptic message, hoping I'd understand. All those years it was there—"

"It's over now," Sheppard said harshly. "It worked out just like the lad said it would. I thought he was crazy—all these weeks passin', the cops lookin' for me, the risk—but he was right. Brilliant lad. I got to hand it to him. Psychology, he said. The old bitch didn't know nothin'. *You* didn't know nothin'. There was no one else, so we had to play the game, make the calls, jostle your memory, wait. It worked just like he said it would. I was gettin' pretty impatient—"

"You—you won't get away with it," I stammered. "The police will—"

"The police are goin' around in circles. We've seen to that. A fellow claimed he saw me in Liverpool, couple of weeks later I was reported seen in Bristol. Now they think I'm in Wales. We threw up a nice smokescreen. The lad thought of that. He's shrewd, real shrewd. I got to hand it to him. He figured this whole thing out. A brilliant mind—"

I had thought the puzzle complete, but I knew now that one piece was missing, the one that tied everything together. I shook my head, refusing to admit it, refusing to allow the final truth to dawn. No. No. *It couldn't be.* I was mistaken. *It couldn't be.* I pushed the image back, shaken by that brief glimpse, knowing I couldn't even consider it, for my last ray of hope would be gone, and I had to cling to it.

Sheppard reached into his pocket and pulled out the map. Unfolding it, he held it with both hands and studied it, chin lowered, brows furrowed, oblivious to me. I took a cautious step backward . . . another. He looked up, then let the map drop to the table. It drifted like a withered leaf, landing on top of the letters beside the broken box. He looked at me. He looked down at his hands, and that fiendish anticipation burned in his eyes again. I couldn't stall him off any longer. He ran the tip of his tongue around his thick lips. He chuckled. His eyes held mine, and I was paralyzed with terror.

"It's time, Lynn baby. You realize that, don't you?"

"No," I whispered hoarsely. "No—"

"You've been doomed for weeks. You just didn't know it. Relax. Make it easy on yourself."

Slowly, he moved toward me, savoring my terror, savoring his power.

Both of us heard the car at the same time, the sound quite distinct in spite of the deluge of rain. Sheppard paused, not more than four yards away from me. He turned his head, listening. I saw the tall porcelain vase on the table at my side. Summoning every ounce of strength, I threw off the paralysis. A car door slammed outside. Sheppard turned back to me.

"I was worried there for a minute, then I realized who it must be. He said he was comin'. I'd better get this over with quickly. He might not want me to kill you, and I ain't gonna be cheated."

He raised his hands, curled his fingers, grinning. I seized the vase, smashing it across his forehead with all my might. He let out a yell and staggered backward. Bright red blood poured down over his eyes. I turned. I ran, stumbling, knocking over a table, as he lunged after me. I reached the hall, my heart pounding, threatening to burst, my legs giving way. I ran blindly up the stairs. My foot slipped, and I fell against the wall, halfway up. Sheppard tore into the hall. He saw me. He clambered up the stairs toward me, the steps creaking under his weight, his face a mask of maniacal rage. I watched, limp, slipping down the wall, darkness clouding my mind.

A deafening explosion rang in my ears, and I saw the look of total incredulity spread over Sheppard's face. His shoulder seemed to splinter. He grabbed at it with both hands. His knees folded, and he tumbled backward, landing with a heavy thud in almost exactly the same spot where Aunt Daphne had died.

Strong, familiar arms pulled me up, supported me, held me tightly, as I looked up, half unconscious.

"I just winged him good," Bart said casually. "He isn't dead."

"How—"

"You were never in danger," he said, "not for a moment. I've been here all along."

"I don't under—"

"Hush, love. It's not quite over yet."

Holding me up, Bart wrapped one arm tightly about my waist. Confused, bewildered, disbelieving, I fought back the waves of blackness skirting over the surface of my mind. As though in a dream, I saw Lloyd step into the hall and point a gun directly at us.

"Drop it!" he said harshly.

"Certainly," Bart replied.

He dropped the gun. It clattered down the steps with a series of loud metallic thumps, finally coming to rest a few steps from the bottom. Lloyd made no effort to get it. Without expression, he looked at Sheppard's unconscious body lying like a giant rag doll at his feet, blood gushing from the left shoulder. Lifting his eyes, the man I had never known stared up at us, his face as hard as granite. The dark brown eyes were level, and the hand holding the gun was very steady. His coppery hair was wet, his dark tan corduroy overcoat speckled with raindrops. I noticed that the hand at his side clutched the map. He must have picked it up as he came through the parlor.

"Lloyd," I whispered.

"Surprised?" Bart asked.

"It can't be—"

"Oh, but it is," Bart said airily. "We haven't met, Raymond, but I'm sure you know who I am."

"I know," Lloyd said.

"Lynn's told me quite a lot about you, old chap.

Raved about you, in fact. I kept telling her she was making a mistake, that I was the only man for her, but she simply wouldn't listen."

Bart seemed totally unaware of any danger, paying no heed whatsoever to the gun Lloyd held with such a steady grip. From Bart's manner, we might have been standing on the stairs at a party, making idle chitchat with another guest. As I stared at Lloyd, the shock wore off, and I was amazed that I hadn't suspected sooner. He was a stranger. He had always been. Even when it had seemed we were closest, there had been a remoteness, a wall between us.

"Let's face it, Lynn," Bart continued in the same chatty vein, "you're a rotten judge of character. You thought he was a paragon, thought I was a cad. You're a bright, lovable girl, but when it comes to men you're extremely naive. Let this be a lesson."

"Why?" I asked, looking into Lloyd's eyes.

"For this," he replied, holding up the map, keeping the gun leveled at us. "There's a fortune in uncut gems. I intend to have them. I've been planning this for a long time."

"I was just a—a tool?"

"You were part of the plan."

"You—you made those phone calls?"

He nodded brusquely.

"I don't believe it." I paused, looking at that cold, hard face and trying to find some sign of the Lloyd I had known. "How could you be associated with an animal like that?"

"Blood is thicker than water," Bart said breezily. "Lloyd is a very devoted nephew—at least, he became one after he grew up and discovered that Uncle Herb took part in a spectacular robbery twenty years ago and that a fortune in uncut jewels was still missing. He made several dutiful visits to Uncle in prison, and when Uncle broke out it was only natural he should make a beeline for his devoted nephew."

"You seem to know quite a lot," Lloyd remarked.

"Oh, I know it all. Rest assured. You gave Uncle Herb a hiding place. Kept him in your own flat, didn't you? Who'd ever think of looking for a hardened criminal in the flat of such an ultra-respectable lawyer, a nephew who told the police he was mortified by the relationship, feared it would wreck his career if it ever came out? Right? Right. First thing Herbie did after he found a safe place to hide was drive to Devon to see the sister of his old friend and colleague. When he was convinced that she knew nothing about the missing jewels, he thought about killing her but was afraid it would call attention to the past, so he merely terrorized her. He went back to nephew Lloyd, bewildered. It seemed *no* one knew where the jewels were—and then he remembered the little girl, the daughter who was six years old at the time."

Bart paused dramatically, clearly enjoying himself. Lloyd stood at the foot of the stairs with the gun in his hand, his hard, handsome face a stony mask. I knew that he was as dangerous as Sheppard, coldly determined to kill us now that he had the map. Bart seemed totally unconcerned. Blithe, chatty, confident, audacious, he wrapped his other arm around my waist, peering over my shoulder at Lloyd. This might all be a jolly lark, a party game the three of us were playing.

"This is where it gets interesting," he said. "Complicated, too. Your noble hero here made a point of meeting you, overwhelming you with his sincerity and sober charm. He soon discovered you knew nothing, at least not consciously, but he knew quite a lot about psychology. You believed your father had gone to Australia, but there was a chance that he might have said something to you when you were a child, something you'd long since forgotten. So Lloyd devised his plan. It would take time, and it would take a lot of patience, but a fortune was at stake. He couldn't come right out and *ask* you anything—that would give the whole show away—so he started making the phone calls. After each one, he talked to you, questioned you about your father, hoping against hope you'd dredge up some memory that would lead him to the jewels. Am I right, Raymond?"

"Right."

"It might have gone on indefinitely, but Herbie got anxious. Lloyd might be willing to bide his time, but not Herbie. He came back here, and when Daphne got out of hand he murdered her. Actually, it was a stroke of luck, for if you hadn't come here and remembered the box, the jewels might never have been located. They'd been missing for two decades. Experts had failed to find them. After your father died, not a living soul knew where they were. Lloyd's idea was brilliant—rather farfetched, and complicated as hell—but it bloody well worked."

"It worked," Lloyd said. "It took three months, but it worked. I've got what I wanted."

"A lot of this was my own reconstruction. I was right, then?"

"In every detail. It's almost uncanny."

"I'm pretty good at this sort of thing—you might say it's the way I make my living. I'd like to take all the credit, but actually I had some remarkable and quite unexpected help. I picked up a point or two as I listened to Herbie there chat with Lynn. Of course, *she* deserves the real applause for finding the map. That came as a complete surprise. You'll have to tell me how you discovered it was there, love."

"I'm afraid there's no time," Lloyd said grimly.

"No? I see. You've got the map, you'll get the jewels, and now you intend to murder us."

"Right again."

"You intend to shoot us in cold *blood?*"

"In cold blood."

"That's it!" Bart called. "We've got it all."

The hall was suddenly alive with policemen.

They came swarming noisily from the parlor, from the library, from the back of the house, at least half a dozen of them. One grabbed Lloyd's wrist and wrestled the gun from him; another pounced on him from behind, throwing a blue-clad arm around his throat, pulling him back. I heard the shouts, the pounding footsteps, and saw the struggle. Constable Plimpton stepped into the room, looking flustered and disturbed and all at sea. Lloyd fought desperately, and the policeman who had him by the throat lost his grip. Breaking loose, Lloyd dashed to the door. Another stout bobby made a flying tackle, and both of them crashed to the floor. Two of his colleagues ran to help, and there was a tangle of arms and legs and flying fists. Hopelessly outnumbered, realizing the futility of further struggle, Lloyd finally stood still, his face ashen.

"Pugnacious chap, isn't he?" Bart remarked.

I pulled away from him. "They were here all along. You *knew!* That's why you were so cocky."

"Naturally. I'm not that brave."

"You—you used me as *bait!*"

"More or less," he said amiably.

Leaving me standing there, he moved on down the stairs and stepped nimbly over the unconscious Sheppard. He pulled a tape recorder out from under a heavily carved chair. I was livid, all other emotions eclipsed by the cold, icy rage that surged inside. They had allowed me to be frightened half to death, just so they could get all the facts on tape. They had been hovering nearby, listening, watching, while I went through unspeakable mental torture. I had been kept in the dark. I had been heartlessly used.

As Bart removed the reel of tape, there was pounding on the front door, and one of the bobbies opened it, to admit a severely disapproving Sergeant Duncan. Mandy, of course, was right behind him. She wore his heavy police mackintosh over her pink slack suit, her hair was a mass of wet, tawny gold ringlets, and, naturally, she looked positively ravishing. Arching one brow, she quickly took in the scene in the hall: Sheppard's body, Lloyd being held by three bobbies, Bart with the reel in his hand. Then she saw me standing on the stairs.

"It looks like I've missed all the action," she said dryly. "I insisted Douglas bring me in earlier, but he wouldn't hear of it. It's really shockingly unfair. After all, this was my brainchild. I'm the one who figured everything out, and then Bart hogged in and the police took over and—Lynn, I have so much to *tell* you."

"You certainly do!" I snapped.

15

I STOOD at the back window, looking out at the gray cityscape. Smoke curled, making a blue-gray haze against an already hazy sky, and a lonely pigeon perched on a window ledge, looking discouraged. It had rained for the past four days, and London seemed bleak, all liveliness and vitality dampened by the depressing weather. I felt pensive, a tenuous sadness inside. Thank goodness I was leaving. At last it looked as though I would be able to work. I had rented a small cottage in Cornwall for the summer and, alone, with nothing to distract me, I should be able to finish the book.

My bags were packed. My recently purchased second-hand car was parked out in front of the building under the wet trees. Mandy, crushed that I was leaving, and promising to write faithfully, had already said good-bye and dashed off to rehearsals of the new comedy to open in the West End next month. It wasn't the BBC, alas, nothing so prestigious, and Mandy wouldn't get to play Nell Gwynn, but it was the latest work of one of the most commercially successful playwrights in the business, and a surefire hit. She was wildly enthusiastic about the role, her most important to date.

Although she hated to see me leave, Mandy would have very little time to miss me. She would have her hands full with the play, and with Douglas Duncan, no longer a sergeant. That was Mandy's doing. After seeing him in the dress rehearsal of *She*

Stoops to Conquer at the school auditorium, she had phoned her agent, vowed she'd discovered a fabulous new talent, and insisted he come down for the opening. After seeing the sergeant in action, Herbie had signed him on the spot. I wasn't at all surprised. On stage, Douglas had complete confidence and aplomb, a terrific presence. He seemed to be blessed with a natural gift for acting. He had turned in his uniform, moved to London bag and baggage, taken a flat directly beneath ours in the building, and was already filming a commercial for Male Man shaving lotion. He was also taking voice lessons for his Scots accent. Although Doug seemed rather nonchalant about it, Mandy was elated with his new career, certain he would be a roaring success. They spent all their free time together. No, Mandy wouldn't miss me.

Sighing, I turned away from the window and walked down the hall to the living room. My bags were piled in the center of the floor, the three file boxes, typewriter, bundles of books beside them. Douglas, who had driven Mandy to rehearsal in his battered old car, had promised to help me carry the things down as soon as he got back. It was after one now. He should be back soon. Restless, I stepped to the front window and looked down at the tiny park surrounded by its wrought-iron fence. Even the trees looked dispirited, as if they were huddling together to avoid the drizzle. What a day for starting a motor trip, I thought, but I had put it off long enough. I needed to get away. I needed to get to work.

He hadn't come to see me. He hadn't called, not once. I knew he was here in the city, in his posh flat in Chelsea. Frightfully busy, Mandy had informed me. Oh yes, *she* had seen him. He had been in London for a week. Well, if he did call he would discover I was gone. It was ridiculous for me to stay around, hoping. Everything was over. The house had been sold. Clive, Mandy's antiques-dealer friend, had purchased all the valuable furniture and antiques, paying a more-than-generous sum. The books and the few items I had wanted to keep were in storage, and the rest had been given to the needy in Cooper's Green under Myrtle's dictatorial supervision.

Sheppard and Lloyd were in jail, awaiting trial, and the jewels had been claimed by the insurance company that had reimbursed for their loss twenty years ago. Almost a month had passed since that nightmare night, and I was not going to make a fool of myself simply because Bartholomew Cooper hadn't shown any further interest.

I sat down on the sofa, impatient, wishing Douglas would hurry. Spying the brightly jacketed thriller there on the coffee table in front of me, I picked it up, resentful. The new Brad Carter, just off the press, not even in the stores yet. He had given it to Mandy. I turned it over, studying the photograph on the back of the jacket. Brad Carter, author of a dozen best-selling thrillers, his face incredibly handsome. It was rather sinister here, but that was what the photographer had intended, a matter of lighting and shadow. The eyebrows, comically tilting in real life, arched diabolically in the picture, and that wide, good-natured mouth seemed here to curl in a derisive sneer. His face, yet not his face at all. That's why Mandy had been puzzled when she saw him for the first time.

They had been in league together almost from the first. Sheppard *had* broken into the house that first night, and Bart had discovered signs of it. He had been far more disturbed than he had appeared, so, while I took my walk, he and Mandy had had a long talk. She had learned his true identity, and she had told him all about the phone calls, about Daphne's hysterical call the night she was murdered. Stubbornly convinced that Colonel March had been innocent, Mandy had found a strong ally in Bart, who had never once entertained the thought that the old man could have mur-

dered her. They had agreed to put their heads together, collaborate, so to speak, and both had felt I
would be better off not knowing anything about it.

Myrtle's tale had given Mandy food for thought,
and Bart had phoned one of his police friends in London to request any information available on Bill Morgan. I had gone to the funeral. I had met Cassie in the
square. That afternoon I had met her in the woods
and, on my return, related everything to Lloyd over
the telephone. Eavesdropping, Mandy had thought it
peculiar that Lloyd had told me not to inform the police. His tale about Scotland Yard men had fooled me,
but Mandy had been doubtful. When I had received
another anonymous call that night, she had been convinced that Lloyd was behind it. With the exception of
Herbie, her agent, Lloyd had been the only other person who had known the number.

Bart had gone the next morning, using our quarrel
as an excuse, making a big scene of arriving at the inn
with his baggage, letting it be broadcast that he was no
longer staying at the house. He had had every intention of returning at night, on the sly, hoping to catch
the man who had broken in, who, thinking no male
was around, might be bolder. After we had discovered
the letters, Mandy had begun to add things up. She
had phoned Bart at the inn to explain what had happened. He had had news of his own: His police friend
had uncovered the whole story about the robbery, and
added that Herb Sheppard had escaped from prison
just three months previously and was still at large. Bart
also had been interested to hear that Sheppard's
nephew was an up-and-coming young lawyer, Lloyd
Raymond. Quick as lightning, Mandy, the inveterate
addict of thrillers, and Bart, who wrote them, had understood the whole complicated plot.

They had decided to set a trap.

Mandy had made a second call—to Lloyd. She
had told him that Bart had gone and she was going to

have to leave for London and I would be alone. Could she count on his arriving? She was worried about me, she had said. I had been talking about my father, saying something about a robbery and missing jewels, and, quite frankly, she feared that the strain had been too much for me. She didn't want me to be alone in the house. Lloyd had assured her that he would arrive before nightfall.

Mandy had driven me to the jumble sale, then gone directly to the police station. Bart was already there. Cassie's body had just been discovered, and the place was in chaos. Together, they had explained everything to Constable Plimpton.

Then the police had taken over.

When we had come back from the jumble sale, Mandy had had to draw upon every bit of acting skill she possessed, knowing what she knew, knowing that she was going to have to leave me alone. I had sensed something wrong, so she had told me about my father, hoping that bit of information would keep me from asking more questions. As they had arranged, Bart had called, and she had pretended he was Herbie. During the next hour, she had given a performance that, had it been on film, would surely have won her every award in the book. I had driven her to the station, and she had made sure I left her before the train actually came in. When I had returned to the house, it had been literally full of policemen. Bart had been there too, of course, and it was a wonder I hadn't seen any of them. I had been nervous and tense, waiting for Lloyd, and Myrtle had come and told me about Cassie, and then I had been alone again—or thought I was—and I had begun to figure things out for myself. I had discovered the map, which was something none of them had counted on. Finding the map really had been my only contribution to the whole affair.

Sheppard had been hiding out in an empty cottage in the area. He had kept in touch with Lloyd by telephone. Lloyd evidently had phoned him, told him what Mandy had said and that he himself would be arriving that night. Sheppard had been impatient. He hadn't wanted to wait any longer. As soon as night had fallen, he had left the cottage, driven through the woods, parked his car under the trees, and come to the house . . . I shuddered, remembering the horror. I had been in no real danger, of course, but *I* hadn't known that. I was still angry when I thought about how they'd used me.

Lost in thought, I found that I was still holding the book. I put it down, front side up, hiding that handsome face, which seemed to mock me. Bart had arranged everything with Hampton through his own lawyer, and the second will, Daphne's hasty, impulsive gesture, had been declared void. Despite my reservations about the man, Hampton had proved himself most efficient, finding a buyer for the house in less than a week. I got a most generous amount, which, combined with what I'd received from Clive, would enable me to do exactly as I pleased for a number of years. I had bought the second-hand car, the first I'd ever owned, and through an agency in London I'd rented the cottage in Cornwall for the summer, sight unseen. I was eager to work. Even if this first book proved a failure, I'd be financially free to start another one immediately.

I would immerse myself in work. Work would be wonderful therapy. I'd soon forget those merry blue eyes and dark, improbably tilting eyebrows. He *wasn't* shiftless, a ne'er-do-well living off his brother. I understood now why he had rented the rooms over the carriage house, why he had preferred the quiet and isolation to his flat in London, but, just the same, he was impossible, far too sure of himself. I was glad he hadn't called, I told myself. I didn't want to have my life disrupted by the likes of Bartholomew Cooper, or Brad Carter, or anyone, for that matter.

I glanced at the clock. It was one forty. Douglas should have been back long before now. Men, I thought bitterly, you couldn't depend on any of them. I might just as well load the car myself. Picking up the smallest of the suitcases, I started downstairs and, as luck would have it, ran into Mrs. Wellington in the foyer.

"*There* you are!" she cried, pouncing from behind one of the aspidistras. Plumper than ever, wearing the familiar felt slippers and old print dress, she had her hair in old-fashioned curlers and held a scandal magazine in one hand. "You're leaving *already?*"

"I'm leaving," I said wearily.

"What you'll be doin' way off down there by yourself I have no *idea,*" she said, fanning herself with the magazine. "You could've knocked me over with a feather when I 'eard about it."

"I'll be working, Mrs. Wellington."

"Hump! Sure you aren't meetin' some man, dearie?"

"Quite sure," I snapped. Why did we put up with her?

"Speakin' of men—that Douglas Duncan chap. I'm not *sure* about him. He's paid up in advance—that ain't botherin' me—but it seems like I've seen him before. I've been wrackin' my brain, tryin' to remember. Didn't he call on you once, before you left for Devon? Handsome lad, I'll admit, but so solemn. Never says a word to me, never stops to chat, just stares at me like 'e was a cop or somethin' and intends to raid the place. Your friend Amanda certainly seems to be taken with 'im, doesn't she? I run a respectable 'ouse, and I'm not sure I approve of—"

"I'm really in a bit of a hurry," I protested.

"Since 'e arrived, there ain't been all those other men callin' on 'er day and night," she continued, deaf to my protest. "She never goes out with anyone else. The way 'e looks at 'er, so possessive-like, the way she dotes on it—I wouldn't be surprised if they got married or somethin'—"

"I wouldn't either. I really must—"

"Oh? Are they plannin'—"

Refusing to be pumped, I hurried on outside. My car was parked across the street. I undid the trunk and swung the suitcase inside. As I did so, another car pulled up directly behind me. There was a loud horn blast. I almost jumped out of my skin. He gave me a jolly wave through the windshield and climbed out. He was wearing jeans and jersey, his blue eyes merry, raven locks in tumbled disarray.

"What's this?" he asked jauntily. "Going somewhere?"

"You *would* turn up now."

"Mandy called, actually. Told me you were leaving. I thought I'd better pop over and see what it was all about."

"Not that it's any of your business, but I'm going to Cornwall. I've rented a cottage for the summer."

"Indeed?" He arched one of those improbable brows, looking thoughtful. "How big is it?"

"It's—" I paused. "Why? What could that possibly mat—"

"It should be small enough to be cozy," he said, "but large enough so we won't get in each other's way when we're working. Actually, I intended to rent a place in Scotland, but I suppose Cornwall will do just as well. Modern plumbing, I hope?"

"What on earth are you—"

"I'm going with you, of course."

"You're out of your bloody mind."

"I suppose you could say that. I shouldn't have stayed away so long, I can see. I've wounded your susceptible feelings. I had so much to *do*, you see—one book to finish, proofs of another to read and correct, contracts to negotiate, foreign rights to arrange—and I wanted to get it all done so I could devote full time to my new project."

"Your new project?"

"You," he said, smiling seductively.

"I'm tempted to use some very unladylike language, Mr. Cooper. If you expect me to be overwhelmed—"

"That was the general idea."

"I'm leaving," I said crisply.

"And I'm going with you. We might as well take your car. We'll have to stop by the flat. I'll need to pack some clothes, and I'll have to explain things to my landlady and make a few arrangements, write a couple of quick letters. All in all, I should be ready around four thirty or five."

Exasperated, with him, with myself, I left the car trunk standing open and crossed the street. Bart trotted along behind me. Mrs. Wellington was still standing in the foyer. Her eyes widened in surprise when she saw Bart.

"Who's *he?*" she demanded.

"Hello, old thing," he said chattily. "I'm her lover. We're going to Cornwall together. We're going to spend three months in delicious sin. Isn't that grand?"

I was already halfway up the stairs. He hurried after me and followed me into the flat. Ignoring him, I picked up another suitcase. He took the two that remained. As I went back downstairs, Bart was right behind me, as jaunty and merry as a boy. Mrs. Wellington's brows went shooting up. Her mouth made a round, shocked *o*.

"Eat your heart out," Bart told her.

I put the bag in the trunk. Bart deposited the others beside it, and I slammed the lid down. File, books, and typewriter would go in the back seat.

"This has gone far enough," I said.

"Not *nearly*," he replied.

"Go away!"

"No chance, love."

"You think I'd just go off with you?"

"Why not?"

"You don't know anything, do you?"

"I know I want you. I know you want me."

He stood there with his arms folded across his chest, a faint smile on his lips, but the vivid blue eyes were filled with determination. The pavement glistened with dampness. Above us the tree leaves dripped tears. I was on the verge of tears myself. I turned quickly, before he could see, and hurried across the street. I went back upstairs, and in just a moment or so, he stepped inside.

I refused to look at him. Hands clasped tightly together, I fought back the tears. The sad, weepy feeling vanished, but the anger was still there, and the humiliation. Hundreds of women would have jumped at the chance to go off with him, to spend three months with a man so handsome, so magnetic, so exciting, but I was old-fashioned and strait-laced about sex, and he should have *known* that. It was infuriating and insulting and altogether too much to bear. I turned around, cheeks flushed, and he looked dejected and bewildered and hurt.

"What is all this? Don't you love me? I could have sworn—"

"Just go away!"

He shrugged his shoulders. "Well, at least I can help you carry the rest of your things down."

He started to pick up the files.

"Don't you *dare!*" I cried. "I've finally got them all in order again, and I don't want you to touch them!"

He stepped back, anger mounting.

"Look, do you want me to *marry* you? Is that what you want?"

"Of course it is!"

"That's what I was afraid of!"

"Well?"

"Well all right! I *will!*"

I grew very quiet.

"You're a scheming little vixen! You meant for me to marry you from the very first. You held off, held back, taunted me. You drove me out of my mind! After all these years of caution, all these years of avoiding predatory, marriage-minded females, I had to run into you! It isn't fair. It isn't funny! Don't you dare gloat—"

I didn't. I was most serene.

"It's going to be hell. I can see that right now! We're going to fight like cats and dogs. I warn you, I can get pretty ugly. If you think marriage to me will be a bed of roses—"

"I think it will be divine."

"The minute we met I was a *marked man*—"

"You were," I admitted. "You've lost."

Bart glared at me, brows slanting crazily, and then the scowl disappeared and, suddenly, he began to grin. He came over to me and took hold of my arms and looked down into my eyes.

"Oh no," he said. "You're mistaken. I haven't lost. The victory is all mine."

He was wrong, but it was a minor point. There was really no need to argue about it.